ROGUE KNIGHT

ROGUE KNIGHT

Paperback ISBN: 978-1-5141983-0-8
Print Edition

PRAISE FOR MEDIEVAL WARRIORS:

"This series captures the medieval era perfectly, creating the true sensation of traveling back in time to experience epic, riveting love stories that ignite the imagination. Beautifully written, perfectly paced and action-packed... What more can you ask?"

—*The Book Review*

THE RED WOLF'S PRIZE

"An exciting tale and a passionate love story that brings to life England after the Conquest—medieval romance at its best!"

—*Virginia Henley New York Times Bestselling Author*

ROGUE KNIGHT

"Rogue Knight is yet another brilliant novel from Regan Walker. She is a master of her craft. Her novels instantly draw you in, keep you reading and leave you with a smile on your face."

—*Good Friends, Good Books*

REBEL WARRIOR

"... beautifully layered with true historic figures, facts and authentic history of Scotland woven into a creative and intriguing fictional story. A spectacular, riveting adventure!"

—*Tartan Book Reviews*

KING'S KNIGHT

"A sweeping tale that pulls you in at the very beginning and doesn't let you go. It's medieval romance at its finest. Well done, Regan Walker! Very, very well done!"

—*The Reading Cafe*

AUTHOR'S NOTE

The love story of Sir Geoffroi de Tournai and Emma of York is set in England in 1069-70 during what became known as William the Conqueror's Harrying of the North. While I have used minor artistic license to fit the story, most of the events in *Rogue Knight* actually occurred as I have described them.

At the time of the Norman Conquest of England in 1066, Northumbria in the north was a very different place than Wessex in the south. At one time it was the capital of the Danelaw where the laws of the Danes governed from the 9th into the 11th century. Even after Northumbria was incorporated into England in 954, it was governed by powerful earls and thegns who operated somewhat independently from the king.

In its language and culture, Yorkshire was Anglo-Scandinavian not Saxon. Almost every street in the city of York had the Old Norse suffix "*gata*" or "gate" meaning "street" and most of the personal names would have been Scandinavian.

It is not surprising, then, that in 1068 when William the Conqueror came north and built his first castle in York (as told in *The Red Wolf's Prize*), the people resented his presence and that of his French knights. They did not consider William their king any more than they had the Saxon Harold Godwinson before him. The situation was made worse by the despicable way the Normans treated the people.

Maerleswein, the former Sheriff of Lincolnshire and Emma's father in my story, was a real historic figure and a rich English thegn of noble Danish lineage. He did not fight against William at the Battle of Hastings, but by 1068, he'd had enough of William and his egregious taxes and joined the rebellion.

In 1069 when my story begins, York was the largest city north of London and an important center of commerce with as many as 15,000 residents. It was a city William very much wanted under his control. But it was not to come to him easily.

One indication of the seething resentment of the Northumbrians for the Norman invaders is seen in the fact that the great families—both English and Danish—that had been feuding for hundreds of years, came together in 1069 to fight against William. Given York's history, it was natural for the rebels to look to the Danes for help.

William's vengeance on the North for the ensuing rebellion was so horrible that for decades thereafter, the land between York and Durham remained untilled and no village was inhabited. It would take the North centuries to fully recover.

Orderic Vitalis, the English chronicler and Benedictine monk, said of William's actions, "I dare not commend him. He leveled both the bad and the good in one common ruin by a consuming famine…he was…guilty of wholesale massacre…and barbarous homicide."

Indeed he was.

William of Jumièges, a monk and contemporary of William the Conqueror, said that "from the youngest to the oldest" most of the population of York was killed.

The wolves would have had a great feast on the bodies left lying in the woods where they fell.

It was enough to turn any noble knight rogue.

England, Scotland,
& Wales
1069-70
Scotland
NORTHUMBRIA
Durham
Talisand
York
Humber River
England
MERCIA
Wales
London
WESSEX

CHARACTERS OF NOTE
(BOTH REAL AND FICTIONAL)

Sir Geoffroi de Tournai
Emma of York

At Talisand:

Sir Renaud de Pierrepont, Earl of Talisand
Serena, Countess of Talisand
Maugris the Wise, a seer
Maggie, cook and housekeeper
Mathieu, squire to Sir Geoffroi
Sir Alain de Roux ("the Bear")

In York, the Northumbrians and their allies:

Maerleswein, Emma's father, Danish nobleman and former Sheriff of Lincolnshire
Cospatric, Earl of Bamburgh, former Earl of Northumbria, and cousin to King Malcolm of Scotland
Magnus, Emma's Irish hound (in modern terms, a wolfhound)
Inga, Emma's friend
Feigr, sword-maker and Inga's father
Finna and Ottar, twins, Emma's adopted children
Artur and Sigga, Emma's servants
Edgar Ætheling, Saxon heir to the throne of England
Waltheof, Earl of Huntingdon, cousin to King Swein, King Harold and Earl Cospatric

The Normans in York:

William I, King of England, Duke of Normandy
William Malet de Graville, Sheriff of Yorkshire
Richard FitzRichard, Castellan of York (1st castle)
Gilbert de Ghent, Castellan of York (2nd castle)
William FitzOsbern, Earl of Hereford
Robert, Count of Mortain, half-brother to William the Conqueror

Sir Eude de Fourneaux

The Danes:

King Swein of Denmark
Osbjorn, brother to King Swein

The Scots:

King Malcolm of Scotland
Margaret of Wessex, sister to Edgar Ætheling and betrothed to Malcolm

Where now is the warrior? Where is the warhorse?
Bestowal of treasure, and sharing of feast?
Alas! The bright ale-cup, the mail-clad warrior,
The prince in his splendor—those days are long sped
In the night of the past, as if they never had been!

From the Anglo-Saxon poem *The Wanderer*

CHAPTER 1

York, England, December 1068

The Minster bell tolled loudly as Emma hurried down Coppergate, gripping her green woolen cloak tightly to her chest against the winter chill. The deep folds of her hood hid her flaxen hair. Only the huge gray hound striding beside her told the merchants who it was that passed their open stalls.

A glance at the nearly white sky warned her nightfall would bring snow. She hastened her step. There were things she needed for Christmastide and neither the ominous weather nor the risk of encountering one of the dreaded Normans would keep her from town this day.

Townspeople on either side of her hurried along, their steps displaying the same urgency of last minute tasks.

Nearing her destination, she heard raised voices in French. *Normans.* Her stomach clenched. Where the French knights went, wickedness always followed. They treated the people of York—even the thegns—worse than serfs, freely taking what they wanted often as not. It was why, even with Magnus at her side, she was grateful for the deadly seax at her hip. Both the hound and the knife had been gifts from her father.

She slowed as she approached the altercation and slipped into the shadows in front of the goldsmith's shop, leading the hound with her.

Across the street, four knights wearing mail hauberks crowded around Feigr's stall where the best swords in all of York could be found. At the rear of his shop, smoke billowed from the forge, open to the air.

As was the Norman custom, the knights wore no beards and their hair was shorter than any man of York would deign to wear.

She watched as one of the knights abruptly lifted a sword from those Feigr displayed and strode away, clutching his prize.

Feigr chased after him shouting his protest against the knight's failure to pay.

The three knights who remained laughed.

Emma inwardly seethed, her brows pressing into a frown at yet another incident of treachery from the garrisoned knights. One among many that had angered the people of York. Feigr worked hard for the living he provided for himself and his daughter, Inga. He could ill afford to give away his fine swords.

One of the knights directed a leering gaze at Inga where she stood next to the stall. Garbed in the simple rust-colored tunic she wore when helping her father, Inga was still an appealing young woman, her delicate features and golden hair only adding to her slim body.

And she was now alone with only an old servant.

Magnus moved slightly forward, lowered his head and stared straight ahead at the three knights, a low growl rumbling from his throat. Emma knotted her fingers into the coarse fur of the hound's neck, feeling the tension in his body. Something was about to happen.

The leering knight suddenly reached for Inga, his powerful hand clutching the girl's delicate arm.

Inga shrieked in terror.

Magnus' growl grew louder as his dark eyes narrowed on the Norman who held Inga.

The knight pulled Inga to his chest.

Attempting to break free, Inga tugged her arm back, but she was a frail thing and provided little resistance to the muscular knight.

"I've seen the one who will warm my bed this night," the knight confidently announced in French to his two companions.

"Yea, a fair one," one of the knights tossed back.

Emma gripped the hilt of her seax, her body tensing to move. Beneath her other hand, Magnus tightened his muscles to lunge. She caught the edge of his ear between her fingers and hissed a caution under her breath. The hound quivered but obeyed, remaining by her side. The tall Irish hound was more a threat than she was, for his sharp teeth had brought down more than one wolf in the forests of Yorkshire, but she would not yet let him enter the fray.

The knight who held Inga lifted her long plait of dark golden hair, letting it run over his hand.

Inga let out a wail and then a whimper as tears streaked down her face. "Please, no."

Emma could stay her hand no longer. Anger, building as she had watched the Norman's ill treatment of her friend, now compelled her away from the shadows. She took a step toward the street, Magnus moving with her.

A hand reached out, staying her progress and tugging her back. A familiar voice spoke from behind. "Nay, my lady, leave it be. See, her father returns. The knight must have paid him for the sword."

Recognizing the voice, she guided Magnus back into the shadows. 'Twas Auki, the goldsmith, whose shop had been her destination. She shifted her eyes to where Auki pointed to Inga's father hurrying down the street toward his stall.

Facing Auki, she pulled her arm free. "I cannot let them treat Inga so."

"You would only put yourself in their sights, my lady, were you to do aught. Feigr will protect her, and see, now the townspeople have stopped to watch."

Keeping her hand on Magnus, Emma turned toward the gathering crowd, a frown on every face. It was not the first time the people of York had seen the Normans seize what was not theirs. Since the garrison of knights had come earlier in the year, fear rode the streets of York like an ever-present phantom. But this time there was more than fear in the eyes of the people. There was outrage.

Reaching his stall, Inga's father stepped between his sobbing daughter and the knight, breaking the man's hold on her arm. Though smaller than the knight in stature, long years of working with metal had given Feigr brawny shoulders and arms. He faced the knight, his bearded chin raised in defiance, his stance sure.

The knight clenched his fists and leaned into Feigr, touching the sword-maker's chest with his own, a threat apparent to all.

Emma tensed, worried for Feigr should the three knights attack him together. At her side, Magnus resumed his low growl. Removing her hand from her seax, she stroked the rough fur on his neck to calm him.

The murmurs of the townspeople grew boisterous as they stared at the unfolding drama, their gazes condemning the effrontery of the French knight who dared lay hands on a maiden of York.

One of the knights turned to look at the crowd, then strode to his companion who was confronting Feigr. Placing his hand on the knight's shoulder, he whispered something in his companion's ear.

The knight jerked his shoulder away. "What is one of them to so many of us?" he challenged.

"A crowd gathers. The wench will keep, Eude. We are expected back at the castle."

With a speaking glance at Inga that sent a shiver of fear through Emma, the knight called Eude shrugged and joined his fellow Normans.

As the three of them swaggered away from the stall, Eude made a rude gesture that caused his fellow knights to bellow their laughter.

Rage choked Emma. Had they planned the whole affair taking the sword to lure Feigr away from his shop?

As the French knights sauntered down the street, relief replaced Emma's anger. She was thankful for the crowd of townspeople that had come. Their show of strength had no doubt kept the knights from doing worse.

"Thank God I did not bring Finna and Ottar," she muttered beneath her breath. The last thing she wanted was for the two young orphans who lived under her protection to have witnessed the assault on her friend.

The crowd dispersed, shaking their heads.

With Magnus at her side, Emma rushed across the street to where Inga's father comforted his daughter. Both were clearly shaken by what had happened.

"Oh, Inga. I am so sorry. Are you all right?"

Gray eyes, wide with fear, looked up at Emma. Barely sixteen, Inga had shouldered much since her mother's death two winters before, helping her father with his shop as well as their home. Emma, seven years older, had lost her own mother at a young age and knew well the emptiness it left. She tried to look after the younger woman, for there was no son to help Feigr, no other child.

Not knowing what to say, Emma reached her hand to touch Inga's arm in solace. The gesture brought little comfort, for Inga turned her face into her father's broad chest and sobbed.

Feigr's eyes glared his hatred as his gaze followed the French knights disappearing down the street.

In the distance the tall square tower of the Norman castle loomed over the city like a great vulture's nest.

* * *

Talisand, Lune River Valley, northwest England, February 1069

"'Tis enough!" Sir Geoffroi de Tournai called as he sheathed his sword and strode from the practice yard outside the palisade fence. Passing through the gate, he entered the bailey, heading toward the stairs leading up to the timbered castle, his sweat chilled by the frigid winter air. Having seen the king's messenger ride in through the gate, he was anxious to know what that ominous arrival portended.

Geoff stepped into the great hall where sunlight sifted through the shuttered windows to cast pale streams of light onto the herbed rushes strewn on the floor. Built less than a year before, it still smelled of new wood. But stronger was the spicy aroma of mutton stew. His mouth watered as he imagined tender chunks of meat in rich sauce and butter dripping from a thick slice of bread. Suddenly he was starving.

"I suppose ye have a yearning for some of me stew after all yer swordplay," observed Maggie coming toward him, a twinkle in her green eyes.

As Talisand's cook, the plump Maggie held a special place in his heart. When he and the Red Wolf had arrived to claim Talisand the year before, Maggie was the first of the English to accept them, mayhap the only one at the beginning. That her husband was the blacksmith rendered the pair indispensable. To knights who wore chain mail, fought with blades of steel and rode iron-shod warhorses, the blacksmith was most valuable, a good one, like Maggie's husband, highly prized.

"A picture of your stew has been with me all morn, Maggie, but I must see the Red Wolf before I eat." Sir Renaud de Pierrepont was the Earl of Talisand by King William's decree, but Geoff still thought of him as he'd known him years before, the knight named for the beast he had slain with his bare hands.

Before Geoff could head toward the Red Wolf's chamber, Maugris approached, his ancient blue eyes shining out of his weathered face framed by gray hair that was ever in disarray. A Norman, who had come with them to England more than two years before, Maugris was neither a soldier nor a servant, nor the wizard the people of Talisand had at first thought him. He was a wise man and a seer who directed his own fate. It struck Geoff then, as it always did, how nimble the old man was in both mind and body. Maugris had been the first of them to learn the English tongue.

Geoff's gaze shifted to the door of the bedchamber where the Red Wolf lay.

"Lady Serena is with the earl just now," Maugris informed him. "'Twould be best to eat first."

"I suppose you speak wisdom," Geoff muttered as he stretched his hands toward the hearth fire.

"Why not join me at the table?" Maugris suggested.

Though anxious to see his friend, Geoff grunted his agreement and headed for the high table.

"Sit yerself down," insisted Maggie, "and I'll see ye both have some stew."

He and Maugris took their seats.

"How is he, Maggie?" Geoff inquired, his brow furrowed in worry as he again looked toward the bedchamber where Renaud was recovering from a wound all were concerned could lead to a deadly fever.

"None too pleased, I expect. 'Twas worse than he pretended. He is already growling at being so confined, but Lady Serena rightly insists he stay abed."

Maggie disappeared into the kitchen and a servant brought trenchers with bowls of stew and bread and butter to join the pitchers of ale already on the table.

Geoff speared a piece of mutton from his stew with his knife.

Maugris reached for the bread. "The Red Wolf is not used to being injured or mayhap I should say he is unused to *acknowledging* his injuries. Lady Serena has forced him to do so."

"'Twas a bad riding accident that," muttered Geoff, remembering the fall Renaud had taken from his stallion a few days before when the horse had stepped into a hole and fallen. "His Spanish stallion is none the better for it, either."

"Belasco will recover, as will his master."

"Have you seen that in one of your visions?" Geoff asked, only slightly amused, for he desperately wanted assurance Ren would be well.

Maugris took a sip of his ale. "Nay, but I know the Red Wolf and his Spanish stallion. Both will recover in time."

Knowing Maugris was never wrong, Geoff's spirits lifted. "And I will be thanking God when that day arrives."

He cut a large piece of bread with his knife and slathered it with butter. It was nearly to his mouth when, out of the corner of his eye, he glimpsed Serena, Countess of Talisand, coming toward them from the chamber at the base of the stairs, her flaxen hair covered now that she was wed. Beneath the headcloth were two long plaits trailing down the front of her violet gown.

Round with the child she would deliver in the spring, Serena walked slowly to the dais. "Good day to you both."

Geoff set down his bread and he and Maugris rose as one and bowed.

"My lady," Geoff said, helping her to her seat.

Once settled, Serena rested a hand on the mound of her belly. "'Tis fortuitous my lord cannot climb the stairs and must be confined to the lower chamber as I will soon be unable to climb them myself."

"'Twill not be long now," observed Maugris. "The coming of April will see the Red Wolf with his first cub."

"I look forward to the day he arrives, Maugris," she returned, casting the old man a kindly glance. "I cannot sleep for this babe's kicking in the night."

A servant set a trencher before Serena, but she must have been thinking of her husband, for she only picked at her food.

"What news from the messenger, my lady?" asked Geoff, eager to hear. "Did your husband happen to say?"

"Yea, but I would have him tell you himself. When you finish your meal, he will likely be ready for you and Maugris. Just now his bandage is being changed and he's snarling like the wolf whose name he bears. The leg pains him greatly but he tries to hide it."

Geoff finished his stew quickly, knowing the other knights would soon be coming in for the midday meal. Since the king had left a contingent of knights and men-at-arms with them, it was always crowded in the hall at meals. Rising, he bowed to Serena, "With your permission—"

She waved him off. "Go. He will be shouting for you soon enough."

"Come, wise one," said Geoff turning to Maugris. "Your counsel will surely be needed."

"Do not be in such haste to hear unpleasant news," chided the old one as he slowly rose from the table, the folds of his dark woolen tunic loose about his thin frame.

"I did not need your visions to know it would be unpleasant," Geoff protested. "When I saw the messenger ride in through the gate, the hair stood up on the back of my neck. Things around here have too long been quiet."

Together they crossed the hall and entered the bedchamber sometimes used for visiting nobles. The king himself had stayed there only last year. At one end of the chamber was a large velvet-curtained bed where the Red Wolf was propped up on a mound of pillows, staring out the unshuttered window, frowning.

"Ren?"

The Red Wolf turned his glower on Geoff. "'Tis a dark day that has brought me news from Durham. It will take you back to York, my friend."

"York?" blurted Geoff. "It has not been a year since we were there and William built his castle. What has happened in Durham that would take me back to York?"

Ren lifted himself onto the pillows, wincing. His chestnut hair fell over his forehead as he slowly let out a breath. "It was as I suspected when we left York last year. The Northumbrians slinked away into the forests, taking their will to rebel with them."

"Have they returned?" asked Geoff.

"Not to York as far as I know but I believe 'twill be soon. When William replaced Cospatric with Robert de Comines as Earl of Northumbria, it appears our sire made a bad choice."

"He is a Fleming," muttered Geoff. "We have seen what the Flemish mercenaries did in the South. They came not to settle as we did, but to pillage."

"Aye, 'twould seem Robert de Comines' men were of the same cloth," declared Ren. "A fortnight ago, the new earl and his mercenaries cut a swath of misery and death on their way north to Durham."

"*Mon Dieu*," Geoff hissed. "Northumbria will again be in turmoil."

"The news is worse." Ren's frown deepened. "When the word of Comines' ravaging the countryside reached the men of Durham, they thought to flee but a heavy snow blocked their retreat, forcing them to fight. They set fire to the house where Comines was staying. Those of the earl's retinue that did not perish in the blaze died by the sword—including the earl."

"*Merde*!" Geoff cursed. "What a fool Comines was to let his mercenaries loose on the town. 'Tis no surprise the people rose against him."

"The messenger hinted of rumors that have spread following the uprising. Edgar Ætheling, the man the English consider heir to the throne, is on the move. Word has it he has left his refuge in Scotland, accompanied by Cospatric and that rich Dane, Maerleswein." Ren shook his head. "I suppose they are encouraged by what happened in Durham."

"Did the messenger say where they were headed?"

"The rumors say York."

Maugris, who had been silently listening, spoke, his wizened voice sounding like a harbinger of doom. "Ancient enemies have come together to rise against a common foe."

"So it would seem," Geoff murmured in resigned acceptance. "And we Frenchmen are the foe."

"As you might expect," said Ren, "William summons us to York, along with his knights and men-at-arms we shelter. You must lead them, Geoff, for I cannot."

Regret flickered in the eyes of his friend. Geoff recognized it for he would have felt the same had he been forced to stay behind. "I will gladly go in your stead."

The Red Wolf nodded his acceptance of what he could not change. "Do you remember William Malet, my old friend who fought with us at Hastings?"

"Aye, I remember him," replied Geoff. "William appointed him Sheriff of York just as we left the city last year."

"No doubt he will be pleased to see you with what he is facing." Ren stared into space once again, seeing something Geoff did not. "His hands will be full if the Northumbrians rise under Edgar's banner. The thegns of York have been waiting for the young Ætheling to return. He will draw many to their cause."

"William will stand for no king in England save himself," Geoff insisted.

Ren shook his head in dismay. "Yea, and York is important to our sovereign. The messenger said William already marches north. He will have a battle on his hands when he gets there. I thought it a possibility when his victory at York last year came too easily. The Northumbrians with their Danish connections may yet hope to carve out a northern kingdom as they did in the past."

"If that be true, the people of York have much to fear," replied Geoff. "It will not be pleasant for them when William arrives to exact his revenge. Does Lady Serena know?"

"Aye, she knows, and is none too pleased that the people of York are threatened by William's army. You know well how she feels about our sire."

From behind Geoff, Maugris spoke. "William is a great king, but terrible in his wrath. He cares more for his crown and his treasures than the people he would rule. I fear for him on Judgment Day when the Master of the Heavens holds him accountable for his cruelty and his slaying of little ones."

"Little ones?" Geoff protested. "I have yet to see William's knights raise their swords against children."

Maugris' eyes fixed on some unknown point as he gazed out the window. "In my visions I have seen it. And though horrible, it did not surprise me. When defied, William can become a great destroyer, ripping off limbs, blinding eyes and laying waste to all in his path. This time, William will show the people of York no mercy."

Geoff knew Maugris saw things the rest of them did not, but he remembered the mercy William had shown the year before when he entered York and left behind a castle and a garrison of knights. "I hope such can be avoided."

"I have seen a great wasteland," Maugris intoned, "where nothing grows." As he spoke, the old man appeared taller, his voice enduing him with power. "Vacant land strewn with the dead, both young ones and old."

"For once, wise one, I hope your vision is wrong," said the Red Wolf.

Troubled by Maugris' ominous words, Geoff gripped the hilt of his sword. "I will prepare to ride."

"Tomorrow is soon enough," Ren insisted. "Take Mathieu along as your squire. He is nearly a knight and grows impatient for action."

"Yea, I will." Geoff was happy to have Mathieu join his company, for the squire had served the Red Wolf well. "His sword arm is strong. I welcome his service."

"With me limping around, you'd best leave my few knights, save Alain. The Bear will guard your back as he has guarded mine, though he will not be anxious to return to York where he got that scar that adorns his jaw."

Geoff remembered the fight the year before when the knight, dubbed "the Bear" for his size, had taken a blade across his jaw. "I would gladly have Alain with me. What about the others?"

"Take all the knights William has quartered here. Serena will be glad to see them go. She nearly sank an arrow into one for grabbing a servant girl, and that in *her* condition!"

Geoff chuckled at the picture of Lady Serena, heavy with child, wielding a bow and arrow. Her state would not stop her from defending the maidens of Talisand. "I will do as you say, Ren. Rest if you can bring yourself to do so. We want you in the practice yard again."

"Godspeed," said Ren as they left the chamber. Geoff heard concern in his voice but there was nothing for it. They must heed the king's summons.

Early the next day, a good meal under his belt, Geoff mounted Athos, his chestnut stallion. The air was chilled even though the pale sun was shining on the winter landscape. He was glad it was not raining. His helm and shield tied to his saddle, Geoff gave the signal to ride.

Mathieu followed on his palfrey, leading Geoff's black destrier, the squire's brown hair blowing about his face. A few years in Ren's service had given him a proud bearing and a confident look, more like a knight than a squire.

Behind Mathieu rode Alain and the long line of William's knights who would accompany them to York.

Geoff guided Athos toward the gate, but before he could pass through the wide opening, Maugris called him back.

"Sir Geoffroi!"

Geoff brought the column to a halt and circled back to the old man whose face bore an expression more serious than his normal mien.

Looking up at Geoff, Maugris said, "I have had another vision..."

Geoff swallowed and waited, his stomach tightening into a knot as he anticipated what the seer's vision might have told him.

"You will have to face the fear you have carried from your youth, the one you keep hidden even from the Red Wolf that has nothing to do with battle. But mayhap you will find these words encouraging: You will give help to those who would otherwise fall and you will find an ally where you least expect it. But if need be, you must have courage to stand alone."

From atop his horse, Geoff stared down at the wise one, wondering at the cryptic message. How could the old man know of something Geoff had shared with no one?

"I do not suppose you would care to elaborate?"

"All will be clear in time," Maugris assured him with a knowing grin.

So the old man's remarks were to remain a mystery. "All right," he reluctantly agreed. "I shall try to do as you say. Take care of the earl and his lady."

As Geoff turned his horse, he glimpsed the Red Wolf standing in the open doorway of the old manor in the bailey, his arm around Serena's shoulders, whether in affection or for support Geoff could not tell. Mayhap both, for Ren loved his lady and his stance told Geoff he was favoring his wounded leg. That he had managed to walk given the pain he was in was a tribute to both his strength and his resolve.

Geoff tipped his head to him and, as he did, noted Serena looking around the bailey, searching, he knew, for her friend, Eawyn. Ren's wife had hoped Geoff would one day wed the beautiful widow. He was relieved to see Eawyn had stayed away. She had not warmed to his advances as he had hoped. What he had thought was a growing affection had turned out to be merely a friendship on her part. She was still in love with her dead English husband. Mayhap she always would be.

When he returned, he would have to make it clear to Serena there was no hope for the match.

A look of frustration crossed Ren's face as he raised a hand to Geoff in farewell. Geoff knew its source. It was the first time the Red Wolf had failed to heed the call of his sire.

The first time Geoff rode alone.

CHAPTER 2

By the light from the fire in the hearth, Emma sat bent over her embroidery, lost in her thoughts. A loud pounding on the front door made her start. She thrust the needle into the linen and stood.

Magnus clambered up from where he'd been lounging next to the hearth and trotted to the door, reaching it before her. She was glad for his presence. An unwelcome visitor would think twice before forcing entry. But this time the hound's prodigious tail wagged furiously, telling her the visitor was most welcome indeed.

She unlatched the door to see Maerleswein, her tall, proud father, standing there grinning, his golden hair loose about his shoulders, his mustache and beard neatly trimmed.

"Daughter!"

She had not seen him for nearly a year. "Father, you look well." She reached out to embrace him. "It has been too long."

Before she could say more, he gave her a quick hug, planted a kiss on her forehead and strode over the threshold, crushing the rushes under his large feet. Behind him was a man she recognized from many past meetings, Cospatric, the handsome Earl of Bamburgh. Unlike most Danish and English men, he was clean-shaven and his dark brown hair extended only to the base of his neck.

"My lady," Cospatric bowed, his brown eyes twinkling. Straightening, he took her hand and brought it to his lips. "You are beautiful as ever and a most welcome sight."

"And you, my lord, are too kind. Do come in." He walked past her and she closed the door. Emma smiled to herself. The charming nobleman who had once been the Earl of Northumbria had always been wont to flatter her.

Magnus followed the two men into the room. It was large enough to provide seating for several people around the fire burning in the central hearth where smoke ascended to a hole in the roof. Firelight illuminated the tapestries gracing the whitewashed walls, tapestries that had been in her family for generations.

Artur, her manservant, and his wife Sigga, hurried in from the kitchen door at the far end of the room on the other side of the table where the family dined. "Welcome, my lord," said Artur, taking the cloaks of the two men and hanging them on pegs near the door.

"Greetings, to you, Artur, Sigga," replied her father. "As you see, I come with a guest, Earl Cospatric. You might recall him from the last time I was in York."

"Aye, I do," said Artur. "My lord." He bowed to Cospatric. At Artur's side, Sigga curtsied.

Magnus sniffed Cospatric as he would anyone coming with her father.

"May I bring you something to drink?" asked Sigga, looking at her father.

"Aye, 'tis cold with more snow coming," observed Maerleswein, reaching his hands to the hearth fire.

"Best warm the mead, Sigga," instructed Emma.

"Yea, mistress." Sigga dipped her head and retreated toward the kitchen along with her husband. They had been with Emma a long time and knew her preference to make guests feel welcome as soon as they entered.

"I see that great beast I gave you has grown," remarked her father. "His chest deepens."

As if knowing he was the topic of discussion, Magnus rose from where he had been sitting, nuzzled her father's hand and wagged his considerable tail. Her father patted the coarse fur of the hound's head without having to stoop, for the dog was that tall.

"He remembers you from when he was only a whelp," she said.

With an answering chuckle, her father scratched Magnus behind the ears. "Wise hound. Does he yet hunt?"

"Oh, indeed," she confirmed, smiling at Cospatric who watched, amused. "But the hares he brings to my door often arrive a bit mangled."

Her father laughed, a deep belly laugh, his voice resonating through the house.

Ottar bounded into the room from the kitchen. While not her natural son, Ottar and his sister, Finna, nine-year-old twins, might have been for all the love she gave them. Orphaned three years ago at the same time she had miscarried her own child upon hearing the news of her husband's death, she'd taken them in. They had brought each other comfort during that painful time and now they were a family.

"Godfather!" shouted Ottar hugging Maerleswein about his hips.

"Aye, 'tis me," he teased, wrapping his powerful arms around the boy's shoulders and mussing his hair. "Is that your sister I see?"

Peeking into the room from the doorway to the kitchen, Finna gave Emma's father a shy smile. She was a beautiful child and, like her brother, her brown hair was streaked with sunlight, but whereas her brother had dark gray eyes, hers were a soft brown.

"Greetings to you, Godfather," she said, coming slowly forward. When she got close, Maerleswein snaked his arm out to draw her to him to hug her in turn.

"And this," explained her father, gesturing to Cospatric, "is my friend the Earl of Bamburgh."

Ottar bowed and Finna did a small curtsy as Emma had taught her.

"I remember you, sir," Finna shyly admitted.

Cospatric looked pleased.

The twins returned their attention to Emma's father, whom they adored. Once the Sheriff of Lincolnshire, a man of wealth with eight manors, he had been stripped of his title and his lands once he joined the rebellion. The cursed Norman invader had given those to one of his loyal followers. But her father still had his noble Danish blood and much of his wealth. And he still had the love of the people of York.

"Come sit." Emma gestured to the benches near the hearth fire. "'Tis certain you are tired."

The men sat on one of the benches and Magnus settled himself on the floor at her father's feet.

Finna and Ottar, detecting an adult conversation about to commence, retreated to the kitchen where Sigga was preparing their meal. The smell of the spices Sigga added to the mead, cinnamon and cloves, wafted from the kitchen.

Emma sat on the bench opposite the men and directed her question to her father. "Not that I am not pleased to see you and Earl Cospatric, but why have you left Scotland? Is it safe with the Conqueror's knights still garrisoned in York?"

"Then you have not heard," said her father.

"Heard what?"

"The news from the North," Cospatric finished.

Emma looked at them, puzzled.

Sigga returned with tankards of heated mead and Emma accepted the one offered her. "Drink your mead," said Emma, "but tell me what has happened."

She waited until her father and Cospatric had downed some of the honeyed wine, then with eager anticipation, asked, "Well?"

Holding his tankard between his two large hands, her father leaned forward. "Durham has been retaken by the Northumbrians." He sat back, grinning. "William's latest earl, Comines, was slain along with his hundreds of raiding mercenaries. Good riddance, I say."

Emma looked from her father to Cospatric whose countenance had suddenly grown serious. "What can it mean for *us*?" she asked.

Cospatric shifted his gaze to her father.

A confident smile crossed her father's face. She had not seen him so pleased since before the Norman Bastard had come to England. "A chance to regain the North, Emma."

"Can it be true?" she asked, afraid to hope.

Cospatric nodded, apparently sharing her father's favorable outlook.

It was her most fervent desire, and that of the people of York, to see the city freed of the Norman yoke, but it seemed only a dream when the Norman Bastard had thousands of knights at his disposal. While York had thousands of people living within its city walls, they were unarmed and mostly merchants, craftsmen and shopkeepers, along with the people they served, the freemen, farmers and villeins—not warriors.

"Yea, for we do not come alone, Emma. Earl Cospatric brings with him the Northumbrians from the House of Bamburgh."

"And the sons of Karli of the Danes of York," added the earl.

"But the sons of Karli are your enemies," Emma protested.

"Ah, they *were*," said the dark-haired Cospatric with a slow smile spreading on his face.

"The enemies of our enemy have become our friends," her father explained.

"Ah, I see." She was surprised that after so many years of feuding, the great families of the North had banded together. Mayhap her father was right and there was hope. "But will that be enough with so many French knights and soldiers at the Norman king's disposal?"

"We have sent word to King Swein of Denmark, asking for his aid."

"The Danes..." Her voice trailed off as she pondered the possibility of the powerful warriors and their dragon ships sailing to York. "Will he come?"

"I cannot imagine he will not," said her father. "He could hardly give up what was once the capital of the Danelaw to a French bastard, now could he?"

Cospatric took a deep breath and let it out. "The question is *when* he might come, not *if*, Emma. Your father and I are prepared to go to Denmark to plead our cause to King Swein if we must."

She turned to her father. "What will it mean for the people of York if you are successful? They have experienced so much loss already."

"Freedom from the yoke of the Normans, I trust," her father boldly stated.

Emma observed the two men were pleased with the plans they were making. She only hoped their confidence was not misplaced. She, too, hated the Normans and their garrison of knights, but like any woman, she worried about the death the battles would bring, worried about Finna and Ottar and the children of York.

* * *

It should have taken Geoff and his knights two days to reach York but, much to his dismay, the winter storms slowed their pace. Freezing rain sliced through their clothing as their horses slogged through the deep mud. Nights on the cold ground were often sleepless. At the end of the third day, they arrived at the castle, cold, tired and covered with mud.

Followed by his men, Geoff rode his horse toward the bridge that led over the moat to the timbered castle at the junction of the Rivers Ouse and Foss.

The citizens of York, who had been milling about outside the castle moat, stopped and watched. The men with their long hair and full beards looked askance at the newly arriving knights. As Geoff's procession passed by, the people began to mutter amongst themselves, their voices rising in anger and their expressions dour.

Geoff drew his brows together, puzzling over the people's reaction to their arrival. He would have thought by now they would be used to Normans in their city. Mayhap they had heard of Robert de Comines' ravaging of Durham. Whatever it was, this reception did not bode well.

Just as he was about to cross the bridge, his eye was drawn to a cloaked figure moving swiftly through the crowd and a huge dark gray dog striding apace. The gown showing beneath the cloak told him it was a woman. A sudden gust of wind threw back her hood to reveal flaxen hair and a nearly perfect face marred only by a scowl directed at him and his knights. The image of a Valkyrie arose in his mind, a handmaiden of the Norse god Odin tasked with choosing which warriors would live and which would die. 'Twas a tale he had once heard around the hearth fire.

Captivated by the strength the woman exuded, he paused to watch her and the hound before turning away to proceed into the bailey crowded with knights and men-at-arms.

Buildings he did not recall from the year before were scattered around the periphery of the palisade fence of wooden stakes that surrounded the large bailey. No doubt the new buildings served the hundreds of knights and men-at-arms now garrisoned here. There would be workshops, an armory, a blacksmith and stables and possibly a chapel. He hoped it had a good kitchen and a good cook.

He dismounted, pulling off his gloves to stroke Athos' neck. The chestnut stallion nickered and tossed its head. "You did well, my boy." At Mathieu's approach, Geoff handed the stallion's reins to the squire. "Mathieu, see that Athos gets some extra oats while I find the castellan to let him know we have arrived."

"Yea, sir," said Mathieu and, with Geoff's two horses and Mathieu's own in tow, the squire headed toward what appeared to be stables at the far edge of the bailey.

Turning to Alain, who was sliding from his great horse, Geoff said, "Best see the men are settled." He glanced at the sky. "Gloaming is not far off. The men may be relegated to pallets in the castle's hall or they may be accommodated in shelters in the bailey. Whichever the case, I will meet you in the castle. I go to seek out the castellan, FitzRichard."

Alain nodded and set off about the task, his stride slower than normal. The large knight was weary. All of them were tired and hungry after three days on the road eating cold fare and enduring the freezing rain that had turned to snow as they traveled east. They would welcome dry clothing, hot food and a fire.

Geoff walked through the melting snow toward the stairs leading up to the castle that sat atop the motte, the mound of dirt nearly thirty feet tall. Snorting horses, knights in conversation and others brandishing swords in a practice yard set to one side of the bailey made for a noisy place. The bailey was like a small town and, after the quiet of the countryside, loud with the clash of arms and the hoarse voices of men.

"Ho! Sir Geoffroi!" The shout came from behind him just as he reached the base of the stairs. Geoff turned to see William Malet striding toward him and was struck again by the man's fair appearance. Older than Geoff by more than a decade, Malet was half-Saxon and related to the former King Harold by marriage. Still, the man had fought with William at Hastings and was now in a position of trust. More importantly to Geoff, the Red Wolf counted him a friend.

"Judging by your appearance," remarked Malet, "I would say you traveled the same roads I did."

Geoff laughed. Admittedly his condition was foul and Malet fared no better. "Aye, I am surprised you recognized me under all this mud."

Malet's seeking gaze reached behind Geoff. "Where is the Earl of Talisand?"

"Recovering from a fall and a bad gash in his leg. He was most disappointed not to be able to rise to William's summons."

"We could use his sword arm for what I fear may be coming."

"So I hear."

Malet paused and looked toward the open gate. "I assume you noticed the discontent of the locals as you entered the city."

Geoff remembered the hostile looks the men of York had given them. "I did. Angrier faces I have not seen before."

"The situation is worse than when I left," advised Malet. "York is like a kettle of stew left too long on the fire." At Geoff's raised brows, the sheriff added, "There will be time to speak of it over the evening meal. In the meantime, we could both use a bath if one can be found in this throng."

"From whence did you come?" Geoff inquired.

"I was in the south of Yorkshire and most recently in my lands in Holderness, east of York. I have returned to see about matters in York. Helise and my two sons are with me. But I am thinking mayhap I should have left them in Holderness. I have concerns about FitzRichard's ability to control William's men garrisoned here. The city is rife with discontent.

And now this trouble in Durham…"

"I did not know about FitzRichard but I observed for myself the unhappy state of the people. While I was still at Talisand, a messenger came with news of the slaying of Earl Robert."

"A conversation best shared over good French wine. Walk with me. The servants are local serfs and continually overtaxed as you might suppose, but since we will be housed in the tower, as soon as we find our chambers, we'll have our baths."

Geoff followed Malet up the stairs that led from the bailey to the top of the motte, his spurs jangling on the steps. At the top, a great square tower rose three stories into the air, providing a strategic view of the surrounding countryside and the forest beyond.

Once inside the tower, FitzRichard came to greet them in the main hall. "Welcome, Sir Geoffroi. 'Tis glad I am to see you. Has Malet told you the news?"

"Yea, and unwelcome news it is."

"We can talk after you are settled in your chambers. You and Malet are housed on this level." To Malet he said, "Your lady wife awaits you." Then taking a long perusal of them, he added, "By the look of you, a bath is in order. I shall see each of you has one, but best to be quick. Supper will soon be served."

Geoff and Malet thanked FitzRichard for his hospitality and followed the summoned servants who showed them to their chambers.

Geoff was relieved to shut the door on the confusion of the main hall. He unbuckled his sword belt, laid the scabbard on the small table and slumped onto the bench by the brazier that warmed the chamber. He unfastened his spurs and pulled off his short leather boots, shaking off the mud.

A knock sounded and he rose and opened the door to see two servants carrying a large copper tub, followed by lads carrying buckets, steam rising from the water. A bath was a rare privilege and he would not fail to avail himself of it after days of slogging through mud.

When the servants had gone, he stripped off his clothes and sank into the hot water, leaning his head against the metal edge. He closed his eyes with a sigh. As he did, the faces of the people of York returned to his mind, one beautiful woman's in particular.

Angry faces all.

CHAPTER 3

She floated above the forest, the sounds of battle ringing in her ears. In a clearing below her, men fought, their swords clashing then sliding against each other, the sound of metal against metal loud in her ears. Grunts and moans filled the air as sword points encountered unmailed chests and necks and sank into vulnerable flesh. Flashes of red streaked across her vision. Blood. So much blood. Bright crimson against white snow. Flashes of light laced with blue sliced through the air. When the bright light was gone and the sounds died away, all that remained were corpses carelessly strewn about the clearing. Wind stirred in the surrounding trees, sounding like souls ascending to Heaven.

Loud shouts roused Emma from her dream. She woke startled, her heart pounding in her chest as she tried to clear her mind. For a moment, she stared at the roof, listening, as she forced her heart to calm and the terrifying images faded. But the shouts did not.

Fully awake, she sat up and gazed about her chamber. Light seeped around the edges of the hide that covered the window, telling her it was morning although the sun rose later in the winter months. The air was chilled, the coals in the brazier, having been banked, gave little warmth. Throwing off the cover, she reached for her fur-lined robe and slipped on her leather shoes. As she stood, Magnus roused from the floor at the foot of her bed and came to greet her, his tail wagging, his large eyes gazing at her expectantly.

She pulled on her robe, looking down at the hound. "Do not look at me as if I know what is causing the clamor outside. I do not."

Hurriedly, she left her bedchamber and descended the stairs with

Magnus close on her heels. The hearth fire was already a steady blaze. Near the door, her father was strapping on his sword belt.

"What is it, Father? What is happening?"

"It sounds like the thegns mean to start the uprising without me. My men, along with those of Cospatric and Edgar, are camped outside the city, but from the sounds of it, the men of York have had enough of the Normans. Or mayhap the men from Durham have arrived." He shrugged. "Either way, it has begun. I would have waited for the Danes, but it was not to be." He gave her a kiss on her forehead and unlatched the door.

He stepped through the doorway. The din was louder but she could not see any men in the street.

"I will be back as soon as I can," he assured her.

With that, he was gone.

Emma let Magnus out and waited for him to return, shivering as she stood in the open doorway, listening to the shouting coming from the center of town. She drew her robe more tightly around her, relieved when the hound quickly returned. She shut the door behind him and paced before the hearth fire, considering what to do. She was anxious to see for herself what was happening in the city. But there were Ottar and Finna to worry about. She would check on the children first.

She ascended the stairs to her chamber, hurriedly donning a linen shift, blue woolen gown, warm stockings and her soft leather half boots. With Magnus by her side, she hastened to the twins' chamber. Soundlessly, she pulled open the door. In one bed Finna slept with her little fist curled under her chin. Emma's eyes shifted to the next bed. The cover was tossed aside, the bed empty. She quickly scanned the room but Ottar was not there. Her father had said nothing about the boy when he left. Mayhap he woke hungry and went to the kitchen for bread and honey.

She rushed downstairs, passing the hearth and the large table, as she headed toward the kitchen. Ottar was nowhere in sight. Worry was beginning to creep into her thoughts when she knocked on the servants' bedchamber door on the other side of the kitchen. How they had slept through the tumult in the streets, she did not know.

The door creaked open and Artur's bleary-eyed face appeared, his brown hair tousled. "M'lady?"

"Do you not hear it, Artur? There is a great uproar in the city. My father has gone to see the cause of it for himself. He believes an uprising has begun. Do you know where Ottar is?"

His face took on a puzzled expression.

"No, I can see you do not. I wonder if he may have followed my father into the streets."

Now more awake, Artur mumbled, "You know he is always wanting to be with the men, my lady."

"This is not a day for him to be out there alone, especially if my father has no idea Ottar may be trailing him."

"Should I go in search of him?" asked Artur.

"Nay. I will go myself but you must keep Finna safe while I am gone."

His forehead creased with worry as he came fully awake. "My lady, no! If there is trouble in the city, the streets will not be safe for a… a… gentlewoman such as you."

"Then the streets are not safe for a child. I cannot sit around wondering where Ottar might be."

She was gratified to see the look of resignation on his face.

"You will take Magnus with you?" he asked.

"I will. Do not worry." Knowing that he would, she added, "I will stay away from the fray."

"Come, Magnus," she commanded the hound as she walked to the front door and reached for her cloak. "We must find Ottar."

The sky was a pale blue when she stepped into the street coated with fresh snow and headed toward the source of the rising noise.

Several streets from her house, Emma encountered large numbers of York men, carrying spears and swords, moving from all parts of the city in one direction: toward the Norman castle. Hugging the buildings, she moved in the same direction, near enough to the crowd to observe, but not so close as to become embroiled in any fighting. All the while, she desperately searched for Ottar, but did not see him among the men.

Following the crowd, she drew near to the mass of rioters waving their weapons in front of the Norman edifice.

A shout rose above the din. "Kill the castellan!"

In the distance, ahead of the crowd, a mounted Norman, richly attired, tried to control his panicked horse. A small group of mounted knights surrounded him, attempting to force the crowd away from the noble. The press of the mob caused the knights' horses to rear. One knight drew his sword to slash at a man on the ground, but as he did, another man ran the knight through with a spear. When the knight fell, his throat was slit, blood spattering the crowd.

Emma was stunned by how suddenly death had come to the Norman.

The mass of shouting men engulfed the other Normans. She heard the knights' cries as they were pulled from their horses, followed by mockery from the rebels as they hacked at the bodies, taking their vengeance.

The richly attired Norman was the last to be pulled from his horse as the bloodthirsty crowd closed in on him. She did not see his end. Hearing his cries had been enough.

Emma turned away, shocked at the violence, her stomach sickened by the sight of so much blood. She understood the anger that had led to the scene she had witnessed. But she could not love it and hoped with all her heart Ottar had not seen the slaying of the noble and the knights. She shuddered to think of the Normans' revenge that would surely come in its wake.

* * *

Geoff stood in the great hall of the castle as chaos ensued following the killing of the castellan. Knights reached for weapons. Captains roared orders to their men-at-arms. Geoff looked for Malet. Spotting the sheriff across the room, he headed in that direction when Alain came to tell him the men were prepared for battle and awaited him in the bailey.

"I will join you as soon as I can," he assured Alain and continued his path toward the table where Malet sat with some of his knights.

"Fool!" Malet exclaimed, pounding his fist on the table, causing tankards of ale to dance, their contents splashing onto the wood. "Whatever compelled FitzRichard to leave the castle at first light? He was aware of the angry mood of the people yesterday. What could he have been thinking?"

"He paid for his rash move with his life," admonished Geoff. "No need to find fault with him now." Roused from his bed by the shouts outside the castle, Geoff had witnessed the slaughter himself. None, save the foolish castellan and his personal guard of knights, had ventured out of the gates. Why they had done so no one knew. If FitzRichard had set forth with hundreds of knights instead of a few, the loss could have been avoided.

In the aftermath of FitzRichard's slaying, men prepared for battle as servants hurriedly set about lighting candles on the table where Geoff and a small group of knights now gathered with Malet in the great hall.

"I want the gates kept shut until the king arrives!" Malet ordered. The sheriff's senior knight moved to obey. Malet raised a hand. "Wait!"

The knight paused and turned toward Malet with a questioning look.

"Send two men out the postern gate to ride south and warn the king of the rebels' action," ordered the sheriff.

"Yea, my lord." The knight bowed and departed.

"William cannot be far," Geoff assured Malet. "We received word he was marching north before I left Talisand."

"Nay, not far," Malet murmured as he anxiously chewed his bottom lip. "Knowing William as I do, he will be most displeased when he arrives for I have failed to keep the peace."

"'Tis not clear any could," said Geoff. "The Northumbrians will not easily accept a king they do not see as theirs."

"You know the king as well as I. He will make them accept him no matter the lengths he must go to in order to see it done."

Maugris' words echoed in Geoff's mind. *William is a great king, but terrible in his wrath.*

* * *

That afternoon, from the top of the tower Geoff stared into the distance as the large army flowed over the land toward the castle like locusts out of season covering the winter landscape. William had arrived and was mowing down the rebels outside the walls of York.

Once the king's forces were in sight, the main gate was thrown open. Geoff tore down the stairs from the motte to the bailey, anxious to be engaged in the fight. Too long he had been relegated to swordplay with his own men.

Mathieu handed him his helm and waited until Geoff mounted his destrier, then passed him his shield and lance. Geoff and his knights were among the first to leave the confines of the castle, their horses' hooves sending up a great clatter as they raced over the bridge that spanned the moat. Alain was at his back, followed by the knights from Talisand. They formed a formidable force to meet the rebels fleeing William's army back toward the city.

Northumbrians wielding spears, pikes and swords scattered in all directions at the thundering hooves of the knights' warhorses. But some stood and fought. Caught between William's army moving north and the knights from York moving south, the rebels had not a chance. They were slain by the hundreds.

Geoff turned his destrier to confront a spear-wielding rebel, his sword raised for a crushing blow. A glint of metal at his side caught his eye. With a quick change in his aim, he sliced first at the man coming alongside his horse, a long seax gripped in the rebel's fist. Blood splashed onto Geoff's leggings, the crimson liquid dripping onto his leather boots. With a quick turn, he directed his horse toward the rebel with the spear. The destrier knocked the man to the side, allowing Geoff a swift slash to his throat. Blood splattered onto his mail. The man's shocked eyes stared at him for a moment before he crashed to the ground.

The sounds of battle surrounded him as he plunged into the throng of fighting men. He did his share of killing, cutting down all who faced his sword, uncaring of the blood splashing onto his hauberk.

The youngest of seven sons, he had fought for all he had ever claimed as his. A page at seven, a squire at fourteen and a knight at seventeen, he had proved to all he could take his place with the best of Duke William's knights. It made up for his youth in which he had ever borne the brunt of his brothers' taunts. Before he had gained his height, they had thought him a weakling. Mayhap their merciless harassment had made him who he was. Even before he had sailed for England, years of fighting in Normandy at the Red Wolf's side had honed his skills to a sharp edge. The Northumbrians, untrained and undisciplined, were no match for the experienced knights.

At his back, Alain fought with a strength few men possessed, like the vicious bear that had gained him his name.

When they had dispatched the last rebel, Geoff glimpsed William's banner waving in the distance, two golden leopards on a field of red. He took off his helm and wiped the sweat from his brow. Putting it back on, he raised his arm to gesture his knights toward the king.

William sat atop his dark bay warhorse, the Iberian stallion he had ridden at the Battle of Hastings when they had first assaulted England's shores. Surrounding the king was his guard and behind them, his army.

Geoff brought his knights to a halt and walked his horse toward the king.

"Sire," he bowed his head. "'Tis Sir Geoffroi of Talisand. Your presence is most welcome."

Beneath his conical helm graced by a golden crown, the breeze stirred the king's short brown hair. "We can see that it is, sir knight. We are pleased we were able to surprise the rebels south of the city." Then in a harsh tone, "But what of our castellan FitzRichard and Malet, our sheriff—and our hundreds of knights? Why have they not kept the peace?"

"FitzRichard fell to the rebels this morning, sire, cruelly murdered. Malet is well, as far as I know. I left him in the castle ere I came to join you. As for the knights, based on what I have seen, I cannot say whether they have helped or hurt the peace of the city. I have not been here long enough to rightly judge."

"Malet has much to account for."

In the face of William's ire Geoff remained silent.

"And what of our wolf? Where is he?"

"Recovering in Talisand from a grievous wound, My Lord. He was most disappointed to be forced to remain behind."

The king frowned, then raised his brow. "He will recover?"

"Yea, My Lord. His lady tends him."

William nodded, apparently satisfied. "We remember well the beautiful archer who guards our wolf. A bit too free with her arrows, we think."

Geoff smiled at the king's recollection of the Lady Serena. It was true Serena would fight any who threatened one she loved. He turned his horse in a circle to take his place next to the king as the two of them proceeded to walk their horses toward York.

The Talisand knights circled their horses to join William's army behind the king's guard.

Slain Northumbrians and Normans lay on either side of their path. The king gave them scant attention. "Have you captured many of the rebels?"

"Some, My Lord, but many fled when confronted with our longer swords."

"We suspect the leaders have slipped through our net once again," said the king with narrowed brows. "That apostate, Earl Cospatric, is likely one of them. Any word of the Ætheling?"

Geoff saw the worry in the king's face and knew William feared a rebel plan to have the young Edgar crowned king here in York. Archbishop Ealdred of York certainly had the authority. "Nay, sire."

They were almost to the castle when the king paused and looked up at the tower. "We are of a mind to build a second castle in York to remind the populace we reign here as we do in the rest of England."

Given William's propensity toward building the symbols of his domination, Geoff was unsurprised. "Might I take my leave of you here, sire? I'd like to scout the countryside for rebel stragglers and wounded before returning."

"Go, Sir Geoffroi. Leave none to escape. We will see you at the evening meal."

At Geoff's signal, Alain and Mathieu peeled off from William's army and followed him into the forest. He could only wonder what he might find.

* * *

Emma emerged from the dense stand of trees, shocked by the tragic scene before her. Despite her search, she had not found Ottar and, disbelieving what was shouted in the streets, had come to see for herself. But not even her dream had prepared her for the slaughter that had awaited her here.

Dear God.

She crossed herself and covered her mouth, fighting the urge to spew at the sight of so much blood and so many bodies strewn about the clearing, blood congealed on their clothing, their vacant eyes staring into space. Some of the blood had pooled on the ground to catch the rays of the sun. The metallic scent of it, carried by the wind, rose in her nostrils.

At her side, the hound whimpered.

So many.

Until the Normans had come, Yorkshire had been a place of gentle hills, forests and thatched cottages circling a glistening jewel of a city set between two winding rivers. A place of children's voices at play, some of those voices now silenced forever, for among the bodies lying on the cold ground were mere boys, their corpses cast aside like broken playthings.

At the sound of heavy footfalls on the snow-crusted ground, she jerked her head around, her heart pounding in her chest.

A figure emerged from the trees, so close she could have touched him.

She cringed. *A Norman.*

A tall giant of a knight, his blood-splattered mail a dull gray in the weak winter sun, ripped off his silvered helm and expelled an oath as he surveyed the dozens of dead. The sword in his hand still dripped the blood of those he had slain. He was no youth this one, at least thirty. His fair appearance made her think of Lucifer, the fallen angel of light. *A seasoned warrior of death who has taken many lives.*

Had he killed people she knew? Her heart raced as fear rose in her chest.

Would she be next?

The wind blew his straw-colored hair about his face as he turned from the field of bodies to stare at her.

She backed away as their gazes met and a frown creased his forehead, a puzzled look flickering in his stark blue eyes. Was he surprised to find a living soul among the dead? Or was it because she was a woman?

Beneath her cloak, her hand went to her seax, her mind screaming for retribution even as fear rose in her throat. Magnus came to her side but, to her surprise, did not growl at the threatening warrior.

The knight's eyes shifted to where her hand gripped the hilt of her knife. "Still your hand, lady. I mean you no harm." He had spoken in English.

Wiping his sword on his leg, he sheathed the weapon in a leather scabbard attached to his belt.

"No harm?" she blurted out. Taking her hand from the hilt of her blade, she swept it in a wide arc over the bodies. "Is this not harm enough?" Her voice dripped with the sarcasm and hatred she felt for the Norman Bastard and his soldiers.

"The rebels brought this on themselves."

Before she could answer, Magnus let out a sudden bark and bolted across the clearing to where a mere youth, blood spattered on his tunic, lay on the snow-covered ground. The hound licked the boy's face and she heard the boy groan. A sudden dread came over her when she spotted the familiar tunic and sun-streaked hair. "Ottar!"

She flew across the clearing and knelt beside him. Magnus pressed his nose to the boy's cheek.

"Ottar!"

His eyes were closed and his face was as pale as the snow he lay upon. Desperation rose in her mind. Placing her ear on his chest, she heard the sound of a heartbeat. *He lives!*

Ignoring the knight behind her, she gathered Ottar into her arms and tried to stand, anxious to take him home. But the lad was heavy and she faltered.

The knight's shadow fell across her. "I will carry him."

She reached her arm protectively over Ottar. "You'll nay touch him, Norman scum."

"You have no choice but to allow me. 'Tis obvious you cannot bear his weight."

"Have you and your kind not done enough?"

He bent and scooped up the boy. "Do not be foolish, woman. You have my word no harm will come to you or the lad."

What was the word of a Norman to her? She hesitated, hating to accept his help but there was the town to cross and she was not certain she could carry Ottar the distance she must. Nor could she leave him to freeze on the icy ground. "All right."

With her words, into the clearing stepped two Normans, one very large knight holding the reins of a great, gray horse. His dark hair and the scar on his face rendered his visage frightening. The other man was younger, his appearance almost boyish, but he held himself proud and erect. He led two horses, not as large as the gray. Both were black. *A squire.*

The blond knight carried Ottar toward the larger Norman and signaled him to mount, then placed the boy in his arms. "You carry the lad, Alain. I'll take the woman."

The large knight grunted his acceptance and cradled the boy in one arm, holding the reins in the other. Despite his frightening visage, he handled Ottar with a gentleness that belied his great size and appearance.

To the younger one, the blond knight said, "Mathieu, check to see if any others are alive."

Emma was saddened by the deaths yet relieved not to have recognized any of the others who had fallen there. She was particularly glad not to have seen her father among the dead.

Her attention focused on Ottar, she experienced a tremor of fear at seeing his eyes still closed. She was about to object to being separated from him when the blond knight mounted his black warhorse, brought it swiftly to her side and reached down to sweep her into his lap.

She shrieked in protest. "Where are you taking us?"

"Wherever you like, lady. Lead on."

She breathed a sigh of relief, anxious to get Ottar home. But what if her father were there? She dismissed the thought. It mattered little at this point. For whatever reason, this knight, this Lucifer wanted to help. She must see the boy to his bed, no matter it would be a Norman who brought him there. No matter what payment he might expect.

The young one named Mathieu finished checking the bodies and called out to the blond knight, "The boy is the only one living, sir."

Grateful Ottar might survive and eager to get him home, once they were inside the city's walls, Emma directed them down winding alleys and paths that were away from the main streets. She had no wish to encounter either Normans or the rebel fighters.

CHAPTER 4

Geoff guided his horse as the woman directed. The large hound trailed beside the destrier, the dog's dark eyes anxiously watching its mistress. Geoff remembered the woman and her hound from the first day he'd entered York. He had never seen a more beautiful woman nor a dog so large. Even then, the image of them striding along together through the crowd had captured his attention. He was certain it was the same woman the hound stared at so intently. But this was not a day for her to be wandering outside of the city, even with such an escort. What had brought her to the clearing where a battle had raged? Mayhap she had been searching for the lad. Or a husband? Her headcloth told him she was married. Even so, it was foolishness for the woman to risk so much.

She had the most incredible eyes he had ever seen, even when they flashed in anger. Blue-green like the waters of the River Lune on a sun-filled day. She sat before him, wisps of her pale hair, freed from its plait, blowing across his face like gentle rain. With his arms on either side of her, leaving his hands free to direct his difficult warhorse chafing at its bit, she was forced to sit with her back tight against his chest. Her scent was fresh, like delicate herbs, reminding him the Danes bathed often.

He had not had a woman in his arms for a very long while, not since London in the days after the Conquest. Talisand had few wenches available for sport and Eawyn had never invited him to her bed. Now he had one of York's women in his lap, her buttocks tight against his groin, her female scent rousing his senses and causing his loins to swell. A woman he should not be drawn to but was. There was beauty in her face and spirit in her heart but he saw hatred in her eyes.

The city was quiet as they made their way through the back alleys and streets she directed him to take. The rebels that had survived William's army would be lying low now that York was once again in Norman hands with more than a thousand knights to maintain order.

They took a narrow passage between buildings that emptied onto a street of fine manor homes, much larger than the cottages he had seen elsewhere. "Stop here," she said when he nearly passed a large, two-story home.

"You live *here*?"

"Yea."

It was not the home of a peasant or a common villager. This was a rich man's home, on a street of rich men's homes. "This is your husband's?"

"'Tis mine," she said defiantly. "My husband is three years dead."

A widow. A beautiful, young widow. Was she, too, in love with her dead husband as Eawyn was?

He dismounted and reached his arms to lift her from the saddle. Reluctantly, or so it appeared to him, she accepted his help, putting her hands on his shoulders. Once she was standing, he took the lad from Alain and followed her to the front door.

Alain and Mathieu dismounted.

She knocked on the door. A man in his fourth decade answered and, by his simple tunic and leggings, Geoff judged him a servant. The man pulled the door wide and paled when his gaze fell upon Geoff standing behind the woman, holding the boy in his arms.

"Praise God you are safe, Mistress, but what has happened to the boy?"

Her voice wavering, she said, "Ottar is hurt. Prepare his bedchamber, Artur, and hurry."

The servant hastened to do her bidding.

With the lad in his arms, Geoff turned to Mathieu and Alain. "Take care of the horses, Mathieu, then come inside. 'Tis too cold to remain out here."

"There is a stable in the back," the woman said.

The squire nodded and headed for the rear of the house, the horses in tow.

To Alain, who stood silently waiting, Geoff said in a low voice, "'Twould be best if you, too, wait within."

Geoff followed the woman into the house and trudged up the stairs behind her and the hound to the upper floor where she led him to a chamber with two narrow beds. A small table was set between them, a chest at the end of each bed. It was simple in decoration but clean and the rushes, smelling of lavender, were fresh. Hanging on the wall were two tapestries picturing children in a field of flowers.

"You can lay him here," she directed, pointing to the bed with the cover turned back.

The servant he had seen earlier added a piece of wood to the fire that burned in the brazier and stirred the glowing coals. "'Twill be warmer soon, Mistress."

The hound settled himself next to the source of warmth, resting his head on his paws.

Once Geoff had laid the boy on the bed, he sat on its edge and began inspecting the boy for wounds.

"What are you doing?" the woman asked, her beautiful eyes shouting her concern as she removed her cloak and set it aside. Beneath it, she wore a deep blue gown that fit snuggly to her breasts and hips. Despite the anger in her eyes, she was an alluring sight.

He forced his attention back to the unconscious boy. "I am looking for wounds." He had seen the blood splattered on the lad's clothes, but no tear in the cloth. "The blood on his tunic is not his." He began to examine the rest of the boy, beginning at the top of his head. An egg-sized lump protruded from the side and Geoff's searching fingers found blood underneath the boy's hair. "I believe he was hit by the broad side of a sword. See the dried blood there and the large bump?"

She leaned closer and tenderly touched the spot. Turning to the servant, she said, "Artur, get me ice. It will be clean in the back of the house. And tell Sigga I will need water, salve and bandages."

"Aye, Mistress." He dipped his head and departed.

The woman began to undress the lad. When he was freed of the bloodstained garments, she threw them to the floor and walked to the chest at the end of the bed, drawing out a clean nightshirt. Seeing her intent, Geoff carefully lifted the boy's shoulders so she could pull the shirt over his head.

Her eyes flashed a protest but she did not stop him. He knew instinctively she would tolerate his presence, and his help, if only for the sake of the boy.

"Why do you help a boy your fellow knights left for dead?"

Why indeed? Had it been the woman? He might have noticed the lad was alive and taken him back to the castle, yet it was the woman he had rushed to help. "I would not see children die with men. He should not have been in the fighting."

"On that, at least, we agree."

A small girl peeked her head around the open doorway, a worried expression on her young face. "What is wrong with Ottar, Emma?"

Ah, the young widow's name is Emma.

"Ottar has been hurt, Finna, and I am caring for him." Her voice was much different when she addressed the child. It was the tender voice of a mother taking time to explain to her young daughter. But why did the child call her Emma and not Mama?

The servant, Artur, returned with the items Emma had requested. The little girl followed him into the room, stopping to pat the head of the giant hound, unafraid. The hound licked at her hand.

Bent to her work, Emma cleaned the boy's wound of dried blood, applied salve from a clay jar and wrapped a bandage around his head. The little girl walked to the bed and took the boy's hand in hers, her brow wrinkled in worry, a tear falling from her eye. The sweet gesture made him smile.

Geoff stole a glance at Emma as she leaned over the boy, concentrating on the last wrap of the bandage. The glow from the brazier caused tendrils of her hair to glimmer a pale gold. Her skin was the color of cream, her full lips enticing. Her waist was narrow and her breasts rounded and full. He did not doubt she was lovely beneath the gown.

She ignored him, occasionally shifting her gaze to the large hound as if she expected him to rise up and growl. But the hound lay content, not at all disturbed by Geoff being near her or the children. He had always liked animals and in his father's demesne in Tournai, hounds abounded, but none as large as this one.

Geoff was about to leave when the little girl came to stand beside him, her big brown eyes focused on his bloodstained hauberk. She glanced from his mail to his eyes, seemingly unafraid. "Are you the Norman Bastard Emma talks about?"

He held back a laugh, but his lips curved into a smile, his eyes darting to Emma. She fumbled with the bandages in her lap, keeping her head down. Because of the innocence with which the question had been spoken, Geoff was not offended, not even for his king. "Nay, Finna, I am merely one of his knights."

"Oh," she breathed, returning his smile. The child was charming.

Emma shot him a glance, her expression stern. "You should leave."

He rose. Mayhap he had stayed overlong.

She stood. Slowly she raised her head as if gathering her courage. "You have my thanks for bringing the boy home when I could not." It was clear she had been raised a lady, and her breeding would not allow her to be ungracious to one who had rendered help, even if he were someone she hated. Still, her hostility made it easier to take his leave. Had his reception been otherwise, he might have been tempted to pursue her. A strange thought given he was not looking for such a woman.

But he, too, could be gracious. He bowed before her. "Sir Geoffroi de Tournai at your service, my lady." He took a few steps toward the door, then paused and looked back. "These are perilous times. Should you ever have need of me, remember my name."

He turned on his heels and strode through the door, his spurs sounding loud in his ears in the silence that filled the chamber as he left.

⋆ ⋆ ⋆

Emma took a deep drink of her mead and let out a sigh as she stared at the pot of stew Sigga stirred over the kitchen fire while humming a Nordic folk tune as she worked. In her mind, Emma saw only the tall, fair-haired knight. She had not expected kindness from a Norman. Perhaps he felt guilt for the children slain? Had her father been one of those he had slain that day? Might it have been her father's blood on the knight's mail?

Sigga paused in her singing to dish out the stew.

Emma spoke her thought aloud. "I am glad my father was not here."

"Aye," agreed Sigga, her dark eyes shadowed by her head cloth, "'twould nay have been pleasant."

"But where is he? Many men from York have been killed and he has not returned."

"He will be fine, Mistress. Maerleswein is a strong man, good with a sword and a wise leader of men."

Emma stared at the shelves that held earthen vessels and baskets of herbs Sigga used in cooking, but she was thinking of her father. "Yea, and a leader of the rebellion, too," she said. "He would have been in the front of the fighting."

Sigga glanced up from the bowls of stew set before her. "Have no worry, Mistress, you will see him ere long."

Emma drew comfort from Sigga's words and idly looked around for Artur, not having seen him since the Normans left some time ago. In the morning, he was often with his wife.

Sigga's gaze met hers. "Artur has gone to the Minster to see how the old archbishop fares."

"I had not thought to worry about a man of God. Might the Normans seek to harm him or the church?"

"They will be taking vengeance wherever they can find it," said Sigga. "The Minster is large and will draw their attention. And some of the rebels may seek sanctuary there. We are fortunate to be so far from the center of town."

Emma shuddered at the possibility of harm coming to the church and the archbishop. While there were other churches in the city, to the people, the Minster was the most significant, the focus of their daily lives and their hopes for the next life.

Sigga offered her a bowl of the steaming stew. "Here, 'twill do you good. 'Tis cool enough to eat now."

Emma accepted the dish, warming her hands around it as she sat on a stool. Her strength was spent and the aroma of beef, thyme and coriander roused her hunger. It was the first food she had eaten all day.

"I can take some broth to Ottar and a bowl of stew for Finna while you eat," offered Sigga. "How is the lad?"

Emma had remained by Ottar's side until the boy roused. "He is awake but says little. No doubt his head pains him. Mayhap you can take him some willow bark tea with the broth. I will wait to question him until he is stronger." She took a spoonful of the rich meaty stew into her mouth. "'Tis good, Sigga."

The servant smiled her thanks as she went about fixing the tea. "All the boy talked about yesterday was wanting to see Maerleswein and his men."

"I suspected it was so," Emma murmured. "He must have followed my father to the battle outside the city walls. The lad admires him so. We will have to keep the twins from the streets. The Norman knights are everywhere now. I fear they are not done with their vengeance for the slaying of the noble."

"Aye, I will watch the children more closely."

Catching Sigga's eye, Emma remarked, "I saw the flag of their king and his army of knights with him." She shuddered at the memory of so many mail-clad mounted knights headed toward the city. "More Normans," she complained. "Mayhap thousands."

"Would they were all like the one who brought Ottar home," Sigga said thoughtfully. "A handsome one, he was, and kind."

"They are all Normans, Sigga. I would have none in our city and none in my home."

* * *

From the trestle table where he sat with Alain eating the evening meal, Geoff gazed beyond the crackling hearth fire and the ascending smoke to where Malet sat at the head table with his wife, Helise, and their two young sons. The hall was crowded with knights eating a dinner of roasted lamb. The low rumble of male voices in conversation filled the large space.

Helise's face, normally serene, was lined with worry. Geoff did not wonder at her concern, given what must have transpired between William and her husband. Mayhap Malet would not long hold the position of Sheriff of Yorkshire.

Alain shifted in his seat, his eyes following the object of Geoff's interest. "William appeared none too happy when he took his seat at the dais and now he glares at Malet between sips of wine."

Geoff looked at his friend. "You speak uncommonly much this night." The knight the Red Wolf had dubbed "the Bear" for his size was known for speaking in grunts and growls more often than words.

"I speak when I have something to say."

"Which is not often," Geoff teased. "But I do not doubt the truth of your words. 'Tis certain Malet earned a stern rebuke, though being a friend of the king, I expect it was delivered in private."

"Likely while we were seeing the injured lad home."

"Yea, likely so." Suddenly the vision of the beautiful York widow ministering to the boy returned to Geoff's mind. Despite her hostility, he was anxious about her living alone with only children and servants while the streets of York swarmed with knights, men-at-arms and mercenaries looking for trouble, looking for women to ease their battle lust.

Returning his attention to his meal, he stabbed a large piece of meat and brought it to his trencher. She would not have listened to him had he tried to counsel her.

The Bear slid him a mischievous glance. "From what I observed, that woman you aided did not like you much."

Geoff tossed a piece of bread at Alain's chest. "She liked me well enough for a Norman, you dolt."

"She could use your protection were you to give it," said Alain, more seriously. "With William's army combing the streets, there will not be a woman left untouched in York."

Geoff let out a breath. "Leave it be, Alain. I want no woman and Emma of York would have no Norman." *Though I would give her my protection whether she asked for it or not.*

"None of the English women want Norman husbands," argued Alain, "but Serena accepted the Red Wolf and my own Aethel was finally persuaded to wed with me. In time, there will be many such matches."

"The York widow would be near impossible to win."

"That which comes with much effort is more highly prized," Alain declared thoughtfully.

"You begin to sound like Maugris, my friend."

"I have learned a few truths since coming to England."

"Oh?"

"It does nay take Maugris to see the only wives for French knights are English unless the women come from France, like Helise Malet."

Geoff cast a glance at the woman sitting beside her husband. "'Twould be a rare knight who brought a wife with him." He laughed at what came to his mind. "We brought only horses and squires."

Geoff drank his wine in silence after that, watching the king and his companions on the dais. It appeared that William had recovered from his dour mood. He was now in jovial spirits laughing with his friends.

"I heard talk of William building a second castle," said Alain, his eyes on the king.

"Yea, William spoke of it as we rode toward the city. I imagine the good people of York who were not killed in the fighting or escaped into the woods will be pressed into the work."

"'Tis his way," observed Alain.

"Did you happen to notice who is sitting at the dais with the king?"

Alain glanced at the table at the front of the hall. "Aye, I recognize the older one, William FitzOsbern, the Earl of Hereford. He is the companion of the king who came with him to Talisand last year. But I do not know the other."

"The younger one is Gilbert de Ghent. I encountered the Fleming as I was going to my chamber when I returned from the widow's. He told me he's being sent by the king to Durham with a group of his Flemish mercenaries to chase down the rebels fleeing north."

"No good can come of that," observed Alain. "Like wraiths, the rebels can hide in the woods. 'Tis what they always do."

"No matter. William is intent on chasing them down."

* * *

It was night when the knock came at the front door. The sound was faint and Emma, who had been sorting through some tapestries in her chamber by candlelight, was not even certain she had heard it until Magnus scrambled from the floor beside her and went to scratch at her chamber door.

"All right. I am coming." She threw on her robe and opened the door of her chamber. Magnus raced down the stairs and scratched at the front door.

This time the knock was a mere thump and then a sound like something falling against the door.

Emma took one look at Magnus and realized whoever was on the other side of the door was someone he knew. He whined and did not growl, so the late hour visitor could not be a Norman soldier.

She unlatched the door and a sobbing Inga fell into her arms.

"Inga!"

The girl trembled as she clutched her cloak tightly to her body.

Emma wrapped her arms around her. "What is it, Inga? What has happened?"

One look at Inga's face told her questions would have to come later. The girl's eyes were wide with fear, her cheeks tear-stained. She was incapable of speech.

Still holding Inga, Emma shut the door, making sure it was locked. Wrapping an arm around the girl's waist, Emma helped her to the stairs. "Come, I will take you to my chamber."

Together, they stumbled up the steps, Emma helping the young woman whose strength appeared to be at an end. As they neared the top, Inga tripped and nearly fell. Emma gripped her more securely and together they managed to reach her chamber. Magnus followed closely behind. He had known Inga since he was a whelp. She was family.

Emma helped the girl to the bed, gently laying her upon it. Inga mumbled, "He returned... oh, Emma, he came back."

"Who returned, Inga? Who?"

Inga's terror-filled eyes fastened on Emma, telling her without words who it was. She remembered the French knight from the day he had accosted her friend outside Feigr's shop on Coppergate. Eude, the tall, burly Norman with dark hair and a heavy jaw. A sudden loathing came over Emma, fueling her rising fury. Seeing the bruise on Inga's face, Emma could imagine what had happened.

Artur had apparently heard the commotion, bringing him to her chamber. "What has happened, Mistress? Do you need help?"

"Aye, I need Sigga's hemlock and wormwood potion that warms and brings sleep. Inga is hurt and needs rest."

He took one look at Inga, curled into herself on the bed, and departed.

Emma took off her fur-lined robe and draped it over the young woman, then sat on the bed next to her, holding her hand, waiting for the potion to arrive. "Inga, can you speak?"

Inga's hand was cold despite the heat from the coals in the brazier and the warm robe covering her. "My father... Oh, Emma. The Norman was not alone. The men with him beat my father when he tried to protect me, before the Norman...." She broke off and shut her eyes tightly as if trying not to see the images that haunted her. "The knights who came with him took my father prisoner. I am afraid of what they will do to him." Then with a shudder, she added, "At least he did not see my shame."

"Oh, Inga." *It was as I feared.*

On the young woman's face, the bruise seemed to darken. She had obviously been struck. Her heavy, golden hair, always neatly confined to a long plait, was loose and tangled.

Artur returned with the potion, a bowl of water and a clean cloth. "Thank you, Artur. I had not thought to ask for the water and cloth, but they are needed. I must bathe the dirt from her face." Emma would not mention what had happened to her friend. Artur was a man who had lived long enough to understand what a young woman like Inga might have suffered but he would say nothing. The terrible truth would remain a secret.

"Do you need aught else, Mistress?"

"Yea." A plan was already forming in her mind. "Once Inga is asleep I will need to borrow a gown and cloak from Sigga. And then I would ask Sigga to sit with Inga. I am going out but I will let you know when I leave."

"You would leave the house tonight?" He sounded aghast.

"I must."

"Do you want me to go with you?"

"Nay."

"You must take care. The Normans will spare no one. Keep to the shadows." His countenance fell in resignation as he turned to go.

She called after him, "Artur?"

He paused at the door. "Yea?"

"Do not mention what you have seen here to anyone save Sigga."

He nodded and left, closing the door behind him.

Emma helped the stunned girl to drink the potion that would send her to sweet oblivion. Then she waited for it to take effect.

Once she was certain Inga was deep in sleep, Emma removed the robe she had placed over Inga. Carefully, she peeled back the edges of Inga's cloak and gasped. Inga's tunic and shift had been torn from neck to the hem, leaving her naked and exposed. The girl would have been no match for the Norman. "He forced you, the bastard," she hissed under her breath. Inga's small breasts were bruised and there were more bruises on her hips and slim thighs. And blood. It was caked in streaks on her skin from her woman's center halfway down her thighs. The rampaging beast had hurt her, hurt her badly.

A sudden rage rose within Emma. *He will pay for this.* If she could find a way, she would see him dead for what he had done.

As tenderly as she could, Emma cleaned the blood from Inga's young skin and wiped the streaks of dried tears from her cheeks.

Once she had finished bathing Inga, she gently pulled the torn gown from under the girl and took one of her own shifts from the chest at the foot of the bed. After some difficulty, she was able to put it on Inga, thinking it would be best if she did not wake to see the bruises on her breasts and hips. She would surely feel them, but at least she would not have the sight of them to remind her.

The torn and soiled garments Emma took downstairs and burned in the hearth fire. She was standing over the fire, watching the soiled clothing turn to ash, when Sigga met her with the tunic and the cloak that would disguise Emma as a servant.

"The clothes you asked for, Mistress."

"Thank you, Sigga. I will return them."

"Are you certain you are doing the right thing, my lady?"

"Aye, I must save Feigr if I can."

Sigga's gaze followed Emma as she climbed the stairs to her chamber. Setting the clothing aside, she carefully combed the tangles from Inga's hair using her own carved wooden comb, then tucked the cover around the girl and smoothed the hair from her forehead.

Tears fell as Emma faced the stark reality: Inga might look innocent in her sleep, but her innocence was no more.

Once she had made Inga as comfortable as possible, Emma dressed in the servant's clothing. Sigga had given her the best tunic she had, a crimson one she kept for special days. It was so like Sigga not to want her mistress to be seen in the ones the servant used to prepare their meals. Still, it would serve. It was looser than her own fine gowns and would mask her slender curves.

Wrapping Sigga's cloak around her against the cold night air, she set forth, bidding Magnus to stay. She would not take him with her lest he growl at some knight and be slain. Her errand was one of mercy.

Sir Geoffroi had offered her his service. She would test the sincerity of his offer, risking much to save Inga's father. Even entering the den of Lucifer himself.

CHAPTER 5

For some reason he could not explain, instead of returning to his chamber after the evening meal, Geoff lingered to observe the knights and men-at-arms gathered in the hall. Leaning against the rear wall, not far from his chamber, he crossed his arms over his chest, and watched the men dicing, drinking and telling stories of their encounters with the rebels that day.

They were a rough lot, some having newly joined William's army, among them Flemish mercenaries who came for the plunder and the freedom to pillage. They were the most dangerous of William's men for they cared not what destruction they left behind them. Surely they had been the ones responsible for the boys who had been killed.

A cloaked figure moved in and out of the shadows, drawing Geoff's attention. Though the hood mostly covered her head, he could see it was a woman. By her apparel, a serving wench, but she carried herself like a lady. As he studied her more carefully, there was something familiar about her. It was the way she walked with confidence, her head up, her shoulders back. *The young widow... Emma*! The only thing missing was the hound. Why had she come to the castle where so much danger threatened a woman alone?

In the flickering light of the torches, she gazed anxiously around the hall, searching the faces of the men as if looking for someone. Suddenly her eyes fixed upon one of the mercenaries and she froze. Like the Valkyrie he had first imagined her, she glared at the knight as her hand moved slowly beneath her cloak to her hip. In the same manner she had reached for her knife that morning when he'd come upon her in the clearing.

Geoff knew the mercenary she was staring at, a man he heartily disliked, a braggart whose mouth was never silent. Sir Eude de Fourneaux.

It took him but a moment to realize her intent.

Striding toward her, Geoff grabbed her arm beneath her cloak. Their eyes met and at once he discerned her intent. "Do not, lady. Else he would see you dead."

"I did not come for him, though I would kill him if I could. I came to seek your help if your offer is still good."

Before he could assure her it was, the man whom she had stalked focused his attention on them.

"What vision is this, Sir Geoffroi? We could happily use another wench this night. One to sheathe my most worthy sword." Eude's words were slurred with the drink he had consumed, but his meaning was clear enough.

Eude's friends laughed and shouted for Geoff to remove Emma's cloak. "Let us see the prize you have there!"

Without taking his eyes from Emma, Geoff said, "I saw her first, Eude."

"You could share," came the lazy retort.

In her eyes, Geoff saw both fear and determination. She would not shy from murder, but with the knights' attention drawn to her, she knew she was in grievous danger. Conversations broke off as men at the tables paused to observe the confrontation.

Into the silence, he said in a commanding voice, "I never share."

The mercenary rose, a few of his companions with him. Geoff reached for Emma, pulling her against his chest. She was slender and her resistance fleeting against his knight's strength. "If you would be spared their lust, do not fight me," he whispered.

He claimed her mouth as an act of possession, a demonstration to the assembled knights that she was his. But when their lips touched, it was he who was claimed. Her mouth was soft and inviting, the taste of her as sweet as summer wine. The attraction he had felt for her before now surged in his veins. Urging her lips open, his tongue found the warmth within. She responded. In the honey of her kiss, his rising passion was echoed in his loins. Alone in their own world, the kiss continued.

Hearing the jeers behind him, he broke the embrace, though it cost him to do so. Breathing heavily, he stared into her beautiful blue-green eyes.

She shifted her passion-filled gaze to the floor.

Turning to the knights, who had slowed their approach, he announced, "As you see, the lady is mine, I have claimed her."

"Leave off, Eude," urged one of the man's friends. "'Tis Sir Geoffroi you challenge, a favorite of the king. He is the right arm of the Red Wolf and his sword is just as deadly."

At his words, Eude and his companions lost interest in their mission and returned to their table.

"There are plenty of wenches in the city," Eude blustered.

At Geoff's side, Emma stiffened.

He waited until he was certain the other knights would not pursue them, then escorted her to his chamber, his arm tight around her shoulder.

Once inside his chamber, he dropped his arm, walked to the table near the brazier and poured her a goblet of wine. "Here," he said, handing it to her.

With unsteady hands, she took it and drank, her chest rising and falling with apparent emotion. She had been more nervous than he had initially thought. Mayhap more afraid. Or was she also moved by the kiss they had shared?

No matter the cause, her presence worried him. Such a beautiful woman should not be out alone, much less in a castle full of men with too few whores to share. He took in her clothing, that of a servant and ill fitting. "What could you have been thinking to come to the castle? And how did you gain admittance?"

Holding the goblet between her hands, she stepped to the brazier as if seeking its heat. "I came as a servant. The guards gave me a bit of trouble but apparently the need for serving wenches is great. I answered their questions and they admitted me."

His brows drew together at the ridiculous notion. "No one would see you as a servant, even in those clothes."

"Your guards are not so discerning as you," she said dismissively. "And mayhap not so sober."

"Where is that great beast that usually follows at your heels?"

"I left him at home. I feared he might be speared by one of your French swords."

"And so he might have been. As might you." It concerned him that she had been so foolish. "Why did you come?"

"To seek your help in saving the life of a man taken prisoner. But when I saw the knight called Eude, I could think of nothing else but to kill him for what he has done." When he raised his brows, she explained, "He raped my friend, Inga, the daughter of Feigr, the sword-maker. When her father tried to protect her, Eude's companions beat him and took him prisoner. I assumed they brought him here. I would free him and see Eude dead."

"And your life would be lost in the process had you been successful with the mercenary."

"My anger has cooled but only just," she said, setting down the goblet and turning to pace. "The man deserves to die!"

"Aye, likely he does. I would not put rape past him. I like him not."

She paused in her pacing to gaze at him. "Inga was young, untouched," she explained, her distress showing on her face. "Feigr's only child and much loved."

"What would you have me do?"

Her beautiful, tear-filled eyes fixed on him, desperation in their depths. "Find Feigr, save him, protect him, as I will now protect Inga."

Seeing her tears, he could deny her nothing. "All right. But you must stay here until I locate him."

"My family will worry. Ottar is still recovering and now I have Inga to see to."

"I will send my squire to tell them you are safe. Latch the door after I leave. When I return, listen for three knocks. I myself will take you home."

He went first to Mathieu to dispatch him to Emma's house, to tell her servants she was safe. Once that was done, he went looking for the sword-maker. He found him with the other prisoners who had been taken that day, now sequestered in a building in the outer bailey.

* * *

Emma paced in Sir Geoffroi's small chamber, keenly aware she was confined inside the Norman castle where the French knights gathered like wasps around a hive.

The smell of metal, leather and horses filled the room, a masculine smell she recognized as belonging to the blond knight from when he had carried her home from the clearing earlier in the day. The candles set about the chamber made it seem somehow intimate and, because it was the abode of a Norman knight, more threatening. Could she trust him to find Feigr and bring him to safety? Did she have a choice? She could not very well leave on her own now that the creature Eude knew she was here. To approach him had been a mistake. She would not have succeeded in killing him. Sir Geoffroi was right to scold her. Surely if she had killed Eude, the other knights would have killed her. But the mad impulse had seized her when she recognized the monster who had raped her friend.

She touched her fingers to her lips, still swollen with Sir Geoffroi's kiss. Since his reason for kissing her had been to protect her, she did not resent it. But she had not expected to like it so well. His mouth had been gentle on hers and his tongue… *Oh God.* The memory of his seductive tongue exploring her mouth made her tremble even now. Had it only been for show? Mayhap he had kissed many women. The thought did not please her.

When he had taken her into his arms, she had felt protected, not threatened. It disturbed her that she should find a Norman so desirable. She did not like that her reaction to him seemed to steal away the hatred that gave her the strength to fight. She did not like the way her body still craved his touch.

Her pacing stopped. Would he help her to take vengeance on the one called Sir Eude? She suspected the answer was no. But if she could leave with Feigr, if he were still alive, then she would have accomplished her purpose in coming. The rest she could see to another time.

Some minutes later, three knocks sounded at the door. She unlatched it and pulled it open.

Sir Geoffroi strode into the chamber.

Closing the door behind him, she asked, "Where is Feigr?"

"You did not expect me to bring a rebel prisoner to the hall where the king himself dines?"

"No, I suppose not," she said, disappointed. "But did you find him?"

"Yea. Alain is guarding him now. We will collect him when we leave the tower. He is too weak to ride alone."

She inhaled sharply. "Will he live?"

"I cannot say what injuries lie beneath his skin. He has been badly beaten and his body is all cuts and scrapes. He might have a broken arm as well, for he cradles it close to his chest. I have asked the king's physic to see what can be done."

"Poor Feigr. He was only trying to protect his daughter. Inga will be despondent."

"William does not countenance rape but even he cannot control so many knights and men-at-arms. Some are mercenaries with no care for anything save what they can gain. 'Tis a bad time to try to protect a young woman in York."

She could tell by his expression he included her in his statement. As she considered what had happened after the battle the full scope of the truth came to her. Inga was likely not the only woman raped by the Normans this day. She shuddered. "When do we leave?"

"Now if you like, but we may have to wait for the physic to complete his work."

She drew her cloak around her, eager to leave and wanting to assure herself Feigr would be well.

"Keep your hood pulled over your head, stay close to me and do not look at the men."

Emma was only too happy to oblige. She had seen the lust in the knights' eyes when they had discovered her in the hall. Never did she want to draw their leers again. They were like the hungry wolves that hid in the forest.

When they reached the part of the bailey where prisoners were housed, the knight with the scarred face, the one called Sir Alain, waited for them with horses. Torches illuminated the bailey and the face of the huge knight. He no longer appeared so formidable to her, his scar now merely part of a familiar face.

"The physic is near finished," he informed Sir Geoffroi. "The arm was broken, but not the flesh. The physic has set the bone."

With anxious eyes, Emma looked up at the huge knight. "What does the healer say about Feigr? Will he recover?"

"If it is God's will, lady. Only time will reveal the outcome." His voice was surprisingly kind. "Some of the sword-maker's wounds are inside, but the physic was encouraging. You should know he does not usually see prisoners, but Sir Geoffroi asked on your behalf and, given the circumstances, he did not refuse."

Emma turned her gaze to the blond knight. "You have come to my aid once again. Why, I cannot imagine."

"Can you not?" he whispered. His blue eyes teased but she detected a seriousness there that belied the laughter in his eyes.

"If your interest is in me, sir knight, it is misplaced."

He took her hand and kissed her knuckles, sending a shiver coursing through her, making her breasts tingle. "We will see, my lady."

She turned her eyes from his intense regard and pulled back her hand. "No matter, I am in your debt once again. Thank you."

"I will always come to your aid," he said.

The connection with the French knight embarrassed her. She had sought his help so she could hardly fail to thank him, but there was more between them than his kindness and her gratitude. There was that kiss she could not forget and the unmistakable attraction that grew with his nearness. She was more conscious of his presence than other men.

She waited until the Norman physic was done and the knights had collected Feigr. They rode across the bridge over the castle's moat, she in front of Sir Geoffroi on his chestnut stallion and Feigr with Sir Alain on his huge gray horse. Mathieu, the squire, had returned from his messenger duty to ride with them.

Sir Geoffroi's mailed chest was hard at her back and his powerful arms braced her as he held the reins of his horse. His head was so close to hers she could feel his breath on her temple. She had not been this close to a man, save her father, since her husband, Halden. Remembering Sir Geoffroi's kiss, her heart quickened its pace. Halden had loved her but had not kissed her like that.

A moan from Feigr drew her attention to where he slumped against the chest of the huge knight. The sword-maker's eyes were closed and his bandaged arm rested in a sling across his chest. Only the arm of the knight kept Inga's father from falling.

Before they had left the castle, she had explained to Feigr that Sir Geoffroi and his companions had aided her and were taking him to her home. But his eyes had been glazed from the pain-dulling potion the physic had given him and she could not be certain he had understood her words.

She was grateful for the blond knight's help. Whether his motives were pure she did not question. For now, she needed him and so did Feigr. She would take him at his word and hope he did not betray her.

As they rode through the city, an eerie silence pervaded the town. The only sound was that from the horses crushing snow and ice beneath their hooves. Above them the stars appeared like sparkling jewels scattered over a midnight blue cloth. In its center was a pale half-moon.

There were no townspeople on the streets, no laughter from taverns, no light from cottages. The men of York who had not been killed had escaped into the woods or were in hiding, their homes closed to all. She did not dare think of the women.

Now that the tension she had held inside for so long had subsided, exhaustion overtook her. The wind blowing off the ice made her shiver despite Sigga's cloak. Sir Geoffroi must have felt it for he drew her back against his chest and wrapped the edges of his cloak tightly around her. It was a caring gesture, one she had not expected from the enemy. She gave in to her desire to be sheltered in his arms and rested her head on his shoulder. *What makes him so different than the others?*

The street was dark when they arrived at her home. No light came from behind the window coverings of her neighbors' dwellings.

Artur admitted them and Magnus came to nuzzle her hand. "Sorry, old boy, but it was safer for you here."

Standing next to her husband, Sigga raised her brows. "Safer for him mayhap, but we were worried when we saw you had left the hound behind. The squire, Mathieu, brought us word you were well and with his master."

"I could not take Magnus where I was going," she said, as Sir Geoffroi followed her inside.

Sigga looked from Sir Geoffroi to Emma and raised her brows with what Emma knew to be a fellow woman's insight. Sigga and Artur might be servants but they were her family, too.

Sir Alain carried Feigr into the house. She was impressed with the huge knight's strength for Feigr was not a small man. Her two servants raised their candles high and stared wide-eyed as Sir Alain passed them.

Emma directed him up the stairs and to the chamber her father used. The knight laid the sword-maker on the bed and stood back.

Artur and Sigga then went to work, first lighting candles and stirring the fire in the brazier, then stripping the soiled and bloodstained clothes from Feigr, carefully lifting his bandaged arm. He moaned when they touched it.

"His arm was broken," she said to Artur, "but Sir Geoffroi asked the physic at the castle to tend him. He set the bone and gave Feigr a sleeping potion."

Magnus strolled into the room and sat at her side, his dark eyes watching the servants.

Neither of the Norman knights commented on the few things her father had left behind in the room he usually occupied, but they had to wonder at the extra shield, a pair of boots and a few pieces of his gold jewelry he had left on the shelf. The light from the candles made the gold glisten. Of course, there were more of his things they could not see in the chest at the foot of the bed.

Emma turned to Sir Geoffroi. "I must see how Inga fares. You need not stay." She knew her servants would be uncomfortable with the Normans in their home. Emma was not at ease with their presence either, though she was coming to realize Sir Geoffroi presented no threat.

"I will remain until I am assured all is well," he remarked and sent his fellow knight, Sir Alain, to wait below with the squire.

Emma slowly walked to her chamber and opened the door, keenly aware Sir Geoffroi followed close behind her. A warm light from the coals in the brazier allowed her to see Inga still slept. She paused for a moment and then closed the door.

"When she wakes," she said to Sir Geoffroi, "it will comfort her to know her father is near and his wounds have been tended. Once again, I am in your debt. You have carried those I love to safety."

"As I told you, my lady, you may call upon me anytime."

In the dim light of the passage, his blue eyes appeared like pools of dark water, his lips curved in a seductive smile. Against her will, she was drawn to him, attracted to his courage and his kindness, no matter he was a Norman. When he smiled, as he did now, his chiseled jaw softened, along with the look in his eyes. Underneath his smile, she sensed there lay a man of unfailing strength and an iron resolve.

Her husband, Halden, had been a free-spirited adventurer who loved the sea. Sir Geoffroi was a steady river whose waters ran deep.

"I hope I will not need to ask you for aid in future," she told him. Pulling her thoughts away from his eyes and his lips, she walked toward the twins' chamber. Weariness settled into her bones, but she had to look in on them before she retired.

"Do you know if the sword-maker was among those fighting today?" he asked.

"I doubt it. Feigr may be a supplier of swords but as far as I know, he has yet to raise one against anyone, let alone a French knight. He is an artist, devoted to his craft and to his daughter. But after what happened to Inga, he may have a new use for his swords." Even to her own ears the words sounded like an accusation. She was frustrated she had not been able to sink her blade into the flesh of the man responsible.

The knight was silent for a moment, then his gaze met hers. "I am sorry for what happened to your friend. Any of the Red Wolf's knights would feel the same, but then Talisand is a very different place."

"Talisand?" She could not recall hearing the name before.

"My home, two days' ride west of here. 'Tis a very pleasant shire where both English and Normans live together in peace."

"I cannot imagine it."

"Given the violence you have witnessed, I can well understand."

Reaching the twins' chamber, she silently opened the door and peeked in, Sir Geoffroi looking over her shoulder. Magnus, who had followed them, padded in and sniffed at the children. Both slept, the white bandage around Ottar's head clearly visible in the light of the glowing coals in the brazier. She tiptoed into the room and kissed each child. Retreating quietly to the open door where the knight stood, she waited for Magnus to join her and then pulled the door closed.

Sir Geoffroi scratched Magnus' ears in a gesture that was oddly reminiscent of her father's affection for the hound.

"'Tis good the children sleep," she whispered.

"How is the lad?"

"He seems to be well. I have chided him for following after the men. I do not think he will be so foolish again. Not after he endured his sister's tears. They are twins, you know."

"Nay, I did not know but I did observe they were about the same age."

The light in the narrow space in which they stood was dim and the knight was very close, his shoulders nearly spanning the corridor. When he dropped his gaze to her lips, without thinking she opened her mouth to expel a breath. Heat flowed between them. He wanted to kiss her, she could feel it. For a long moment, neither said a word.

"You are very beautiful, Emma. Be careful." Then he clenched his jaw and turned, walking toward the stairs. She was amazed when Magnus followed him.

She did not move at first, but watched him walk away and felt a pain in her heart she had not felt in years. A remembered parting. The memory of saying goodbye to Halden the last day she would ever see him as he blithely stepped onto his ship and sailed away. Would she see Sir Geoffroi again? Did she want to? He was a Norman, after all, one who had killed some of her countrymen this very day. Yet he was an enemy who had shown her kindness. No other man had caused her to want again something she had once lost.

She and Halden had been young when they came to realize their love for each other. They had wanted to marry then, but her father had bid them wait. And they had. They were wed but a year when Halden died. A trader whose other loves were his ships and the sea, it had been those other loves that had taken him from her. When his ship was lost in a storm, she had been so distraught, she lost their babe she had only recently become aware was growing within her. Halden was her only love and she had thought not to wed again. With Ottar and Finna, she believed her life full. Now she had to wonder.

She followed the knight to the stairs. As she had once missed Halden, she would miss Sir Geoffroi and the sound of his knight's spurs in her home. The realization was troubling. She hardly knew him.

Suddenly curious to know what his king would do in York, she asked, "What will happen now?"

He paused and looked over his shoulder. "William would have another castle."

A sigh of frustration escaped her lips. She hated the wooden edifice that stood above the river at the south end of the city, a symbol of the hated Norman king. "A castle the people of York will no doubt be forced to build."

He ignored her statement and paused at the top of the stairs. "Stay away from town for the next few days, Emma. William's army will be seeking revenge for the death of FitzRichard and until they are gone, no woman will be safe."

She thought of her friend lying hurt and defiled in the bed where she herself would sleep this night. "Your advice is well-taken."

"In war, not many innocents are spared," he said with a glance in her direction as he descended the stairs to where his men waited, the sound of his spurs on the steps ringing in her ears.

She watched them leave, wondering if she would see the blond knight again.

The Normans had just departed when a knock sounded. She unlatched the door, thinking it might be Sir Geoffroi returned but, instead, her father suddenly loomed before her, looking exasperated.

He crossed the threshold with a long stride. "I thought they would never leave! I saw their horses and have been huddling in the freezing cold, waiting. Why were the French knights here? Did they threaten you?"

She kissed her father on the cheek. "Nay, they did not. 'Tis late and you look tired." Letting her eyes rove over his tunic, stained with Norman blood, she added, "You will want to wash. Why not do that while I fetch you some mead and find you somewhere to sleep. Feigr is in your bed. Then I will tell you what has happened. Tomorrow you must tell me what you have seen. I've been worried."

* * *

"Did you notice the things scattered about the chamber where I laid the sword-maker?" asked Alain when they had returned to the castle. Geoff had called for wine that he, Alain and Mathieu now shared.

The hall was nearly vacant, only a few knights and men-at-arms lingered over their wine, having finished their evening meal. The celebration of the day's victory was largely over.

Geoff turned his goblet in his hands, the rich ruby color of the wine reminding him of the tunic she had worn.

"Yea, I saw them. 'Twould appear the servant, Artur, is not the only man living there."

"Has the woman mentioned a husband?" Alain asked.

Geoff took a drink of his wine and set down his goblet, his gaze meeting Alain's. "She told me she is three years widowed. But now I am forced to consider she harbors a man in her home, mayhap one of the rebels."

"A lover?" questioned Alain.

Geoff felt a scowl building on his face.

"Or a brother," suggested Mathieu. "He occupies a separate bedchamber, does he not?"

A brother! Geoff remembered what he'd seen in the room and his frown returned. Emma now shared a bed with Inga, mayhap to bring the girl comfort. "Whoever he is, he is a large man."

"How do you know that?" asked Alain.

"The shoes he left behind were as long as mine."

"What do you know of her?" asked Alain.

"In truth," admitted Geoff, "very little. By her appearance, I would judge she is in some part Danish. Emma of Normandy, you will recall, married the Dane who became King of England."

"Aye," said Alain. "And this Emma must be a woman of some wealth to have such a fine home. 'Tis twice the size of any cottage and with many bedchambers."

"And there is a stable, but 'tis not large," added Mathieu.

"She is also a caring sort," observed Geoff. "The children who live with her are not hers. She has obviously taken them in. And the girl, Inga, and the sword-maker are now under her care as well. 'Tis a house of the recovering and she the one who graciously cares for them out of her charity. Not many would help strangers with such open hands."

"The lad I carried back from the forest, is he one of the children?" asked Alain.

Geoff pictured in his mind Ottar and his twin. "Yea, and you have yet to see his sister. She is a shy little angel."

"Would William be angry if he knew we had helped the lady?" asked Mathieu.

"Aye, if she houses a rebel," said Geoff. *And if the king knew his knight would willingly help her no matter she did.*

* * *

"What of the uprising, Father?" Emma sat on a stool at his feet by the hearth fire, her chin resting on her upturned hands, her elbows on her knees. They had just finished breaking their fast. Finna was with her brother, who was still recovering, and Inga was with Feigr. They had not been able to speak over the meal, but now they were alone and Emma was eager to hear his version of the events of the day before. "Tell me what happened."

He sat back, running his hand through his long hair, bleached by the sun. He wore a fresh tunic of dark green, belted with fine leather to which was affixed his seax, a longer one than her own. In his hand was a goblet of mead.

"We were not ready," he said with a sigh. "The retreat that followed the first encounter was disorderly, an embarrassment. Many were killed." He took a drink of the honey wine.

She reached out a hand and touched his arm. "I am saddened for their families." She remembered the bodies she had seen in the clearing and shuddered. Mayhap some who were killed in the fighting had been those she knew. "Have we lost so soon?"

"Nay, Daughter, 'tis not over." He took another drink.

"What will you do?"

"Today Cospatric and I leave on my ship, anchored in the Humber, for King Swein's court. We will urge him to send the ships we asked for. Edgar has agreed to join us. From there, we will go to Scotland to see King Malcolm and gather new recruits to our cause."

"So there will be more trouble in York." She spoke with mixed feelings, knowing more battles would mean more dead, yet wanting desperately to see her people shake off the Normans, for they had all been made serfs with the coming of the Conqueror.

"If we are to gain our freedom, Daughter, how can it be otherwise?"

Seeing his goblet was empty, she got up and poured him some more. "I suppose you are right," Emma admitted, worried for him and the people she cared for. "How long will you be gone?" She sat again on the stool.

He fingered his beard. "I cannot say. Mayhap for the summer. Look for me when the grain grows ripe."

Her spirits fell. "So long?"

"It will require time to sail to Denmark and then to Scotland. And more time to bring order to our purpose. We cannot risk another defeat. We must draw our allies to us."

"You mean the Danes?" Though he had been an English high sheriff and a wealthy thegn, Emma knew they traced their lineage to the Danish kings so it was not surprising her father would seek his allies among them.

"Yea, the Danes. We must have King Swein's ships and men. And there will be others who will join us. Even now Edgar prepares messages he will send all over England, urging rebellion." At her concerned look, he hastily added, "The Danes will come, Emma. You will see. Swein believes he was promised the throne of England. York was once the capital of the Danish lands. He will not give that up so easily."

Her gaze drifted to the flames in the hearth. "Kings and their promises! Too easily given, too easily withdrawn. It seems Edward the Confessor promised many the throne of England, including the Norman Bastard who vexes York. At least he claims it was promised to him."

"Aye, well there are many opinions on that. Besides, York is special to the Danes. The other Yorkshire thegns and I are fortifying sites on the Humber to be ready to receive them."

His face exuded confidence now, no longer was he the discouraged man he had been for some time.

"Father, how much more can the people endure?" She was thinking of Feigr and Inga when she asked, but also of Ottar's young body on the snow-covered ground and the other dead she had seen. "So many have been wounded, so many gone from this life."

"They will have to endure more if we are to have our freedom. The Normans have ravaged York, Emma. Even the Minster has been made the object of scorn for they violated sanctuary to take some of our men. A church, by God! You told me yourself what Inga and her father have suffered. I have heard worse tales of the Normans' brutality. We cannot allow such outrage to continue."

She dropped her gaze in resignation. He was right, she knew it.

"Yesterday," her father continued, "after the Normans defiled the Minster, the archbishop still urged us to submit. It was a pathetic and wasted entreaty. None of the men who were there would agree. Ask Artur. He was among them."

"I believe you, given what I have seen… Ottar, Inga and Feigr." How could they submit to those who would hurt innocents?

"They will be avenged, Daughter. Do not lose hope."

Emma rose. "If you must leave today, at least I can see you have clean clothes and a hearty meal to take with you."

CHAPTER 6

Two days later, in the cold, chill air of a morning without sun, Geoff watched from the top of the motte as the building of the second castle began, this one on Baille Hill on the opposite bank of the River Ouse. They were close enough he could hear men shouting orders to the workers as they formed a huge pile of dirt into the mound from which the square tower would rise. Behind him in the bailey of the older castle, the loud clash of metal and shields sounded from the practice yard.

Seeing Northumbrians forced to join in the building of the new castle, he remembered Emma's words. And the regret in her beautiful eyes as she spoke of her people being forced to build yet another symbol of William's reign.

In her home lived a man who was more than a servant. A tall man, most likely for there had been a shield. Could such a man defend her against knights like Sir Eude? He banished a sudden image of a man sharing her bed. Nay, whoever the man in her home was, Mathieu must have the right of it—'twas a brother she had failed to mention. If not a brother, mayhap an uncle or a cousin.

Emma was three years widowed. 'Twas possible her husband had died before the Battle of Hastings. If that were true, at least she would not hold Geoff responsible. Was it not time for her to marry again? He thought of Eawyn, so different from Emma of York, and yet both widows. And both had suffered at the hands of those seeking to conquer England. If he were to pursue the beautiful York widow, would she rebuff him, as Eawyn had? He would not vie with a ghost for her attention.

In the distance, hundreds of men swarmed over the mound that would become the new motte like ants on honey, moving dirt to the desired shape. Emma would be pleased to know it was not only Northumbrians who had been forced into the work. Some of the men were from William's army. To one side of the men working, piles of new wood were neatly stacked. Such a horde of workers would soon make use of the timber. The king was obviously in a hurry.

At the sound of boots crushing the thin layer of snow, he turned to see Malet coming toward him. Geoff raised his head in greeting and gestured to the work underway. "'Tis a furious pace the men set to build William's new castle," he remarked to the sheriff.

Malet nodded and took his place beside Geoff to watch the construction. "William expects the castle to be finished before he leaves for Winchester where he would celebrate Easter."

Geoff shook his head. "That leaves little time."

"Less than a fortnight before he must depart for the South."

As he looked out over the city, Geoff pondered what the people of York might be thinking. "William demands the people of York accept his rule," he mused. "Do you believe they will?"

Malet crossed his arms over his chest and looked beyond the rising castle. "I know not, but having seen the stubborn resistance in their eyes, I doubt it. Many of the rebels have fled into the woods where they hide among the trees. We believe some went north to Durham. Their leaders remain at large."

"The rebels and their leaders will no doubt return." The realization made Geoff lose hope for peace in York.

"Mayhap even this year," Malet added in a somber tone.

"I understand William has sent Gilbert and a group of Flemings to Durham to root out the rebels there."

Malet shrugged. "You can hardly blame him. Durham supplied men, arms and money to the rebels in York. The king would see them all dead."

"Mayhap Gilbert will be successful and the rebels will no longer trouble us."

"We will see," said the sheriff. "In any event, William has made Gil the new castellan, so he will remain in York when he returns."

"The king needed another after FitzRichard's murder." Geoff remembered the morning the foolish castellan had been killed by the angry rebel throng and ruefully wondered if the men from Durham had done the deed.

Malet looked at him with sudden interest. "What about you, Sir Geoffroi? What task is yours?"

"I am to hunt with my knights to add to the storehouse of meat for William's army. Sir Alain readies the men even now."

"Feeding William's army is a worthy task and will keep you busy with so many mouths to satisfy. The pigs and cattle from the surrounding countryside will soon be exhausted. Roast venison, boar and hare stew will be welcomed by the men."

Geoff loved to hunt but he didn't relish being the supplier of food for so great an army. "Others will surely hunt as well. Not all William's men will be building the new castle or searching out rebels."

"You can be glad the king will leave within a fortnight, taking his army with him. Will you go as well?"

"My men and I are to remain in York," said Geoff, not unhappy at the prospect because of Emma.

Malet grinned. "Then I shall look forward to seeing more of you."

"Aye." Geoff said, as he waved his goodbye and headed toward the bailey.

* * *

Emma stole a glance at Inga as they broke their fast together. Days had passed since the rape, and while the girl's body was recovering and the bruise on her face was fading, she still woke at night screaming in terror. Though hidden from view, the violent taking of Inga's innocence would leave scars that would remain forever. It was those deeper wounds of the soul Emma feared the most for her friend.

Inga drew her arms tightly around her body as she stared at the bread before her, trembling even now, mayhap tormented by thoughts of that night.

Emma reached out and touched her hand. "You are safe here, Inga. And your father recovers. In time, you will both be well, you will see." Knowing Inga worried about her father's livelihood, she added, "Artur has seen that Feigr's shop is secure and your servant knows you and your father are here."

Inga turned, her gray eyes looking at Emma. "You have been kind to do so much for us. I only wish the terrible dreams would leave me. I wake in the night with frightening pictures in my mind, my body drenched in sweat. Oh, Emma, I shall never forget."

She would not lie to her friend. In her experience, the truth, while painful, was better handled than a lie. So it had been when she was told of Halden's death. "No, I do not expect you will. But, in time, that memory will fade, replaced by other, happier ones."

Inga reached for some bread. Emma was glad to see she was eating. In the first days after the rape she had refused food.

Watching the young woman with her emerging beauty, Emma recalled the young men of York who had flirted with Inga when her father's head was turned. The flirting had been a harmless foreshadowing of the courting that would soon follow. Inga was pretty and many young men had noticed. Would those young men still want Inga now that her innocence had been taken and her body befouled by one of the French knights? Or, would they pity her but refuse to take her to wife? Emma was determined they would not know, for it was certain they would reject Inga if they did. She had seen it happen before. Inga had been an innocent victim, but no decent man would want as a wife a tainted woman.

Sigga entered the room carrying a tray laden with bowls of steaming gruel. "'Tis well your hound hunts, my lady. Even if Artur would allow me to go to market, I hear the stalls are bare. What the fleeing rebels did not take, the Norman soldiers devour."

Emma was thankful for the provisions they had stored and the meat her hound put on their table. "It's as if Magnus knows to do his part. He keeps us well stocked with hares. As long as our few chickens lay eggs, we'll have those, too. When the weather warms, we can plant vegetables."

"We've enough stored for stew till then," said the cook. "And there is hope the Norman king and his army will leave. Surely he has business elsewhere. Saxons to slaughter in Wessex mayhap." The last of her words had been spoken sarcastically, Emma knew. None of them wished the Norman king on the English in the South.

"I imagine half of England is in rebellion against him," Emma said, glancing at Inga eating her gruel. She did not have to remind the girl that Eude would likely remain when the army left since he had been garrisoned in York with the building of the first castle.

Suddenly, Ottar exploded into the room, followed by Finna at a slower pace. They climbed onto the bench seat at the large trestle table across from the two women. Ottar's eyes roved over the steaming oatmeal and his countenance fell. "Gruel again?"

"'Tis what we have now," Finna chided her brother. "At least you have food."

Emma marveled at the wisdom coming from one so young, but Finna had always been older than her years. Smiling at the girl as her brother dove into his gruel, Emma said to Ottar, "There is plenty of fresh bread and butter. We'll have hare stew for dinner and tomorrow there will be eggs."

His eyes fastening on the pot of thick golden syrup on one side of the table, Ottar shouted, "And honey!"

"Aye," said Inga, seemingly cheered by the young ones. Directing an encouraging smile at Finna, she added, "And honey."

* * *

A sennight passed and to no one's surprise, not the least of which was Geoff's, the king announced he would see the new castle rise on Baille Hill before he took his army south. Thus spurred on, the building proceeded at a furious pace and Geoff and his knights were ordered to continue their daily hunts in the forests of York.

They had been hunting nearly all day when Alain, looking at the ever darkening sky, remarked, "'Twill be gloaming soon. What say you we take the four deer, the hares and the boar we have and retire from the field?"

Geoff chuckled and turned to see Mathieu with one of the red deer strapped behind his saddle. "Yea, I have been seeing a goblet of wine and a juicy slice of venison in my mind for the last hour."

With his raised arm, Geoff drew the men to a halt. Just as he did, the wailing sound of a wounded animal rent the air, sending an eerie shiver down his spine.

"What in the name of Saint Peter is that?" bellowed Alain.

"'Tis not far, sir," observed Mathieu. "Do you want me to go see?"

Geoff hesitated, thinking. The sound had been an eerie one, not easily identified. He remembered that rebels hid in this same forest.

"Hold, Mathieu. Let us go together. I would see this for myself." Geoff ordered the other knights to take their bounty back to the castle, while he, Alain and Mathieu remained. He waited until the sound of thundering of hooves died away, then urged his companions deeper into the woods. "Come, let us see what beast cries from the forest."

They walked the horses through the underbrush of the dense stands of pine. The wail turned into a long trailing howl as the beast shrieked its suffering.

"There!" shouted Mathieu. "Across that dense hedge, 'tis a wolf caught in a trap."

Through the thick foliage, Geoff caught a glimpse of fur, a rough, dark gray coat of a large animal. "'Tis no wolf," he said, "'tis Magnus, Emma's hound, or one just like it. Looks like his leg is caught in a snare."

Geoff cautiously walked Athos nearer to where the giant hound was desperately gnawing at the snare around its back leg. Between them was a thick hedge of tangled undergrowth. With every movement of the hound, he imagined the snare tightening, causing the hound more pain as it cut into his leg. Already, blood dripped from where the wire had sliced into its flesh.

"Poor beast," murmured Mathieu from behind him.

"Aye," acknowledged Alain. "If we had not found him, the hound might have chewed off his leg trying to escape. Wild animals do, you know."

"Or the wolves may have taken their revenge," suggested Geoff, dismounting and slowly walking toward the hedge that was between him and the hound. He would have to crawl through the underbrush. Dropping to his hands and knees, he began to push his shoulders through the hedge. A wave of anxiety flowed over him as the darkness of the thick bushes closed about him. He hated places that were closed in with no light. It reminded him of that time when he was a boy. Refusing to think of it, he closed his eyes and pushed through. Thankfully, after only a short distance, he emerged into light.

Rising, he took off his gloves and tucked them into his belt. The experience in the dense bushes had left him sweating. Aware his companions were watching, he wiped the sweat from his brow and walked to the hound and knelt. He reached out his hand, still uncertain if it was Magnus. The hound's eyes were wild with fright. If it were Magnus, he hardly looked himself.

From behind him, Alain urged caution. "Best be careful, he may bite. He looks mad with terror."

"Magnus," Geoff softly spoke to the hound. "You know me, Magnus. Do not fear. I will free you."

At his voice, the hound calmed. His dark eyes, looking more like those of Magnus, intelligent and keen, followed Geoff's every move.

He extended his bare hand to the hound's nose, letting him sniff. A wet tongue lapped at his fingers, telling Geoff he'd found Emma's dog. Pleased at the trust shown him, Geoff patted the rough fur on Magnus' head. "'Tis all right, boy, I will soon have you free."

"You've a way with the creature, sir," Mathieu said, dismounting. "May I help?"

"First, I must free him and see the damage the snare has wrought."

Geoff looked at the bloody leg just above the rear paw. He drew his knife from his waist and sliced through the thin wire. Magnus whimpered and when the hound realized he was free, tried to rise, but unsteady on his wounded leg, he fell to the ground with a groan and commenced licking the wound.

Geoff sat and lifted the leg onto his lap. "Let me see, Magnus." The hound did not resist but moaned. The wound was bad and if not tended, could result in the hound losing the leg, or worse.

Alain circled around the bushes and forced his way through the thick underbrush. He came to Geoff's side and crouched, handing Geoff a cloth. "Here, take this for the bleeding."

Geoff wrapped the cloth snugly around the hound's leg, all the while speaking encouraging words as Magnus watched him with his dark, trusting eyes.

"Mathieu, hold Athos." With a huff, Geoff lifted the large hound into his arms. "He's as heavy as his mistress."

Alain's mouth twitched up on one side. "Surely that can be no burden."

Geoff rolled his eyes.

Content now that he had been rescued, the hound lay pliant, resting his large head over Geoff's shoulder.

"Aye, Magnus, you are among friends," Geoff said, avoiding another wet kiss from the beast. He followed Alain through the opening the huge knight had found in the thick brush. Walking to Athos, Geoff said, "If Magnus will allow you to hold him, I can mount and then take him."

At Alain's nod, Geoff carefully handed Magnus to him. The hound allowed it as if he knew what they were about.

Geoff quickly mounted and accepted the hound across the saddle, settling him onto his lap. "We shall return Magnus to his mistress." With his free hand, he turned his horse back toward the walled city.

"Emma will be grateful," observed Mathieu.

"That was my fervent hope," Geoff mumbled, a grin forming on his face.

* * *

Emma paced in front of the hearth fire, her eyes darting from Magnus' empty pallet to where her cloak hung on a peg near the door. "I must search for him," she said to Artur, who stood close by, as worried as she was. "He has never stayed away so long. It will soon be dark. Something must have happened."

"I can go, Mistress," Artur bravely offered.

"You cannot ride. And I may have to go a great distance to find him in the forest. 'Tis best I go."

Making a decision, she grabbed her cloak from the peg near the door. "I cannot say how long I will be gone, for I know not where he hunts. You and Sigga feed the others their supper while I am away."

"Do you want me to saddle Thyra?"

"Nay," said Emma, "I can do it."

Artur shot her a concerned glance that told her he wanted to scold her for going out at this hour, but he did not. He had been with her long enough to know when her mind was made up there was no stopping her.

She unlatched the door and heard the sound of pounding hooves. Stepping out of the door, she saw three knights riding toward her, slowing their horses as they approached. *Normans.* One had the straw-colored hair of Sir Geoffroi for he wore no helm. Across his lap he carried... *Magnus!* She nearly cried out with relief. Tears filling her eyes, she ran to meet the three men.

"Magnus! Oh, Sir Geoffroi, you found him!"

Magnus gave out a bark and joy filled her heart. The hound was alive. But the blood-soaked cloth around his leg told her he was hurt.

The one she recognized as Sir Alain dismounted and came around to Sir Geoffroi's horse to accept Magnus into his arms. Sir Geoffroi swung his leg over his saddle and slid off his horse, reclaiming the hound.

The squire, who had also dismounted, gathered the reins of the three horses.

"I think you know where the stable is at the back of the house," she told him. He nodded and headed around the house.

"What happened?" she asked Sir Geoffroi as he carried Magnus through the door she held open.

"Caught his leg in a snare."

"Oh, Magnus," she murmured softly, reaching out her hand to stroke his head.

Sir Geoffroi asked, "Where do you want him?"

"You can lay him on the pallet next to the hearth where I can see to his injury."

He and Sir Alain entered and she pointed to the straw-filled pallet near the fire. "Just there."

Sir Geoffroi laid Magnus on the pallet and she closed the door behind the men as the twins came bounding down the stairs.

"'Tis Sir Geoffroi," said Finna.

"The one who carried me home?" Ottar asked, his gaze taking in the tall mail-clad men. Emma had explained to the boy that it was Sir Geoffroi who had brought him home from the clearing and that the knight was a most unusual Norman.

"'Tis him," said Finna. "He is one of the Bastard's knights. He told me so himself."

Sir Alain covered a cough with his hand.

"Finna!" exclaimed Emma. She had forgotten to tell Finna not to use that name for the Norman king even if it was truth.

Sir Geoffroi chuckled. "Hello, Ottar, Finna." Pointing to Alain, he said, "This is my friend, Sir Alain. I do not think you met him Finna but he was with me when we brought Ottar home."

Finna nodded shyly.

"What happened to Magnus?" inquired Ottar as he stared at the blood-soaked bandage on the hound's leg.

"He caught his leg in a snare," said Sir Geoffroi. Rubbing his lower back, he remarked, "That beast is no light thing."

"Yea," Emma admitted, kneeling next to the dog, "he's full grown now and large even for an Irish hound."

Magnus' tail thumped the ground as his mistress stroked him and the children came to watch.

Emma liked how Sir Geoffroi was with the twins, more tender than she would have expected a hardened knight to be. And he had carried her beloved hound back to her. He might be a Norman but she was now thrice in his debt. How could she be so ungracious as to not welcome him into her home?

"Sit," she said from where she knelt next to Magnus, gesturing to a bench by the hearth. She sent Sigga, who had come into the room, for some mead. To the knights, she said, "You must stay and share some mead."

Sir Geoffroi cast a glance at his companion who nodded. "Aye, we will gladly stay."

Emma shrugged. Normans were in her home again. And for some reason their presence this time did not disturb her. Thank God her father was on his way to Denmark. He would never have accepted the fact there were French knights who did not live to rape and kill.

* * *

Geoff drank deeply of the sweet honey wine Emma's servant had brought him, warming his body in front of the hearth fire. The French did not prefer the drink but they had served it at Talisand a few times.

Mathieu returned from seeing to the horses and joined them.

The hound looked up at him from where he lay on the pallet with his sad, dark eyes, apparently content with Emma's attention as she lovingly removed the cloth around his leg and inspected the wound.

Magnus whimpered.

Emma gasped. "The cut is deep."

The twins leaned over the hound's leg. "Will he be all right?" Ottar asked.

"It has not cut into the bone," she assured the lad. "If I can stop the bleeding, and the wound does not fester, he will heal."

Geoff did not envy the hound the nasty gash but he did envy the attention it was getting from the fair, young widow. Seeing how skillfully she cleaned and dressed the wound, he was reminded of how she had tended Ottar. "You seem to know what you are about."

Not looking up from where she worked on the dog's leg, she replied, "I have tended a man's wounds more than once."

He was curious to know what man she had tended. The one with the large feet? Or, mayhap her husband. But he did not ask. "Your hound is a strong one," he remarked, watching her plait catch the light of the fire, turning it golden. The thick braid flowed down the back of her dark blue gown as she bent over her hound. He imagined her flaxen hair coming unraveled as he took her in his arms and kissed her. His body responded, his loins swelling with desire. Shaking off his wandering thoughts, he reminded himself that despite his attraction to her, she was a proud Northumbrian woman. And, at the moment, they were sitting in her home, surrounded by her family.

When Emma finished tending the hound, the twins took her place on either side of the beast, and began stroking its fur. Magnus laid his head in Finna's lap and closed his eyes.

Emma came to sit beside Geoff, which pleased him greatly. Alain sat on his other side and Mathieu next to Alain. Her eyes fixed on the twins and the hound, she said, "Thank you again for bringing him home. I was not sure I could find him."

He could not have explained it if asked, but Geoff felt very protective of her even though she was not his to protect, even though she harbored hatred for his king. "I would not have you wandering through the forest in search of the beast. 'Twould not be safe, especially this late in the day."

She turned her beautiful eyes on him. "I did not want to go, knowing it would soon be dark, but I could not leave him alone thinking he might be hurt."

"Does he often hunt in the forest?" he asked.

"Yea, more so now that food is needed. He brings home hares nearly every day, proudly dropping them at the door."

"I will gladly supply you with meat, Emma," Geoff said. He would supply her with more, were she to ask. But for now, at least he could see that she and her household were well fed.

The servant, Sigga, refilled their goblets.

Mathieu took a drink as Geoff said to him, "Before we leave, take the deer from your horse and give it to the lady's manservant."

"Aye, sir, I will."

After all, Geoff mused, he and his men were doing the hunting for the king. It would not be difficult to see this family had sufficient meat to sustain them. And it would give him an excuse to see her again.

"We are grateful for the deer," said Emma, "but will your king allow you to feed a York family?"

"My knights and I hunt each day," he told her. "You can have the deer. We took others my men carried back to the castle. 'Tis not like we are feeding rebels." Something flickered in her eyes just then, causing him to wonder. Could the man she harbored be a rebel? Could she be one herself? He remembered the knife she would have wielded against Eude. But from what he had seen, there had been no women among the rebels. "The king would not object to my providing meat for women and children as long as I continue to feed his army."

"Will you and your men stay for the evening meal?" she asked. Then with an amused smile, "We've plenty of hares for stew."

He shot an inquiring glance at Alain and Mathieu. They had expected to eat venison, but the deer they would give Emma would take too long to prepare. He was hungry, as always, and happy to see Alain and Mathieu nodding.

Geoff turned his attention back to Emma. "Aye, and thank you."

She rose, crossing before him, her enticing curves drawing his attention. A woman of her character and beauty was rare. London had its beautiful women and he had not been unmindful of their charms directed at him. There were available women at Talisand, too, but none were like Emma of York.

"Feigr is still abed with his injuries," she informed him. "'Tis best he not know I entertain Normans. I will ask his daughter, Inga, to join us, but I must first tell her you and your men were the ones who rescued her father, else the sight of a French knight will make her fearful, as you can imagine."

"Yea, I can. Are you certain we should stay?" He had no wish to upset the young woman.

"It may not be easy for her, but 'twould be best if she meets you. I have already told her not all Normans are like the one who attacked her."

"I am glad to hear you say that, my lady." He remembered their first meeting in the clearing when she had been angry and spiteful. "It gives me encouragement."

She did not see the smile that came to his lips. Instead, she turned and, without a word, went up the stairs, leaving him to wonder if the missing man whose large shoes he'd seen would also be joining them for the evening meal.

* * *

Emma returned to the hearth room with Inga. Sir Geoffroi knelt beside Magnus with the twins on either side of him. The children listened attentively as he explained where he had found the hound and how he had freed Magnus from the snare. Her heart warmed. *Such an unusual knight.*

She introduced Inga, who was shy around the men, but walked with Emma to the table. In one corner of the room was a bowl of water set on a small table. Next to it was a clean linen cloth.

"Wash up, children," said Emma.

Finna obediently stepped to the bowl and washed, then dried her small hands.

Ottar followed. Shooting a glance at Sir Geoffroi who had come to the table, he said, "She makes us take a bath every Saturday, too."

"*Everyone* takes a bath on Saturday," Finna reminded her brother.

When Emma and Inga washed their hands, Sir Geoffroi announced, "We will wash our hands as well, Ottar. 'Tis needed." He winked at Finna.

"Here," said Sigga, bringing another bowl from the kitchen, "clean water for you and your men."

Once the hand washing was complete, they took their seats on the benches that were on either side of the table, the knights and the squire on one side and Emma, Inga and the twins on the other. Candles flickered in the center of the table as Sigga dished out the steaming stew into bowls. Artur poured more mead and brought fresh baked bread and butter, making Emma's stomach rumble. She watched covertly as everyone in the room crossed themselves to acknowledge their gratitude before the meal, including the Norman knights. Her heart warmed to see their rough manly courtesy.

"I will be glad when I can once again buy food from the market," remarked Sigga.

Emma nodded her agreement and turned her gaze on Sir Geoffroi, watching him as he spread a generous amount of butter on his bread, licking his lips. He obviously loved to eat. "Venison is a boon we did not anticipate. The deer will keep us in meat for many days."

"My men took several deer and a boar this day," said Sir Geoffroi. "'Twill be no hardship to leave one of the deer with you."

"How long will your king and his army remain in York?" It was the question that had consumed her mind in recent days. She did not doubt it was a question Inga thought of, too. Emma's father would have wanted to know had he been here. She was glad he was not. How could she introduce the knights to her father, a leader of the rebels?

He set down his bread and took a drink of his mead. His sun-streaked hair glistened in the candlelight. Her gaze shifted to his chiseled jaw that softened when he laughed, which was often. She was so absorbed in watching him, when he spoke he startled her.

"'Tis been a sennight since William arrived in York. Word in the castle is that he will depart soon. The king would be in Winchester by Easter."

She picked at the vegetables in her stew, then raised her gaze to meet his. "Who will he leave in charge? The same one as before, William

Malet?"

"Malet is still sheriff and helping with the castellan duties but, because of recent events," he shot a side-glance at his fellow knight, "the king's friend, William FitzOsbern, is now charged with keeping the peace."

How prudent of him not to describe the recent events. "I do not know of him."

"He has long been with the king, but I only met him last year at Talisand."

At the mention of the name she had heard him speak before, she cast a glance at his companions. "Are you also from this place Sir Geoffroi speaks of, this Talisand?"

"Yea, my lady," said Sir Alain, taking another piece of bread to dip into his stew.

Mathieu nodded and, looking at Inga, said, "'Tis a beautiful place with its own river."

Emma had purposely seated Inga across from young Mathieu, who appeared to be a few years older than the sword-maker's daughter, thinking he would be less threatening than the knights. Happily, she was right. The young squire was polite and solicitous of Inga, offering her bread and pouring her wine when her goblet was empty, but speaking little. In some ways, he was as shy as she was. Despite all she had endured, Inga responded to his gentle nature, even offering him an occasional smile. Their exchanges encouraged Emma to believe Inga would one day be able to put behind her the tragic events of the recent days and eventually view men without terror.

When they finished their meal, the knights thanked her and rose to leave. Emma was reluctant to bid Sir Geoffroi goodbye. It was a strange feeling, knowing he was the enemy, yet she found it difficult to think of him as such. His easy laughter and kindness made him seem less an enemy and more a friend. She had not always had such laughter in her life. She had loved Halden, but he had not been a man who laughed easily. Being with Sir Geoffroi was like sitting next to a warm fire on a cold night.

"I am sorry to take your leave, my lady," he said, "but the hour grows late and we will be expected. Hopefully with the king's departure, we will not have to hunt so often, but I promise to keep your table in meat, so you can confine that hound of yours to the house while he heals."

Her gaze drifted to the hearth where Magnus was asleep on his pallet. "Mayhap he has learned his lesson with snares."

Ottar came to bid the knights and their squire good eve, his eyes focused on their swords hanging at their sides. She worried he was a bit too fascinated by the knights' weapons. It had been the boy's longing to see the men fighting that had drawn him into the clearing that terrible day.

Finna gave Sir Geoffroi a small wave from where she stood with Inga several feet from the men. The knight waved back. Sir Geoffroi and Finna had made some kind of connection, just like he had with Magnus. He was the only Norman that Magnus had ever warmed to. To most he was indifferent, to others hostile. The knight's two companions had certainly not drawn the hound's affection as Sir Geoffroi had. It was yet another sign of the knight's being unique.

Once Mathieu and Artur had brought the deer around to the other side of the house for Artur to butcher, the Normans departed. Emma felt a pang of regret as she watched them ride away. If she were honest, she would have to admit Sir Geoffroi was becoming more than a friend.

She closed the door and, sending the twins to their chamber, went to join Inga standing near the hearth. The girl was less pale than she had been in the days following that horrible night. "How are you, Inga?"

"I am all right. He was kind."

Emma knew Inga referred to the squire. "I wanted you to see they are not all alike. Even I have had to learn that among those who would kill and maim are those who would help and heal."

Inga raised her eyes to Emma. In their gray depths, she sensed confusion. "But how is one to know?"

"All men are known by their actions," Emma counseled, inwardly giving herself the same advice. "And observing those takes time. Even with that, we can never forget the French knights are sworn to serve their Norman king."

Inga nodded and her gaze drifted up the stairs. "I think I will look in on Papa. He was sleeping when I left him but he may have heard us talking. He will want to know who was here."

"He would like to see you," said Emma, knowing the girl's father worried about her and did not like for them to be long separated.

"I do not think I will mention your guests were Normans," said Inga thoughtfully. "He would not be pleased to know that."

"Yea, you speak truth. He might try to rise from his bed to claim justice no matter these Normans were the ones who helped him."

Inga nodded her acceptance and turned toward the stairs.

"I will see you in a short while," said Emma. "I want to see if Sigga needs any help and then I will make sure the children are in bed."

Emma's gaze followed her friend as she ascended the stairs to the bedchamber Feigr occupied. Then Emma set about her nightly chores, all the while thinking of Sir Geoffroi. In her mind, she saw the creases that formed at the corner of his eyes when he laughed. She remembered his kiss, too, and it sent warmth rippling through her. His gift of the deer would see them well fed. 'Twas unusual for a knight, hardened by war, to have such a tender side. She thought of the wistful look on his face when his fellow knight and squire spoke of Talisand. Could such a place exist where Normans and English lived together in peace? Surely it was only a dream.

* * *

The next day, Geoff stood at the top of the motte, breathing a sigh of relief at seeing the king's procession pass through the gate. William, apparently satisfied his new castle was rising sufficiently from Baille Hill, left for Winchester with his army and FitzOsbern.

Gilbert de Ghent, the new castellan, departed shortly after with his Flemish mercenaries in tow, bound for Durham. Far better they should stalk armed rebels than the innocent maidens of York.

Once the two contingents of soldiers had gone, Geoff went to the bailey where he was to meet his men.

"I was surprised to see Malet is still sheriff," Geoff said to Alain as they mounted their horses, preparing to leave on a hunt. Today they would hunt wild boar, something they were becoming quite good at.

"Yea, William needs him. But the king is taking no chances on another failure. I overheard him tell FitzOsbern that he is to return here after Easter."

Geoff signaled to his men and led them through the gate. He did not worry overmuch about the comings and goings of William's favorites. There was still a garrison of knights that remained. He hoped the city would soon come back to normal. He and his knights would hunt less often and mayhap he could visit Emma more frequently. The last time he had been to her home had given him hope she might one day entertain his suit. To have a summer wooing the Northumbrian widow was a pleasant thought, bringing a smile to his face as he and his men headed for the forest.

CHAPTER 7

Jelling, Denmark

Maerleswein brushed the snow from his hair and cloak and stepped into King Swein's hall, its ancient timbers glistening with ice. He knew many of the Danes that were gathered around the central hearth fire. He raised his hand in greeting as he drew near to the fire to warm his hands. They had to know why he came. Did they look forward to sailing their ships to England once again?

He watched from that vantage as Cospatric and Edgar bowed before the king, here to answer his questions about the aid they sought for Northumbria.

The Danish king reclined in his throne chair. He was regally attired in a crimson tunic with golden belt, his red-gold hair adorned with a bejeweled crown. His long legs stretched out in front of him like a lion in repose. Yet the king was anything but calm, for as he stroked his beard, his brows drew together in a frown.

Edgar appeared like a young Adonis, his head of fair curls and his wispy short beard reminding all of his youth. Still, he could have been King of England after Harold Godwinson, save for the coming of the Norman Bastard.

Beside Edgar was Cospatric, who still commanded the respect of the Northumbrians, despite the fact he no longer held the title that gave him authority over them. But Cospatric was still Earl of Bamburgh, his ancestral home north of Durham.

King Swein's restless stirrings shouted his growing impatience. "Yea, your messages were received," he said to the two men, "asking for our ships and men. We are well aware of what you need."

"The uprising will fail without your support," explained Cospatric.

The king hesitated. Did he fear the same fate that had befallen his Norwegian ally, Harald Hardrada? Before William arrived in England, the King of Norway had sailed to York to fight Harold of Wessex but the Norwegian king never returned. King Swein had been there to witness Hardrada's death. And while Swein had survived, he now walked with a limp.

It had been three years since Maerleswein had seen the Danish king. At fifty, he appeared to have aged a decade; his red beard was now liberally laced with gray. Mayhap he no longer relished the fight. Maerleswein was not young either, but his body was still that of a warrior and he eagerly anticipated the battle that would set Northumbria free.

"King Edward promised us the throne of England," Swein informed them, "but we have heard he made the same promise to others. It is *his* fault England was left in so much confusion that at Harold Godwinson's death, the Norman Bastard was able to claim the throne. And now," the king looked at young Edgar, "you ask us to carve a kingdom out of what is left and give it to this Ætheling?"

Edgar cringed.

Cospatric, looking aghast, took up the argument. "We ask only for ships and men to free Yorkshire, My Lord."

"The heart of the Danelaw, you mean," said the king.

Maerleswein did not have to remind Swein that while they might speak of Yorkshire and an independent Northumbria, William had claimed all of England. It was on both their minds, for the two of them had shared a private conversation before the public audience began.

"Maerleswein," the king had said as they walked in the falling snow, their cloaks dappled in white, "We like not installing a mere youth in a seat of power with William's unfettered ambition running wild."

"Edgar will unite the people of England, Sire," argued Maerleswein, "and not just the Northumbrians. Rebellion spreads in the south. Hereward, my fellow Lincolnshire thegn, has returned from Flanders, now a soldier. He is appalled at what has happened to England in the years he has been away."

"Hereward has returned?"

"Aye. A Dane proficient with an axe." Maerleswein was certain he detected a glimmer of excitement in the king's eyes at the news of Hereward's becoming involved. Both respected him.

After that, he and the king had walked together for a while, sharing stories of Hereward. It was these Maerleswein was certain the king pondered as he listened to the English nobles now arguing their case.

To Cospatric, King Swein said, "You would have young Edgar standing before us named King of England?" The king's eyes roved over the young, fair-haired Saxon not even twenty yet heir to a throne that might never be his, and then returned his gaze to Cospatric whose noble lineage was apparent in his high forehead and firm jaw and the way he carried himself. "Yea, we can see you do." The king shrugged. "We are not opposed to such an arrangement for the time being. Better you, Edgar, than the French Bastard."

It was a large concession and boded well for the alliance Maerleswein had sought. He was glad he'd spoken to the king privately beforehand.

King Swein leaned forward. "What will you do if we agree to send our ships?"

"Once we have your assurance," said Cospatric, "we will go to Scotland to seek allies in our cause, men who will fight with us, mayhap even King Malcolm."

King Swein's gaze fell upon Maerleswein, his brows raised in question.

Maerleswein stepped forward. "We have many allies there," he assured the king, "including Cospatric's cousin, young Waltheof, Earl of Huntingdon. King Malcolm, too, has been most encouraging."

The king sat back, his chin in his hand as he rested his elbow on the arm of his throne. "You shall have the ships you seek," he said, stroking his beard. "But I will not go."

"Then who?" asked Cospatric in disbelief.

The king surveyed his hall, well decorated with weapons of war and his many sons, fifteen in all but only one born in wedlock. His gaze paused on a man with his same red-gold hair and beard, standing to the side. "I will send my brother, Osbjorn, and my sons, Harald and Cnut, with enough men and ships to assure we have our vengeance for the death of my warriors who fought in King Harold's war."

Osbjorn stepped forward from the shadows, a lesser man than the king in Maerleswein's opinion, for he doubted the brother's resolve. But the two sons in their third decade, who came forward to stand before their father, had his same appearance and were considered worthy fighters. Maerleswein would have to content himself with three blood relatives of the king to vouchsafe the strength of the alliance, though regrettably, the king himself would not attend.

Osbjorn bowed. "It will be as you say, my brother."

"Take with you Christian, the Bishop of Aarhus. He can pray for your venture's success."

Before they left for Scotland, Maerleswein had the king's promise he would send at least two hundred ships by summer's end that would carry his Danish warriors and weapons to York.

"It will take that long to see so many built," King Swein had told him. "Longships of solid oak are not made in a day."

Maerleswein departed with his companions, pleased. *It might just be enough to rid the North of the hated Normans.*

* * *

York, England

Surrounded by a field of yellow and white flowers, Emma stood with Inga on the hillside outside the city walls as the twins happily frolicked nearby with Magnus. Both Ottar and the hound had recovered from their injuries and now wore no bandages. Magnus' movements were as lithe as before yet his leg bore a scar from the snare.

Emma relished the warmth of the morning sun on her face as it rose above the trees of the distant forest like a great beacon. In the distance lay pastures planted with new seed and the apple orchard that would bear a rich bounty in the fall.

A soft breeze blew loose strands of her hair across her face and she brushed them away to watch the flock of curlew birds circling overhead. Spring had finally come to York.

It had rained last night and the ground was still wet. Emma loved the smell of the damp earth and harvest time when that same earth brought forth the life-sustaining grains and fruit. She was a creature of the land, she admitted with a smile, not the sea as Halden had been, yet she had loved him with a young girl's passion.

In the far distance, Emma could see the ewes with their lambs. Just that morning, her villein, Jack, had come to tell her of the new lambs dropping each day. "'Tis a bountiful crop this year, m'lady."

"We will pay you and your good wife a visit this afternoon to see them," she had told him. "They always bring the children great delight."

Weeks had passed since the Norman king had left with his army, raising the spirits of all in York. Yet despite the warm sun, the calm meadow and the promise of seeing the lambs, a passing cloud brought Emma a sense of foreboding, reminding her the peaceful respite could not last, not with her father and Cospatric gathering forces to seize York. Not with the people still chafing at the Norman rule, anxious to join him.

But today she was determined not to think of those things.

Finna, her basket in hand, left Ottar and Magnus and ran to Inga, tugging on her arm. "Come pick flowers with me, Inga!"

It was clear Inga wanted to go but was reticent. She had been particularly shy since the rape. But in some way Emma could not explain, Finna understood Inga's sadness and her need for some lighthearted revelry.

Inga looked to Emma as if seeking her assent. Emma nodded enthusiastically. "Go! But beware, Finna will not be satisfied until you have picked half the field!"

The two ran off together laughing and bent their heads to the task. It cheered Emma to see Inga smiling again. Finna could make anyone feel treasured by her little girl ways. Inga was not immune.

Feigr was recovering, now able to get around and attend his shop, but he was bitter and angry. Inga, who still lived with Emma at Feigr's insistence and Emma's happy agreement, was more fearful than angry. In time, Emma hoped both could leave behind the memory of that horrible night. But she had her doubts.

The church often forced a young woman such as Inga to marry her rapist, but even if he knew, Emma did not believe the archbishop would force Inga to accept such a fate. Ealdred was too old and too weak for the people to follow his advice in such matters. Half the town of York would rise in protest if he even suggested such a thing. If all the maidens who had been taken against their will were avenged, it would become another uprising, mayhap one already in the making.

Emma looked behind her to where she could just see the top of the square tower of the first Norman castle. The Bastard king and his army might be gone but his garrison of knights remained, soon to be spread between the old tower and the new castle that appeared to be nearly finished. Yet in those hated castles dwelled one who was a bright light.

True to his word, Sir Geoffroi had kept them supplied with meat even after the market had reopened and butchers once more cried their wares from their stalls. Besides the boon of food, she liked seeing him and his broad smile at her door more than she would admit. He made no demands upon her, though sometimes she sensed he longed for more than the tentative friendship that had grown between them. Did she, too, want more?

She had shared the meat he provided with her neighbors who complained that Normans had brought it. If her father had not been a leader of the rebels, a man all of York respected, they might have protested more loudly, but as it was, they were happy to have the meat and accepted her explanation she was about her father's business. What could they say to the daughter of the noble Dane whom King Harold had asked to govern Northumbria after the victory at Stamford Bridge? Those days might be past, but the citizens of York had not forgotten either her father or Cospatric who had governed Northumbria for a brief time after her father.

Looking beyond Finna and Inga picking flowers to the land that was hers, Emma remembered the time after Halden's death. Her father had helped her sell her husband's two ships and the warehouse of goods on the Humber River. With the proceeds, he had persuaded Cospatric, who then had the authority as Earl of Northumbria, to sell to her some lands east of the River Ouse, which she now kept in flax and barley. It gave her great joy to see the churls tilling the fields, to watch the life-giving plants rise from the rich earth. But if the Normans remained, she would not continue to own the lands. The Norman king would take them to award to his followers.

Finna and Inga returned with a basket full of flowers and smiles on their faces, eager to show her their prize takings.

Shaking off her troublesome thoughts, Emma looked down at the yellow and white flowers filling the basket. "What wonderful flowers! They will bring spring to our table."

Finna leaped at the idea. "I have a clay jar we could use to hold them!"

Emma looked beyond Inga and Finna and their flowers to see Ottar and Magnus with their heads together bent over something on the ground. "What is it that has captured Ottar's attention?" she asked.

"Oh," said Finna with a look of disgust, "'tis just some old frog."

With a grin, Emma reminded her, "I recall a little girl who found frogs fascinating."

Inga gave Finna a knowing grin. Likely Inga also remembered the time.

"That was when I was small," insisted Finna. "I am ever so much bigger now."

Emma and Inga both laughed at Finna's pronouncement and the innocence in her large brown eyes.

"But not so big you have lost your fondness for berry tarts, hmm?" questioned Emma.

"I am very fond of berry tarts," admitted Finna.

"Well, I know where to find some berries for Sigga to turn into tarts."

"Tarts!" shouted Finna.

Ottar's head lifted from where he was crouched. "Tarts?"

Emma and Inga shared a laugh at the twins' enthusiasm for the sweet treats.

Once Ottar learned of their plans, he was persuaded to leave his frog for the promise of the sweet confection and a visit to see the lambs.

Emma guided her small family to the place where she had seen the red berries growing, Magnus bounding along beside them.

The day was once again golden.

* * *

"Sir Geoffroi!"

At the sound of the familiar voice, Geoff turned from where he was speaking with his men in the bailey to see William Malet striding toward him wearing a broad smile.

"You appear in a jovial mood, my lord sheriff." Mayhap the last few weeks had given Malet reason to believe his position was secure notwithstanding William's earlier displeasure. Geoff had to wonder why Malet would care. He was a nobleman with both title and lands in Normandy; he did not need more in England. But the king had given him manors and lands aplenty. Mayhap his new lands in England meant more to the sheriff than his holdings in Normandy.

"Indeed I am in a good mood. I have an invitation for you. Might you be persuaded to join me and a few others for the evening meal?"

Geoff grinned. "If the event involves food, Malet, you know I will be pleased to attend. I never miss a meal."

"Aye, well, Gil is back from his expedition to Durham. 'Twas a failure as we all suspected 'twould be."

Geoff thought of Alain's prediction that Gilbert's foray into the north would not go well. "'Twas likely lost from the beginning."

"Gil tells me a dense fog he attributes to St. Cuthbert cloaked the rebels and prevented his men from advancing."

Geoff pondered the idea. "'Tis said Cuthbert protects that city."

The sheriff shrugged. "Mayhap you are right. The ways of the saints are not for mortal man to understand. On a brighter note, FitzOsbern has returned from Winchester as well and Gil has decided to hold a feast in the new castle on Baille Hill before he opens it to the garrison."

"The men could use a bit of celebration," said Geoff.

"'Twill be only a small group. Gil has invited Helise and me and FitzOsbern, but he also mentioned wanting you to be one of his guests."

"Me?" Geoff would never have expected an invitation to join what would be a feast for the Norman nobles in York.

"Aye, he thinks much of you and asked me to see to it. He's also invited Archbishop Ealdred, seeking to make amends, I presume."

"Or, given the archbishop's one time support for Edgar the Ætheling, it may be Gil wants to be certain Ealdred is with us. Our sire trusts no Anglo-Saxon, not even a man of the Church."

Malet seemed to ponder the suggestion. "I wonder if William put a word in Gilbert's ear before he left. But no matter, it should be a merry group. It has been a long while since we have had a proper feast."

Geoff gazed across the river to the new wooden structure rising from a motte surrounded by a large bailey and palisade. "I did not realize the new castle was completed."

"'Tis finished, save a few final touches of the hammer. William insisted on haste, you will recall. This evening will be a celebration just for us. Gilbert has already moved in but tomorrow he opens it to the others."

"Will you move to the new castle?"

"Nay. Helise and the boys prefer to stay in the original tower while we are here."

Geoff briefly pondered what Emma might think of the new, larger castle and, suddenly, he knew who he wanted by his side for the evening. When he wasn't with her, he was thinking about her. Whether she knew it or not, whether she wanted it or not, Emma of York held his heart in her delicate hand.

"As long as your wife and the English archbishop will be there, might I bring a lady of York as my guest?"

A frown formed on Malet's face. Given the women who frequented the hall—serving wenches and whores—Geoff understood.

"She is a very *proper* lady, Malet… a virtuous young widow."

"Ah. In that case, I am certain Gil will be pleased to include her. Another citizen of York might put the archbishop at ease. Mayhap he knows of her. And Helise would be delighted to have the company of another woman. Yea, by all means, bring her. I will let Gil know to expect the two of you."

* * *

The enticing smell of berries baking in a crust with honey, cinnamon, black pepper and cloves wafted through the air. It was all Emma could do to keep the twins occupied for she had promised they could share the first of the berry tarts when they were cool enough to eat.

Inga, tired from her morning of picking flowers with Finna, was resting in their shared chamber above.

A knock sounded on the door.

Reminding herself that Artur, who would normally greet visitors, was grooming her horse, Emma wiped her hands on a cloth. "I will see who has come."

Sigga nodded and handed the first of the treats into the twins' open palms.

Magnus, held in rapt attention by the sight of the freshly baked tarts disappearing into their mouths, whimpered.

Emma chuckled at the three of them and headed toward the front door. Magnus was so fixed on the tarts he did not even notice her departure.

She unlatched the door to see Sir Geoffroi standing there in his knight's hauberk. Wisely, she supposed, the Normans rarely left the castle without the protection their chain mail afforded them. Since he wore no helm, his blond locks were in full view like spun gold around his head and his blue eyes were twinkling.

"My lady," he said, bowing. When he straightened, there was a grin on his face.

"You seem happy today."

"I am rarely unhappy," he replied.

"You speak the truth." And he did, for he was ever cheerful. It was one of the things she loved about him. And given he was a soldier, engaged in gruesome endeavors, she considered it remarkable. Glancing behind him, she saw no one. "Are you alone?"

"I am. I had an errand that required haste. I did not want to wait for my men to break free from their swordplay."

She opened the door wide. "Come in."

"What is that heavenly smell?" he asked as he crossed the threshold.

"Berry tarts. You will have to wrestle Ottar, Finna and Magnus for one or wait to share one with me."

He grinned and looked at her lips. "I will wait."

They walked into the kitchen where three mouths stained with berry juice greeted them.

Sir Geoffroi laughed at the sight.

"Sir Geoffroi!" the twins said at the same time, their words muffled by the sweet treats that filled their mouths.

"We've plenty for all," said Sigga with a nod to Sir Geoffroi, as she handed him a tart.

"Did you make these, Sigga?" he asked. "They smell delicious."

"Thank you, Sir Geoffroi." Then turning to Emma, "Will you have one, Mistress?"

"Mayhap later, though they are very tempting, Sigga."

Sir Geoffroi took a large bite, closed his eyes and moaned. The sound was sensual to her ears. Did he make the same sound when he made love? She watched him chewing slowly, savoring every bite. "Oh, my," he said, opening his eyes, his tongue running over his bottom lip. "'Tis food for angels."

Sigga looked pleased. "Artur likes them, too." The servant looked down at Magnus who was licking the berry juice from his mouth and snatching any crumbs that fell to the floor. "And the hound."

The knight laughed at the sight of Magnus begging for more tart from Finna who could not say him nay but handed him a piece of her sweet.

Curious to know what had brought the knight to her door, Emma could wait no longer to ask. "Why are you here, Sir Geoffroi? Surely you did not bring us more meat? We have not even plucked the fowl you brought us earlier."

He swallowed and wiped his mouth on the cloth Sigga handed him, then looked at Emma with a hint of uncertainty. "I have an invitation for you."

Thinking they might need to be private for this conversation, she said, "Come, you can finish your tart at the table."

Leaving the twins to their eating, they walked from the kitchen to the table where the family dined, the knight carrying the remains of his tart. Once they were seated, he licked the berry juice from his fingers before speaking. "The new castellan, Gilbert de Ghent, is hosting a feast tonight. I would ask you to attend as my guest."

She was about to decline, when he held up a hand. "Do not say nay until you hear who will be there. 'Tis a private meal. The castellan has invited William FitzOsbern, the Earl of Hereford, William Malet, the sheriff, Helise, his wife and Archbishop Ealdred. We will have the new hall to ourselves. 'Twould mean much for Helise to have the company of another woman with all the other guests being men."

Emma let out a sigh, feeling her brow furrow. "Except for the archbishop, 'tis a gathering of Normans. What place have I there?"

"You have a place of honor at my side, Emma. It would please me much should you come. Will not you consider it?"

He had done so much for them—for Ottar, Feigr, Magnus and her—and provided food when they were hungry. How could she deny him what was obviously a matter of some importance? Her father would urge her to go, if only to learn of the new castle and its bailey. But this latter thought was not why she decided to accept his invitation. It was the look of hope on his face and the way it cheered her heart to see it. She wanted to be with him, to bring him joy. "I will do more than consider, sir knight. I will go, and gladly."

* * *

Geoff came for Emma with Alain riding at his side. The Bear would not attend the dinner with them, but Alain had asked to accompany Geoff to her house, expressing his discomfort at Geoff's riding alone through the darkened streets of York. Mayhap Alain had the right of it for the looks Geoff saw on the faces of the people reflected their continuing disdain.

The sun was already setting when the two of them arrived at Emma's door. Tied up in front of the house was a white mare.

"A worthy bit of horseflesh," Alain remarked as he dismounted and came around to stroke the horse's neck.

Geoff slid from his horse and joined Alain to examine the beautiful mare. "'Tis a woman's saddle the horse bears. Emma of York is full of surprises." *A fine home and now a fine mare.*

The front door opened, the servant Artur appearing as if summoned.

"'Tis my lady's mare, Thyra," he called to them. "Is she not a beauty?"

Like her mistress, Geoff almost replied. At the sound of its name, the horse lifted its head and nickered. "An intelligent one," Geoff said. The look in the horse's eyes told him the mare was spirited. *Also like her mistress.*

Geoff and Alain walked the short distance to the open door.

Artur beckoned them to enter. "Please wait here," he said, leaving them by the hearth. "My wife tells me her mistress is almost ready."

Geoff took off his gloves to warm his hands by the fire, his thoughts still on the white mare. He had no idea Emma could ride or that she had a horse, much less such a fine one. Mathieu had said nothing when he returned from stabling their horses on their prior visits. Most often, Emma walked in the city, like all the other citizens of York. Tonight, she would ride but not in his lap. Though he was disappointed, he supposed it was proper for a lady to have her own horse to travel to a feast.

Artur had referred to her as his "lady" and Geoff recalled the servant had done so before. There was still much about her he did not know. Whether she was highborn. Who her husband had been. Whose large shoes he had seen. And whether she would look fondly upon a Norman knight who would pay her court. He did not believe she still harbored hatred for him. Normans yes, but not him, or Alain or Mathieu. She had made too many exceptions for them and had shown them too many kindnesses. But did she feel more than gratitude for what he had done?

While he and Alain waited, Geoff stole glances up the stairs, anxious to see her. Minutes passed. Then, at the top of the stairs, he caught a glimmer of green silk edged in gold thread, the kind of gown he might have seen in London at William's court. Slowly she descended the stairs, a smile curving her lips. The gown dipped in front and fitted tightly against her breasts and small waist. At her hips was a belt of green, black and gold brocade. Never before had he seen her so richly attired. Tonight she appeared like a Danish princess. Her pale hair, only partially covered by the headcloth, hung in two long plaits down the front of her gown.

"My lady," Geoff said, "You leave me without breath."

Alain bowed as well but said nothing. Geoff was certain the Bear had been rendered speechless in the face of Emma's beauty so richly adorned.

"You flatter me, Sir Geoffroi. But you must have known that I could hardly wear a plain tunic to a feast for nobility." Then in a teasing manner, she added, "No matter they are French."

"Not all of them," he said. "There is the archbishop."

"Thank God for that," came her mumbled retort.

He chuckled.

Artur handed Geoff her cloak and he draped it over her shoulders.

She fastened it with a round brooch of gold that looked Danish in design, a dark red carnelian stone at its center with carving all around. Facing Artur, she asked, "The others are fed?"

"Yea, Sigga gave them an early supper. The twins are in their chamber with Magnus."

She nodded, lifted her hood over her headcloth and turned to Geoff. "I am ready."

He escorted her to the white mare and lifted her into the saddle. "I am surprised you ride; not many women do."

"The horse was a gift from my husband."

Geoff swung into his saddle, wondering at the wealth of the husband she spoke of, wondering, too, if she still loved him.

He headed down the street toward the other side of the city, passing the other fine homes. Did the neighbors who had peered out their windows to watch the knights upon their arrival make ungracious comments to her about Normans paying her a visit? And if they did, what could she have told them?

CHAPTER 8

Emma endured the disapproving stares of the few people they passed on the streets as the three of them rode down Coppergate toward the new castle. They could have taken another route but this street was wider and allowed them easier passage. She knew some who saw her in the company of the knights would wonder about her. A few would think the worst.

Sir Geoffroi had not worn a hauberk this eve. Instead, he had donned a fine tunic of blue wool, a shade darker than his eyes. The shoulders of his tunic were beautifully embroidered with silver thread making her wonder if a woman of Talisand had made it for him. His belt was fine leather studded with silver, one she had not seen before with a design carved into it, mayhap his family's emblem. When she'd first seen him waiting for her at the bottom of the stairs, he had appeared every bit the nobleman, not merely one of the Bastard's knights.

All three of them wore cloaks of dark wool so the people they passed could not observe how elegantly she and Sir Geoffroi were attired, nor did the people who stared at them know of the feast that was their destination. How could she explain to them that what she did was not improper or treacherous, that even her father, whom the people knew and respected, would have encouraged her to go? No, she could not expect them to understand what she only reluctantly admitted to herself, that not all Normans were alike and that Sir Geoffroi was, in all things, honorable.

Yet she did not forget that he and his fellow knights had killed some of her people.

She was relieved when they finally crossed over the moat, leaving the town and the stares of the people behind. But when they entered the bailey and the palisade walls of the Norman fortress surrounded her, it was fear, not relief that caused her to shudder. She had thought of the square wooden tower built a year ago as Lucifer's den. If 'twas so, this new, mightier castle might be Hell.

A few men-at-arms lingered in the wide open bailey, guards mostly, she assumed. Still, her presence was noted as their heads raised and work stopped, their eyes following her as she passed them. They could not see much of her, cloaked as she was, but they had to wonder at a woman escorted by two knights.

Her gaze was drawn to the stables, larger than those built to support the knights garrisoned in the first tower. The other buildings she assumed were those typical of such castles: the armory, blacksmith and lodging for men who did not sleep in the hall. In one corner, a chapel was nearly finished. It was ironic, indeed, that those who came prepared to kill paid homage to God in building a chapel. Mayhap they thought of their deaths and wanted to be prepared. The archbishop had once told her that the Norman king came to England with the Pope's blessing. She could hardly fathom it.

A groom came to take their horses. Sir Geoffroi dismounted and helped her down, raising his hands to her waist to lift her from her saddle. His touch sent a wave of pleasure coursing through her as his hands slid inside her cloak and he lowered her to the ground. How could such a slight encounter leave her wanting? A flame she had thought long extinguished suddenly ignited within her. When her feet touched the earth in the bailey, she raised her eyes to meet his, darkened with emotion. He, too, had been affected by their closeness.

Sir Alain, still atop his horse, interrupted the moment. "I will return at the end of the eve to go with you when you take the lady home."

Sir Geoffroi inhaled deeply and nodded. Turning to her, he offered his arm. She had only to set her fingers upon his tunic and an unexpected shiver ran down her spine. He must have felt the attraction, for he turned his head to look at her and in his eyes she glimpsed intense interest as he led her toward the open door of the castle. It was not convenient, this attraction between them.

Inside the great hall, a servant accepted their cloaks and Sir Geoffroi introduced their host as Gilbert de Ghent. His clothing and bearing suggested he was a nobleman, landed and wealthy. He had black hair and was not more than thirty, dressed in an emerald green tunic with an ornately jeweled belt. His stance conveyed arrogance and his dark eyes raked her body. *Here is a man who expects women to fall at his feet.*

Gilbert bowed over her hand and gave her an admiring glance. "Had I but known a woman of your grace and beauty lived in York, I would have invited you myself." Then with a wry smile aimed at Sir Geoffroi, their host said, "The Talisand knight is holding some secrets."

Sir Geoffroi reclaimed her hand and placed it on his forearm. "Beware the young rogues of Flanders, Emma. My father's estate in Tournai might be in France, but 'tis close to Flanders. We know them well."

Gilbert laughed and strode off saying he would see them at the feast.

For an instant, she entertained the possibility Sir Geoffroi might be jealous of the handsome Gilbert, but then she reconsidered, knowing he loved to tease. Likely the two knights exchanged barbs often.

They walked farther into the hall. It smelled of new timber, herbed rushes and the dinner being prepared. The large timbered space was not unlike the one in the castle across the river, mayhap larger. Sconces full of candles cast a warm glow about the immense room. Servants hurried in and out with platters and trays, occasionally glancing in her direction. They were Northumbrians, after all. A young minstrel walked about strumming a lute while singing a French song. 'Twas the well-appointed den of her enemy. She had to remind herself she was still in York.

Ahead of them a man and a woman stood together, watching them approach. The faces of the couple bore looks of curiosity as if they had not expected Sir Geoffroi to be accompanied by a woman. Like the others, they were richly clothed in fine velvet embroidered with silver and gold, the woman in a dark red gown, the man in a tunic the color of cloves.

When they reached the couple, Sir Geoffroi said, "Allow me to introduce Emma of York."

Emma curtsied as she had been taught as a young girl in Lincolnshire, the same way she had curtsied before the Saxon King Harold.

"Emma, these are my friends, William Malet, our sheriff, and his wife, Helise."

"Welcome Emma," said Helise Malet, "I am delighted you are here."

Emma returned the smile the woman gave her. Malet's wife was a woman of some years but despite the gray strands in her dark hair, Helise was probably not yet forty. She had a kind face and when she returned Emma's smile, it occurred to her that the woman was, indeed, happy to have another woman to talk to. There were no other women in the hall save the servants.

Emma acknowledged Helise's husband with a nod. His red hair was fair, almost Saxon in appearance. His chin bore a short, well-trimmed tuft of the same red hair. His expression was jovial.

"My lady." He bowed before her.

Malet could not know of her noble Danish blood, nor of her highborn father and mother, so she assumed his use of the title was mere courtesy. She wanted no one to know she was the daughter of a Danish thegn, much less Maerleswein, now a rebel leader. It worried her that the archbishop might inadvertently disclose her identity.

Another man, who looked to be near fifty, confidently strode to Sir Geoffroi and introduced himself to her as William FitzOsbern, the Earl of Hereford. His lined face and gray-streaked dark hair made her think he had seen many battles and his heavy mustache gave him a harsh look. She recalled her father once mentioning that FitzOsbern was a friend of the Norman king.

"My lord," she said curtseying before him. Her father would be amazed at her audacity in joining the Normans in their feasting, but he would also have encouraged her for the information it might provide him.

FitzOsbern smiled at her as she rose and facing Sir Geoffroi, said, "Hiding so lovely a flower from us, Sir Geoffroi? 'Tis brave of you to bring her as your guest, knowing neither Gil nor I have a wife."

The offhanded compliment did not endear him to Emma.

Sir Geoffroi laid his hand over hers where it rested on his arm. "Have no misconceptions, Fitz, the lady is with me."

"Aye, I can see that," FitzOsbern said with an amused expression. "I wish you both a happy feast." Tipping his head to her, he took his leave, saying he had to greet a late arriving guest.

Left alone for the moment, Sir Geoffroi led her toward the place where they would dine.

"Should I be flattered by FitzOsbern's words or would he say the same to any woman?" she asked as they walked toward the table.

"Fitz meant it as a compliment, Emma, but truthfully, there are too few women in England for William's thousands of knights. And none like you."

"Are you teasing me again? You pay me too high a compliment."

"Nay, I do not." Guiding her toward the table, he explained that the table arrangement would be different than she might have expected. Instead of a raised dais set at a right angle to long trestle tables, because there were so few guests, there was a U-shaped table covered with a linen cloth and set around the stone-ringed hearth fire.

Servants had begun setting platters of food and trenchers on the table for the guests. Candles illuminated the many dishes that were sending smells of spices and roast meat into the air.

"Suddenly I am hungry for what should be a memorable meal," said Sir Geoffroi. "Come, Gil urges us to take our seats."

They were about to sit when she spotted FitzOsbern coming toward them with the archbishop at his side.

"Do you know the archbishop?" Sir Geoffroi inquired in a whisper. "I had not thought to ask before."

"I do," she said, smiling at the elderly man of God in rich vestments who slowly ambled toward them as if the effort pained him. His hair was white now and very thin but his beard was still full. He wore a surcoat of rich purple velvet and over his shoulders was a white, fur-trimmed robe, the brooch fastener bejeweled. *Here is the one who crowned both Harold of Wessex and William, Duke of Normandy.*

When FitzOsbern and the archbishop reached them, before anyone could introduce her, she curtsied. "My Lord Archbishop."

"Emma," he said, as she stood. "I was delighted when I was told you would be in attendance." She was relieved he had not called her "Lady Emma". "I've not seen you at Mass in recent weeks."

Her cheeks flushed at the reminder. "I have been remiss."

The archbishop sighed. "'Tis not unexpected. These have not been normal times, so we must make allowances. The Good Lord will surely understand. One need not be in a church to pray."

"You are most understanding, My Lord," she replied, grateful he had not said more. He was a kind man, more like a father to the people of York than another archbishop might have been.

FitzOsbern then introduced Sir Geoffroi and the archbishop welcomed the knight to York. "Do come to Mass when you can."

"I will do that," said Sir Geoffroi, smiling. Shooting a glance at Emma, he added, "Mayhap Emma will come with me."

With that, the group took their seats. On one leg of the U-shaped table, sat William Malet and his wife, Helise. Across from them were Sir Geoffroi, Emma and the archbishop. She was happy to be seated next to

Sir Geoffroi though the attraction she felt for him made his closeness somewhat disturbing.

The middle leg of the U-shaped table, which for the evening was essentially the head table, was where Gilbert and FitzOsbern took their seats. The arrangement was such that all the guests could easily converse with each other.

As the servants poured the red wine and the men filled the trenchers from the platters the servants brought, Emma let her gaze drift around the hall, surprised at the lovely tapestries gracing the walls. In a knights' fortress she would not have expected so much civility. Some were so finely woven they appeared to be made of silk. Others, she was certain, were made of wool and pictured trees, deer and birds in blue, green and crimson thread. Raised in Lincolnshire, where her father had many manors, Emma had been taught to weave and embroider as a young girl before her mother had died. The scenes depicted in these tapestries were different than the ones her mother had made for her father, yet Emma still admired the skill of the weavers.

"Do you enjoy the tapestries?" The question had come from Gilbert, their host.

"They are beautiful." She would not tell him of the others with which she was familiar for it would reveal too much. "And fine work."

"In Flanders, where I come from, we have many makers of tapestry. Not a few of those I've displayed here are made of your fine English wool. I brought some with me to remind me of home."

She forced a smile. Before the Bastard had come to England, trade had prospered. Her husband, Halden, had been among those merchants who sold English wool to the Flemish weavers and then sold the tapestries they made back to the English. Tucked away in a chest in her home, there were many.

Emma glanced at the archbishop on her left, hoping he would say nothing about her parentage or her donations of tapestries to the Minster. He must have caught her meaning for his next words did not give away her identity. "The Minster has been given some fine ones by the wealthier families of York."

"I trust the Minster has recovered from the trouble of a few months ago?" offered FitzOsbern.

The old archbishop let out a sigh. "The Minster has been cleansed, blessed and restored to its proper role, thank the Almighty."

Emma detected regret in his voice and remembered the shame the Minster had suffered when the Normans took their revenge on the rebels. It was all she could do not to say something, particularly when FitzOsbern leaned over to Gilbert and in French made a remark about the "good people" of York needing a lesson and the Minster served well enough.

Hearing the insult, Emma's eyes flashed in anger. She had to bite her lower lip to keep from giving him a scathing rebuke. Surely the archbishop had heard the remark.

"Will you not eat, Emma?" asked Sir Geoffroi looking at the choice pieces of venison he had placed on her side of the trencher.

She stabbed the piece of meat as if it were FitzOsbern himself and brought it to her mouth and bit down hard. But when the succulent juices encountered her tongue she had to praise the food. "'Tis very good."

"The knights do not often dine so well," said Sir Geoffroi. "We buy from the market and the herdsmen and hunt for both deer and boar, but the preparation is usually a simple roast on a spit, not cooked in the well-spiced sauce that has made this venison so tender. And you must try some of the boar," he added, laying a slice on her trencher, along with a large helping of roasted beets, onions and turnips. "'Tis delicious."

Emma was amused. Did he realize he had set enough on her side of the trencher to feed two men? "You will make me fat should you expect me to eat such large servings, sir knight."

He turned his head so that his twinkling blue eyes met hers. "I would see you always well cared for, Emma."

In that moment, she forgot she was sitting in the Norman castle surrounded by her enemies. She thought only of the knight who had been her savior more than once. Her kind Lucifer, who was no fallen angel. More like Gabriel, the bringer of good news. Her gaze lingered on his handsome face, his high cheekbones, his striking blue eyes and his full lips. *Aye, Gabriel.*

The archbishop drew her attention as he began to speak. "I was delighted to see you here, Emma, dining with the new castellan. Mayhap your presence will cause others in York to see that peace is in their interest. We must urge them to submit to William. Further rebellion will only lead to more hardship and death."

The archbishop's voice had grown thinner with age, yet she believed Sir Geoffroi had heard him because he had been listening intently. But, thankfully, the knight could not know why the archbishop thought her presence might send a message to the people of York not to pursue rebellion. "I have little to say about what the people might do, My Lord. They have much to regret and many losses to mourn, not the least of which is their freedom."

The archbishop sighed but said nothing.

* * *

Knowing well the losses Emma spoke of, Geoff was grateful she had accepted his invitation to dine with his fellow Normans. It might be difficult for her but he selfishly enjoyed having her by his side. He was proud of how well she had done, how effortlessly she had moved among the French nobles. And he was surprised.

Mayhap she and her husband had been among the wealthier citizens of York. The home her husband left her certainly bespoke of such status. The tapestries that hung on the walls in her home were as well made as the ones Gil had added to the new hall.

Geoff sat close to her on the bench, his tunic touching her gown, close enough to feel her heat, to smell her fresh scent and to notice her body stiffen at FitzOsbern's remark. Her reaction told him she understood the words Fitz had spoken in French. Since Geoff had learned English in the three years he'd been in England, he did not think it unusual for one as intelligent as Emma to have learned some French in the year William's knights had been garrisoned in York.

There was much he wanted to ask her but the questions never made it to his tongue, for he worried her answers might destroy the delicate trust that had grown between them. He needed time to understand her, time for her to freely tell him of her life. Time in which the budding affection between them could grow. Mayhap with summer's coming and peace, they would have that time.

From across the table, Helise spoke. "Emma, I am thinking of planting a garden for the new castle. Gilbert," she looked toward the castellan, who had stopped talking to listen, "has welcomed my efforts. We've servants enough to do the work, but you know the soil of York better than I, what to plant and where. If I could persuade you to assist me, I would welcome your advice."

"Do help her, Lady Emma," said Malet, "for my lady wife is most determined to make the garden a success before we leave at summer's end for Holderness."

Geoff suspected along with help for her planting, Helise wanted Emma's company. He knew of her kitchen garden behind her home, which she had tenderly cultivated with her servants since the first signs of spring. Helise's garden would be a much larger affair, one to supply a castle. Would Emma want to take on such a task with all she had to do? Would she even know how to begin?

"I would be pleased to help you," Emma said graciously.

"Very good!" exclaimed Malet.

Geoff supposed the sheriff also wanted a woman's companionship for his wife while they were in York, but Geoff had another reason to be glad she had agreed to Helise's request. He would see her more often.

"How fortunate for me," offered Gil, "this garden business will bring you back to the castle I am responsible for."

Geoff held back the curse that nearly slipped from his lips, but allowed the scowl on his face at the thought of the handsome castellan paying court to Emma.

"I detect Sir Geoffroi likes not your coming into my castle's bailey," said Gil.

"'Tis not the castle's bailey, so much as the castellan that concerns me," Geoff said.

"Do not mind the cocks' banter, Emma," advised Helise. "Before the dinner is over and Sir Geoffroi sweeps you into the night, we must plan for your return."

Geoff heard Emma let out a sigh and he reached his hand to hers where it rested between them on the bench, giving her slender fingers a gentle squeeze. "Her sons are here, Emma, and only a bit older than the twins."

She looked across to Helise. "Mayhap I will bring along one day the two children who are my charges."

"I am certain my boys would like to meet them," replied Helise.

Listening to the exchange, Geoff wondered. Had she agreed to help Helise for his sake, or only because she was at heart a gracious woman? He hoped her desire to see him had led to her willingness to help Helise, but however it came about, it pleased him that she would be close to where he was most days, where he could see her more often. With difficulty, he pulled his gaze from her face. In Helise's company, she would also be protected by Malet's guards—and from Gilbert's attentions.

When the last course was served, musicians came forward to entertain the guests, a bard with a triangular-shaped harp and another musician with a dulcimer. They reminded him of Rhodri and the evenings at Talisand when the Welsh bard and Lady Serena had entertained them with song. He missed Talisand and such evenings, but were he to leave York without Emma, he would miss her more.

He glanced beyond Emma to see the music was lulling the old archbishop to sleep.

"Why, Sir Geoffroi," Emma suddenly said, her eyes following the platter the servants set before them. "'Tis strawberry tarts. I have seen wild strawberries growing near the edge of the fields. Knowing your fondness for the sweet treats, you must be eager to partake."

He grinned. "I am." He reached for a tart and placed it on her side of their trencher, then retrieved one for himself, "Yet I do not see how they can rival the ones served by a certain lady of my acquaintance who lives in York."

"Oh, but these you need not share with a hound and two ravenous children."

He laughed at the memory, for it was a pleasant one and not just because of the tarts.

"The sharing of them was half the pleasure," he said. Reminded of Emma's household, the young woman who lived with Emma came to his mind. "How is Inga? I did not see her this day."

"She was resting when you arrived. I think she is recovering, yet sometimes when she is lost in her thoughts, there is a sadness about her. While 'tis understandable, it worries me."

The music faded into the background. The candlelight cast a warm glow on Emma's ivory skin and made her blue-green eyes change to a dark blue. He wanted to reach out and touch her, to claim her as his. To see her at Talisand. "Mayhap a change of place might help her."

"Mayhap…" said Emma.

When the music stopped and the last of the tarts had been consumed, the guests rose. Helise came to engage Emma in conversation about the plans for the new garden.

Malet drew Geoff aside. "Sir Geoffroi," he whispered. "I must tell you after watching your lady this evening I do not think she is just any widow in York."

"I would agree, Malet, she is more comely than the other women of

York and what you do not see is her heart, as beautiful as her face."

"You do not get my meaning," Malet said in apparent frustration. "For one thing, she speaks French. Did you not see her eyes narrow when Fitz made his unwise remark? Helise pinched me she was so annoyed with the man, but it hardly suited for me to take the earl to task in the middle of the feast."

"Aye, I had the same impression. She might speak French. So, what of it? We speak their tongue."

"There is more," Malet counseled. "'Tis clear the archbishop is well acquainted with her and she has the air of a highborn woman. What do you know of her?"

Geoff grew indignant at the sheriff's probing. "I know all I need to. She is beautiful, kind and cares for others. She lives with two orphaned children and a young woman she has taken under her wing who was sorely misused by one of William's more disreputable knights." He said nothing about the man whose large shoes he saw in the chamber where they had laid the sword-maker. He did not want to consider what it might mean, so he dismissed the thought. Emma was all that was good.

"All to her credit, I admit," said Malet. "But I cannot help wondering if she might not be acquainted with the leaders of Northumbria we replaced. Earl Cospatric, comes to mind for one. Could she be a rebel spy?"

"I had heard that Cospatric left Scotland but as yet he's not been seen in England. And no, she is not a rebel spy. What is there to spy upon? There are no secrets here that I know of."

"Mayhap not, but I would suggest you watch her closely."

"I intend to, my lord sheriff," Geoff said with a sly grin, "most closely."

* * *

Emma had not imagined the evening with the Normans would be so enjoyable, though as she considered it, the pleasantness must be attributed more to the knight who had accompanied her than to anything else. She had begun to relax in Sir Geoffroi's presence when her temper had flared at FitzOsbern's remark. The man's arrogance was exceeded only by his ignorance.

Her respect for Sir Geoffroi and fear of disclosing who she was had stilled her tongue. She would not embarrass him nor reveal all she knew. To do so would be to betray the two men she held in highest regard, the knight she had come to trust and her noble father. Oddly, it had been the knight who had come first to her mind. But she would not allow herself to consider that her feelings for Sir Geoffroi might run deeper than merely respect.

When they had taken leave of their host and descended the stairs to the bailey, their horses were waiting, along with Sir Alain.

The huge knight grinned, making his scar seem less formidable. "A pleasant evening, I trust?"

"Most pleasant," said Sir Geoffroi, helping her to mount her mare.

Soon they were retracing their path to her home.

For some time, the three rode along in silence. The streets were darkened, but the waxing moon shining in the star-studded sky was so bright their horses cast dim shadows.

"Thank you for attending the feast," said Sir Geoffroi.

"'Twas the least I could do for all you have done for me and those I love."

Sir Geoffroi chuckled. "And now you have another garden to plant."

"I do not mind. Helise Malet is pleasant enough. And the twins might enjoy her sons, but I cannot promise that Finna will not again refer to your king as a bastard." She smiled at the memory of innocent Finna speaking with the knight.

"William hates the label, but 'tis what he is. You and Serena, Countess of Talisand, have in common your dislike of the king. She, too, once called him that."

"She is English?"

"Aye, and has no love for William, but for the sake of the Red Wolf, she tolerates our sire's presence when he visits."

Emma could not imagine entertaining the Norman king. Serena must be an unusual woman.

They turned down Emma's street. It was quiet with nary a candle she could see, save in her own home where the light flickered behind the skins that covered the windows. She was comforted by the knowledge that the hearth fire would still be burning and the brazier in her chamber would be warming the space. Artur, ever faithful, would have seen to it.

They reached her house and Sir Geoffroi slid off his horse to help her dismount. She placed her hands on his broad shoulders and allowed him to lift her down, her breasts brushing his chest as her feet met the ground. For a moment their gazes met, the moonlight bathing them in its soft glow. His hands still on her waist, he bent his head and kissed her lightly. His lips were warm and as gentle as she had remembered them. Though tender, there was passion in the kiss and when he raised his lips from hers, he was breathing heavily. So was she.

He kissed her forehead and whispered, "That you do not reject my kiss encourages me, Emma. Were we alone, I would not leave you so soon." He pulled back and let out a breath. "Still, I would provide no further display for either Alain or your neighbors who might be curious to know what passes between us."

She was gratified to see Sir Alain stood some distance away on the other side of Sir Geoffroi's stallion, his back to them. "Thank you for protecting my reputation, though I am certain my neighbors already wonder at my behavior."

"I hope they do not cause you concern."

"Nay." She would not change what she had done no matter her neighbors disapproved. She had enjoyed her evening with Sir Geoffroi.

"When are you to meet with Helise Malet to plan the garden?"

"Two days hence."

"If I can, I will be there to bid you welcome."

* * *

The next day, kneeling in her own garden, Emma loosened the dirt around the young plants that had risen from the soil. The smell of the herbs and the rich, tilled earth reminded her of the summer harvest that would come.

The garden was nestled behind the kitchen and surrounded by a reed fence some distance from the stable at the rear of her home. While not nearly the scale of the one her family had cultivated in Lincolnshire, it was of sufficient size that they always had more than enough to share with others. Cabbage, leeks, turnips and kale were among the vegetables she planted, along with herbs for cooking—parsley, sage, chives and dill—and those for healing, like betony and chamomile. She planted flowers, too, both for eating and for healing, though not many. Her small garden did not allow for all she would have liked, but there was always enough.

A shadow fell over the plant she was weeding. She sat back on her heels and lifted her hand to shield her eyes from the sun.

Sigga stood over her, a worried expression on her face. "Mistress, I am concerned about Inga."

Emma set aside her tools and rose, dusting off the tunic she usually wore to dig in the earth. "Why?"

"These past few days she has spewed up her morning meal."

"She is unwell?" Inga had seemed so much happier in recent days. Emma had begun to believe the young woman would be able to look forward to her future.

"No, I do not think she is sick." Sigga hesitated, wringing her hands, as if reluctant to say more.

"What, then?" Emma waited for her servant to speak. Whatever she had to say was obviously causing her pain.

"I believe she is with child."

"Oh, no." Emma's heart sank. She had hoped there would be no child from the rape, no lasting reminder of that night. Her own courses were so erratic she did not note Inga missing one, but she had not inquired. Perhaps she had not let herself consider she might be wrong in her assumption all was well. "If what you believe is true, this changes everything."

"Aye, Mistress. And just now she ran from the house. When I shouted after her, asking where she was going, she said only 'the old tower'."

Emma inhaled sharply.

Sigga said, "Might she go to confront the knight who is responsible?"

"Nay," she said, rising from the ground. "Inga would not want to see him again." Suddenly a thought came to Emma, one so horrible it made her heart speed in panic. "Sigga, the square tower the Normans first built is the highest point in the city, save for the Minster. I pray she does not plan what I fear."

"What?" inquired a concerned Sigga.

"The shame she feels may have impelled her to want to take her own life. I think she means to cast herself down from the ramparts."

Sigga crossed herself. "God and all the angels, no."

Emma raced into the house, Sigga following on her heels. "I must stop her."

"But you will not be admitted to the Norman castle," cautioned the servant. "Neither will Inga."

Reaching the door, Emma grabbed her cloak from the peg. "She has only to persuade them she is a new servant and they will let her in. They did me when I went to see Sir Geoffroi. Keep watch over the twins and do not let Magnus leave. He would only draw unwanted attention and no servant would travel with a hound."

She ran out the door. Once in the street, her gaze searched for Inga but all she saw were people going about their business. It was midday and the streets were crowded. If Inga were running, she would be some distance ahead.

Launching herself into the street, she did not stop running until she reached the castle. She was panting when she spoke to the guard. Using her prior excuse, and the added one of being late, she gained entry and hurried through the bailey to the tower. Seeing a group of knights going in the same direction, she kept her head down.

The hall was full of men eating their midday meal and she was able to move to the stairs as one of the servants. Once there, an older serving woman stopped her.

"What brings such a one as ye to the castle?"

Knowing she did not look the part of a servant even wearing her soiled tunic, the only thing that came to mind was to mention the reason she had come to the tower in recent days. "I am on an errand for Helise Malet."

"Aye, well, she is not usually in the floors above."

"I must see for myself," Emma told the woman and brushed past her, racing up the stairs.

Midway to the highest level, Emma stopped, her chest heaving as a sharp pain stabbed her beneath her ribs. She was not accustomed to running such long distances. A few breaths later, determined to find Inga before it was too late, she resumed the climb, reaching the top of the narrow, curling stairs.

The stairs ended in a wooden door. She opened it and stepped onto the platform on the third story of the tower. The wooden walls of the battlement were solid except for the arrow loops, too narrow for even a woman to jump through. But there was the walk at the top that circled the walls. It was there she found Inga, staring out, her hands gripping the edge of the low wall.

"Inga."

The girl shot a glance at Emma, but then returned her gaze to the vast expanse below the tower. The wind whipped strands of her honey-colored hair about her face as she held her body rigid and leaned slightly forward. Was she preparing to leap?

Cautiously, so as not to cause Inga to make a sudden move, Emma closed the distance between them and whispered, "Inga, you must not." She wanted to grab hold of Inga but feared she might cause the girl to suddenly leap from the wall.

Inga glanced back at her. "All will know. I will be shunned, the child called the bastard of our hated enemy. How will my father bear it?"

Finally reaching out to Inga on the narrow walk, Emma pulled her into her arms and backed them away from the precipice. The girl turned into Emma's chest and sobbed.

"Oh, Emma…"

"Your father will not blame you, Inga."

Inga pulled back, her gray eyes appearing to plead. "But how can I live with such a thing?"

"The child is innocent, a child who will grow to love you. To take such a life and your own would be against God's law. 'Tis worse than murder, Inga. You would be killing not only the body, but also the soul. You could not even be buried in hallowed ground. You and your innocent babe would be barred from Heaven for all eternity." Emma knew the words of the Church's teachings were harsh, and while she did not believe God was so unmerciful, she had to use what she could to dissuade Inga from such a dire action.

Inga shuddered in Emma's arms. "How could I ever love a child who looks like him?" Inga muttered.

"Mayhap the child will have your golden hair and gray eyes. Did you not once tell me that your grandfather's look was clear on all his offspring? You and Feigr have the same look about you. So might the child. And to a mother's love, looks are nothing. The child will be heart of your heart, half your own soul. How could you fail to love it?"

Sniffing, Inga's sobs abated, giving Emma hope.

"What are you doing up here?" a deep voice bellowed behind them.

Emma turned her head to see the Norman guard. "We are just looking at the countryside," the excuse coming to Emma. "The forest is so beautiful it has moved my friend to tears."

"Aye, that may be, but you have no business here." He gave Inga a suspicious look, her tear-stained cheek speaking of things other than surveying the surrounding countryside.

"We will trouble your battlement no longer, good sir. We are leaving."

His eyes followed them as Emma helped Inga down and together they walked to the stairs.

"It will be all right, Inga. I will help you. We will raise your child with the twins."

* * *

"I saw your lady in the bailey today," Mathieu said to Geoff as he left the practice yard in the bailey wiping sweat from his brow.

Geoff paused. "Mayhap she came to see Helise about the garden they plan for the new castle. I am sorry to have missed her."

"I do not think so, sir. She was running, as if for her life."

"What?" *Why would Emma be running across the bailey?* "Was anyone chasing her?"

"Nay, but she appeared fearful. Then I saw her again, a short while later, when she walked with her friend, Inga, to the gate. You were in the midst of sparring with Sir Alain or I would have fetched you. I did not see Inga enter, but they left together."

Geoff could not imagine what the sword-maker's daughter would be doing in the castle where Eude and his companions kept their pallets. He would have to ask Helise if Emma had come today about the garden. Or, better still, he would try and get away to pay Emma a visit and ask her himself. *Why had she been afraid?*

* * *

Emma was focused on her embroidery when she heard Feigr's heavy steps as he trudged down the stairs after one of his many visits to see his daughter. Seeing Emma, he drew up a bench in front of her. "Why does my daughter weep so, my lady?"

He was pale and his face lined with worry. She rose and poured him some mead from the pitcher on the table, dreading the conversation to come. "Let us share some mead."

She resumed her seat with her cup, wondering if he would be able to absorb the news. "Inga recovers, Feigr, but…"

"'Tis still that night she thinks of?" he interrupted. Without waiting for Emma's answer, he gazed into the pale liquid he held in his hands. "I failed to protect her." His eyes narrowed. "But no more! I am training with the warriors now. My own swords will be put to good use killing Normans."

"Oh, Feigr, not you, too?"

"I must," he insisted. "When that cur and his brutes came for Inga, had I known better how to wield my own weapons, I might have stopped them."

"Or, mayhap you would have been killed, Feigr. The knights train from their youth. And think. Inga would have wept all the more had she lost you."

For a moment he said nothing, just stared into his wine. "I would give anything to see the tears gone from my daughter's face."

Emma steeled herself for what she must say. "There is something I must tell you." His eyes were the same gray as his daughter's only more intense. She hoped he would understand. "Inga may not be able to tell you, but because you love her, you must know."

"What?"

"Inga is with child."

Feigr's face froze in shock. Then he expelled an oath and beneath his breath his voice was fierce. "I will kill him!"

"Mayhap you will one day, but for now you must help Inga. She needs you. And this you must not speak of ever again: Inga sought to take her life."

He pulled back, a look of shock on his face. Then his eyes narrowed as his face contorted in anger.

"I stopped her in time, Feigr, but she needs both of us to see her through this ordeal, to give her courage to bear the child."

His anger faded and he slumped. "My poor daughter," he mourned, shaking his head, his eyes revealing his grief. "What have they done to my Inga?"

"You must help her, Feigr. You must let her know you stand beside her. The child will be Inga's, after all. And your grandchild."

"'Twill be the Norman's bastard!"

Emma vowed silently never to again use that word. "The babe will be an innocent, Feigr. I have told Inga I will help her to raise the child. We will be a family, Inga, Ottar, Finna and the child. You, too, Feigr. The child will know nothing but love, I promise."

He looked up at her, his eyes full of unshed tears. "I thank you, my lady. Without you, Inga might be lost to me. Aye, for her sake, it will be as you say. I will let her know she has my love, no matter what comes. But I vow I will kill the Norman scum who did this to her."

CHAPTER 9

It was early in June when Geoff sat in the great hall, breaking his fast, wondering which of the many tasks FitzOsbern had given him he should undertake first. He had wanted to go to Emma since that conversation with Mathieu, but with demands on his time from both Malet and FitzOsbern and the needs of his men, he had been unable to return to her in a sennight. But she was constantly in his thoughts. He longed to hold her, to kiss her. He knew she was well from his conversations with Helise Malet who had told him how pleased she was with Emma's help with the new castle's garden.

Helise, who ate next to him, leaned close and whispered, "I like Emma very much, Sir Geoffroi. She is ever so clever. She knows more than I do about growing things. With her advice, I have chosen well the plants for Gilbert's garden."

Her comments about Emma pleased him and he was delighted to realize Emma had made a friend. "The men will be happy to have the bounty from that garden."

"Aye, and the castle's cook will be pleased. Emma is such an unusual young woman, Sir Geoffroi. Did she lose her husband in the fighting? I dared not ask."

He did not know which battle Malet's wife spoke of, for there had been many since William had come to England. Mayhap she had in mind the battle in York that had taken place the year before. It had not lasted long, but even so, Northumbrians had died before the city surrendered to William. "Nay, she has been a widow longer than that." In truth, he did not know much of her husband. If he had died at the hands of Norman knights in earlier battles, Geoff would not be the one to remind her, but knowing Emma she would have told him had that been the case.

It was an hour later when he and Alain had just finished their morning sword practice that shouts echoed through the bailey.

"Attack! The rebels attack!"

Geoff wiped the sweat from his bare chest and hurriedly donned his tunic and hauberk, calling for Mathieu, who was already racing to his side.

"See to our warhorses. We ride with FitzOsbern!"

The squire bolted for the stables.

"Another rising?" asked Alain as he, too, hurriedly donned his clothes and mail, preparing for battle.

"Aye, and not unexpected. With William's army fighting Harold of Wessex's sons in the South, we have less than half the men we once did. They would seize the advantage if they could."

"Sir Geoffroi!" FitzOsbern pulled his horse up short before the two knights, coming to a stop in a cloud of dust. "Do you ride with me?"

Between the practice yard and the stables, Geoff saw Mathieu coming with their horses, the helms and shields tied to the saddles. "Aye, we do."

Striding to his destrier, Geoff mounted, shoved his helm on his head, took up his shield and let out a huff. *Will York never be at peace?*

Moments later, his lance firmly gripped in his right hand, he gave the signal to his waiting men and followed FitzOsbern out the gate.

Between the castle and Skeldergate, the shield-maker's street, a large crowd of Northumbrians was already engaged in fighting the first mounted knights to confront them. In such close quarters, the battle was intense, men's shouts and the clash of metal sounding loud in his ears.

Geoff entered the fray, piercing one rebel with his lance only to turn and engage another. Soon he turned to his sword, his blade slashing into the unmailed chest of a bearded Northumbrian, cutting a long red swath. Another swing of the steel and he sliced through the skin of the rebel's bared neck.

Blood from Geoff's victim shot into the air. And blood ran in the streets as the brutal fighting continued and both rebels and knights fell.

The battle was fought in quarters too close for the Norman crossbows to do any good. Bodkin arrows shot from the tower's arrow loops might as easily hit a Norman as well as a Northumbrian. Geoff fought on, keenly aware this battle would have to be won without such help.

In a matter of minutes, hundreds of knights from both castles streamed into the fight, hacking at the rebels and backing them to Coppergate where they fled into the city.

Sensing danger at his back, Geoff turned to see a rebel running toward him with a raised sword. A knife sailed through the air to lodge in the man's neck, the sickening sound of metal meeting soft flesh echoing in Geoff's ears. Glancing over his shoulder, he glimpsed Alain on his great gray warhorse, smiling beneath his helm.

Turning his horse, Geoff tipped his head in thanks to the powerful knight and surveyed the remaining rebel forces still fighting. "'Tis nearly over."

"Aye," agreed Alain as they headed into what remained of the battle.

Another hour of brutal work gave them the victory, but it had come at a cost. Scores of knights lay dead. Regrettably, some of the slain had been those who rode with him from Talisand, their bodies mingling with those of the slain rebels.

Geoff thought of Emma and the wedge such a battle would drive between them, particularly if any of her kinsmen had been among the rebels. Would she see his hands as stained by their blood? Would she rise like the Valkyrie he had named her to seek revenge? He needed peace between her people and his for there to be peace between the two of them. He longed to see her, to see if he still found favor in her eyes, but his duties required his presence in the castle.

* * *

Emma studied the tapestry she was working on. The gold and yellow threads formed a brilliantly colored background for the black horse in the center. Keeping her hands busy took her mind from the battle that had been fought a sennight ago between the Normans and the men from Durham who had emerged from the woods where they had been waiting for a chance to reengage.

The fighting, Artur had told her, had not lasted long. FitzOsbern and the mounted knights had quickly beaten back the rebels. The word of the defeat had been carried through the city and the loss keenly felt. The people had hoped for another result.

Knights had died as well as men from Durham. While the battle raged, she had worried for Sir Geoffroi. She was glad when Mathieu, the faithful messenger, brought her word that he and Sir Alain lived. She was conflicted in her loyalties, wanting Sir Geoffroi to live yet also wanting the Northumbrians to be victorious. It could not be.

Rising, she walked to the window and pulled back the animal hide covering to stare out. Two of the women who lived on her street waved to her. She waved back. On the surface, the city appeared to be almost normal again. Though she could not see them from her window, she knew the shops and market were open and the people busy at their pursuits. In the fields, churls and villeins once again tended the new crops.

Yet there remained an undercurrent in York, an unease that hung in the air, as if the city were holding its breath, waiting for worse to come. Emma, of all people, knew well what was coming and, whereas once she would have welcomed her father's plans for an uprising, now those plans only brought her dread. Someone she loved was bound to be hurt, even killed.

Should she warn Sir Geoffroi of the plans for a major rising? Of the Danes whose help they sought? Surely to do so would be a betrayal of her father. How could she choose between them? Nay, she could not. She wanted to see York free of the Normans, but she wanted it to happen without bloodshed. An impossible dream.

Helise had insisted Emma pay her a visit to see the garden they had planted and she was determined not to disappoint Malet's wife. With the sun high in the sky, she grabbed her light cloak off the peg and headed toward the tower castle where they had agreed to meet in the bailey.

Magnus loped at her side. It would be the first time she had taken him to the castle but her errand today was not secret so there was no reason to leave him behind. As she traveled down Coppergate, she bid good day to the merchants she knew. Feigr was busy at his forge when she stopped to greet him. Magnus waited patiently by her side.

"Making new swords?" she inquired. Though that was his primary business, he also made fine knives and an occasional seax.

"'Tis an axe blade I forge today for one of the men who prefers that weapon. How is Inga?"

"She fares well. The twins love her, you know."

His face took on a wistful look as if he were seeing something far away. "Like her mother she is. Good with children. I am glad she is with you."

"Do not worry about her, Feigr."

"I am in your debt for the kindness you have shown her."

"Inga is my friend. I could not do otherwise."

She bid him goodbye but did not mention her destination. He would not have approved. And she did not ask him for whom he forged the new weapon. She did not want to know.

Quickening her pace, she passed the other shops. Sigga would be at the market and Inga with the twins, but she did not want to be away too long.

Helise would welcome her, but given the recent hostilities the Normans would be on their guard for anyone from York entering either of the castles.

She looked forward to seeing Malet's wife. In the making of the garden, they had forged a friendship. When one put a face on the enemy, shared a meal with them and made friends among their ranks, it was difficult to see the sides clearly after that. So it was with Emma. She no longer hated the Normans as she once had. While she wanted the North free of the French and men like Eude gone forever, she did not wish to be free of Sir Geoffroi's kind attentions or Helise's friendship. She had come to see the wisdom in the old archbishop's words. *Further rebellion will only lead to more hardship and death.* She might wish it otherwise, but she was practical enough to know further rebellion was inevitable. The Normans had tormented York for too long, reducing it to a city of serfs and their French lords.

Scattered bloodstains, now dried to nearly black, still appeared in places on the ground near the old castle but the bodies were gone. As before, when Emma was questioned at the gate, she was able to gain entry. There were so few women in the castles, the knights welcomed any who entered, be they servants, whores or the occasional lady. But this time the guard knew her name when she gave it. Helise had told her he would.

"The sheriff's wife expects you," said the burly guard who glared apprehensively at Magnus.

"The hound will not harm you," she said, picking up the skirts of her gown and cloak to cross the bailey. Magnus trailed along, his keen eyes darting from one side of the bailey to the other, watchful and protective.

The sounds of knights sparring rose in her ears causing Emma to glance toward the practice yard. Her heart sped.

Sir Geoffroi.

His bare chest glistened with sweat as he deftly wielded his sword, his muscles flexing with the strain as the metal of his blade clashed with that of the huge knight she recognized as Sir Alain. Despite her desire to stay and watch, she paused only briefly in her progress toward the door of the square tower. A woman alone, even an invited one, might face unwanted attention from the men looking on. She fingered the plain, metal brooch at her neck. The day was fair, but in an attempt to ward off the leers of the Norman soldiers, she had worn a cloak.

She entered the hall and went directly to the sheriff's chamber and knocked on the door. A servant answered, backing away as she stared at Magnus. "My lady waits for you within," she said in a shaky voice.

Helise set aside her stitching and rose to greet her. "You have come at last! And who is this with you?"

"Magnus. He is gentle; you need not fear him. He only growls at those he perceives to be a threat."

Malet's wife looked at Magnus' wagging tail. "Well, then, welcome to you both."

The servant, unconvinced, waited to one side.

"I have only a few things I need," said Helise, bustling about the chamber gathering her cloak and a paper that bore a diagram of sorts. "Then we can be off. Wait until you see our plants, Emma! They are growing."

For the first time, Emma noticed the intricate work the older woman had set on the table. "Do you embroider?"

Helise nodded. "I find it keeps me occupied when my husband is otherwise engaged and the boys are at their lessons. At Holderness, I am often left to my own endeavors."

"Where are your sons today?" Emma asked. She had not seen the two lads Ottar's age when she had entered the hall.

"Watching the knights at their swordplay, I suspect. They are of an age to want to become squires, but Robert is his father's heir, so there are expectations for him that will rule that out."

Emma's gaze momentarily fell to her hands. "I was going to bring the twins but since the situation in the city has worsened, I have kept them close to home."

"I understand, Emma." Helise gave her a look of understanding. "My sons know not to leave the castle. 'Tis too dangerous for them to move about freely after the last attack."

Helise picked up her cloak and Emma helped her to don it. The Norman woman held herself in a dignified manner but beneath the aura of calm, Emma sensed tension. One of Helise's hands nervously twisted the folds of her cloak.

"You must be anxious to leave for Holderness," Emma said.

"Aye, I will be glad to quit York. I jump at every loud noise. But we have a happy task to see to today. Come, let me show you the progress in the garden. You will be amazed! And I believe you will like our escort," she added with a wink.

Emma understood Helise's meaning when they reached the knights who waited to escort them to the other side of the River Ouse. Among them was Sir Geoffroi.

* * *

Geoff had informed Malet's wife that he and Alain were available to accompany her and Emma to the new castle on Baille Hill, so he was unsurprised when the summons came.

He was eager to undertake the task.

When Emma saw him waiting, her smile lit her face, setting his heart pounding. He had missed her. Worried she might harbor resentment for some friend killed in the recent skirmish, he was pleased to see she was neither sullen nor angry. Her face radiated only joy at his coming.

Her hound trotted up to him and nuzzled his hand.

"Magnus, you beast. How are you?" He scratched the hound behind the ears as the dog leaned into him.

"Shameless begging, Magnus," Emma chided.

Helise Malet laughed. "You appear to have won a friend, Sir Geoffroi."

He grinned at Emma. "That was my intent."

Together with a few other knights he had chosen, Geoff and Alain accompanied the two women across the bridge to the opposite bank of the Ouse River where the new castle rose on Baille Hill. The townspeople moved to let them pass but their eyes followed the women closely. On a second glance it seemed to Geoff their gazes followed only Emma.

Once they passed through the gate of the new castle, he left the knights to wait, taking only Alain and Mathieu with him to follow Emma and Helise to the far side of the bailey where a large area had been set apart and protected by a short fence. The hound walked at Emma's side.

Beyond the fence lay the tended earth of a new garden, one large enough to produce sufficient vegetables to add to the food of the knights garrisoned in both castles.

Helise led Emma through a gate in the fence and pointed to one section of the garden where new plants rose from the soil, green and thriving. "See how well the vegetables do?"

Geoff stood to one side with Magnus and Alain, watching as Emma placed her hands on her hips and smiled at the garden's progress. "Those leafy turnip tops and squat radish leaves tell me the garden is doing very well," remarked Emma. "'Tis thriving, Helise!"

Geoff looked not at the plants but at Emma. Young and beautiful with her long flaxen plaits hanging down the front of her gown, she was enough to make any man smile. And he wanted to be that man.

"Over there," Helise directed, "are the garlic and onion plants. In time there will be cabbages and leeks, too." Helise consulted her diagram. "Oh, and I should not forget the herbs you suggested, Emma—parsley, sage, chives, dill and marjoram. I agree with that selection. They will please the cook."

"The special ones?" asked Emma. "The chamomile, yarrow, hemlock and wormwood?"

"Those are in that section, over there." Helise pointed. "I should have forgotten them had you not given me a list."

Emma could read, write? Geoff was surprised to learn of it. Only noblewomen could read and few of them.

"You will need the special herbs to treat the wounds of your knights," Emma said with a side-glance in Geoff's direction.

He chuckled. Aye, they had wounds. It was part of being a knight. Chain mail did not prevent them.

Emma bent over the plants like they were young children in need of encouragement. Her long hair fell onto the plants making him want to wrap the flaxen braids around his hand and draw her near for another kiss. In truth, he wanted more than a kiss. He missed the taste of her, the touch of her. He wanted to slip his hands around her slim waist and draw her near, to feel her womanly curves against him.

Magnus went to sniff at the plants Emma coddled and then sneezed, making her laugh. He liked seeing her in good spirits. He wanted to make her smile often.

He shifted his gaze from Emma to the garden she and Helise had created, admiring it. He approved of the way it was ordered. The rectangular wooden boxes, about four feet on a side, allowed the herbs to be set apart from the vegetables and flowers. "Was it your design, Emma?"

Helise answered for her. "It was! And 'tis very clever with the border of *marygolde* flowers, do you not agree, Sir Geoffroi?"

"I do. 'Tis a marvel," he remarked, but he was looking at Emma. *She* was the marvel.

"You will like it better when there is a harvest to be reaped, sir knight," she tossed back with a smile.

Helise pulled Emma toward a patch of dark, leafy greens. "Over here is where you suggested we plant the kale. See how it grows?"

The women chatted about the plants, Emma providing suggestions for helping them to grow. Geoff watched Emma with not just desire but admiration to think she had conceived it. He inspected the short, palisade-like fence that surrounded the large garden. It was sturdy enough to keep out animals and children.

Where had she learned such a skill? And where had she learned to read?

* * *

Emma was enjoying her time with Helise, particularly because Sir Geoffroi was near. She did not have to look at him to feel his presence. There was a tether between her and the blond knight, an invisible cord that held her to him, a desire that flamed whenever he was near.

She did not even mind that the garden she had helped to create would feed the Norman soldiers, for Sir Geoffroi would be one of them.

Seeing the plants rise from the rich soil gave her pride. The garden was not unlike the one her mother had planted at their manor in Lincolnshire, the largest of her father's manors. She had lost her mother when she was younger than Finna but she had fond memories of the woman with the flaxen hair like hers. Her mother had taught her to read as well as embroider. She wished she could have her mother with her now, but it was a comfort to have a friendship with Helise Malet, who was the same age Emma's mother would have been had she lived.

To Emma, their time in the peaceful garden was like an island of calm in a roiling sea. It could not last, but she was loath to question the good that providence offered her, however short such a time might be. She would enjoy the hours she and Sir Geoffroi spent together, for she knew they would end all too soon.

As they made to leave, her gaze caught Sir Geoffroi's and for a moment neither looked away until Helise's chatter distracted her.

"We can harvest the plants together," the older woman offered.

"That would be nice," Emma agreed.

When they returned to the tower castle on the other side of the river, Sir Geoffroi insisted on seeing her home. She was grateful their goodbye would be delayed.

Even avoiding the well-traveled streets as they did, it was a bit of a procession, her traveling with him and his knights and Magnus loping beside them. People stopped to watch them pass. Some would have recognized Magnus and questioned her being in the company of the knights. She was glad when they arrived at her house without incident.

"Will you and Sir Alain come in?" she asked.

"Aye, gladly," he replied.

"I will wait for you here with the men," announced Sir Alain.

When Sir Geoffroi nodded his acceptance, Emma addressed the one called the Bear. "Then I will send ale for you and the other knights."

Once inside, Magnus flopped on his pallet and Emma asked Artur to take the waiting knights ale to refresh them. She hung her cloak on a peg and went into the kitchen, as the servant poured ale and disappeared with a tray of tankards for the knights.

Sigga was still at the market, leaving Emma alone with Sir Geoffroi. She fetched him a berry tart and a tankard of ale. "I saved one for you when I set aside two for the twins. They will have theirs with supper. Best to eat yours now or Magnus will be begging for it."

"Where are the children?"

"Inga was going to take them to a friend's for play while I was at the castle."

She handed him the tart on her palm, the berry juice running onto her fingers.

His eyes fastened on the juicy treat bulging with cooked berries. "You have my thanks, my lady." Swiftly, he engulfed the sweet and washed it down with a swig of ale.

She laughed, seeing the berry juice dripping from his chin. "You are a sight, Sir Geoffroi." Reaching for a cloth, she was about to wipe the juice from his face when he reached for her hand.

Taking the cloth, he set it on the worktable and brought her fingertips to his mouth, licking the juice. The sensation of his warm tongue stroking her fingertips stirred a heat deep within her. Involuntarily her lips parted and she took in a quick breath, shivers making her nipples harden beneath her tunic as his tongue moved over her fingers.

His blue gaze fixed on her. "You taste better than the tart and I would have more."

She regarded his rugged face, browned by his many days in the summer sun. It made his blue eyes all the more striking. His lips curved in a sensual smile, a spot of berry juice still on his mouth. She had the sudden urge to lick it off but before she could do it, his tongue reached out and lapped up the juice.

He pulled her into his chest and gazed intently into her eyes. "Emma, I have longed to kiss you."

"Then mayhap you should," she whispered, wanting nothing more.

He bent his head to take her mouth and she was lost in his kiss, the warmth of his chest pressed against her, the taste of the berries on his tongue sliding over hers, seducing her to his will. But it was her will, too. She had wanted this from the first time she had seen him that morning, mayhap for days before that. She tilted her head to allow him to kiss her more deeply, entwining her fingers in the hair at the base of his neck.

Their breaths quickened, her heart raced and a pool of warm liquid settled in her woman's center.

Breaking the kiss, he pressed his forehead to hers. "Be my lady, Emma. Let me have you and I promise I will never have another."

She was not shocked at his request, but delighted in his words. Their gazes met and for a time neither spoke. Still, there was much in their eyes. For three years she had been without a man and had wanted none, but she wanted him.

Without a word, she took his rough hand in hers and led him out of the kitchen and up the stairs to her chamber, thinking all the while it was meant to be. Once inside, she closed the door and turned to him. "Your companions wait, so we do not have much time."

"Let them wait," he said, drawing her close to kiss her neck, her face, then her lips. "I want you, Emma."

If they'd had more time, mayhap they would have proceeded more slowly but she did not think so. The passion between them was too intense and had been building for too long. Instead, they tore at each other's clothing, frantic to be free of it, but all they managed before they fell to the bed was to remove his hauberk and her woolen gown. Her headcloth had quickly fallen to the floor on its own.

"Emma, Emma," he murmured as his hands reached for her linen shift, lifting it to her hips and running his palm down her quivering thigh.

Then he kissed her deeply, moving his hand to her breast. It felt blessedly right.

The heavy weight of his sex pressed against her. She tugged at his braies. He helped her slide them down leaving their bodies below the waist touching, hot and ready, flamed by the heat coursing between them.

"Geoffroi, hurry."

He rose up, positioned his sex at her welcoming folds and plunged in more deeply than she could have imagined. "My love," he murmured as he stilled.

She raised her hips to take all of him, welcoming his hot flesh into her tight sheath. It had been years since she had known a man, still she could not remember ever experiencing such fullness, such wonder. There was no ghost to greet her, no image of anyone but Geoffroi, his blue gaze intense when she opened her eyes to see him staring at her.

"Is it well with you, my love?" he asked, concern in the depths of his eyes.

"Yea, but 'twill be better when you begin to move."

"I shall move," he said, thrusting into her. "Oh yes, Emma, I shall move."

Then began a most wondrous coupling, a loving she would never forget. Their bodies fit perfectly to each other, his sex gliding slowly in and out of her welcoming flesh.

She raised her hips to move with him, as together they strove to reach the peak of their passion. When their release came, it was a joining that seemed so right, so destined, she felt no guilt. He had wanted her to give herself to him and she had.

There was no turning back now.

CHAPTER 10

Dunfermline, Scotland

A myriad of flickering candles and blazing torches lighted the great hall where Maerleswein joined the men and women feasting on roasted boar. To him it was a regathering of sorts, for they had all been there the year before, seeking refuge willingly offered by the Scottish monarch.

At the head table sat Malcolm Canmore, King of Scotland, nearly forty and still a vigorous man with a warrior's body and a full head of long, brown hair to go with his mustache and well-kept beard. Watching the king was his betrothed, the lovely Margaret of Wessex, who was nearly half his age. Maerleswein had met her the year before, when she and her brother fled north. Anyone who saw Margaret and Edgar Ætheling together would observe the resemblance. The two shared their fair appearance, their blue-gray eyes and the same delicate features; Edgar's only a masculine version of his sister's.

The king had told Maerleswein that when Edgar, his mother and two sisters had landed in Scotland, Malcolm was there to greet them. Maerleswein could well imagine the scene, the king's eyes devouring young Margaret, as they did this night. 'Twas not surprising when, soon after they met, the king offered to make Margaret his wife. Malcolm had fallen quickly, not just because of her royal Saxon lineage, the same lineage that the Norman Bastard would find disturbing when matched with a Scot, but because Margaret was so much more.

Her gentle spirit permeated the hall. He had heard it said in Dunfermline that she was persuaded to accept the king's offer in order to accomplish a holy purpose, to direct Malcolm from his erring ways and increase God's praise in the land. Mayhap it was so, for, from his own observations, the Scottish people loved her, as did their king.

She did not say much, a word here, a nod there, allowing her betrothed to do the talking. While Malcolm spoke both Gaelic and Saxon, Margaret spoke only Saxon. Yet she did not need to speak for those attending to observe the sweetness of her nature.

With her long flaxen plaits and her pleasant expression, Margaret reminded Maerleswein of his wife, Julianna, at that age. A wave of sadness swept over him. He had lost her so early and, even today, missed her far more than he would ever admit. With a sigh, he shook off the longing for the past. He had his daughter to care for and she was the image of her mother. He had named her for Emma of Normandy, Queen Consort of England, Denmark and Norway. The name seemed fitting since both were strong of character and had overcome loss, though after the Bastard plundered England, mayhap the Norman's connection to the name was best forgotten.

He gazed about the hall, decorated with shields and tapestries belonging to the Scottish royal family and proudly noted that the men sharing the meal with the king were nearly all Northumbrians, many related. None was even thirty, yet much would be expected of them if they were to take back the North. The Danes and their ships would not be enough without leaders like Waltheof, the Earl of Huntingdon, who looked like a Dane with his great height and pale hair. And no wonder, for he was cousin to King Swein of Denmark.

As he thought of it, Waltheof was also cousin to Cospatric, the young Earl of Bamburgh. Now there was a man who would make a fine husband for Emma. Handsome by most women's standards, and more importantly to Maerleswein, Cospatric was wealthy and titled, still powerful with his lands north of Durham.

Emma was too independent, too content with her made up family. She needed children of her own. She'd had enough time to mourn Halden's death. Maerleswein had no intention of allowing his only daughter to remain a widow forever. It was time for her to wed again. He was not pleased with this friendship with a French knight who had helped her with Ottar. The look in her eyes when she spoke of the knight's kindness displayed more than gratitude.

Emma had been alone with women, children and servants for too long. She needed a man, one *her father* approved of.

Hearing the men's conversations, retelling the story of the Normans' routing of the weak Northumbrian forces, reminded him of his mission. He had come to Dunfermline not only to seek Malcolm's aid, as he had King Swein's, but to convince the Scot and the others to join the fight. Even more than men and arms, they needed leaders with a firm resolve to accomplish their purpose. He was still doubtful of Osbjorn's ability to lead hundreds of ships and thousands of Danish warriors. He knew William. The Norman Bastard was fierce and would not be stopped except by men with a tenacity to match his own.

"You are a quiet one this night, Maerleswein," observed the king of the Scots, looking down the table to where Maerleswein sat.

"Aye. I have been contemplating all that must be done by summer's end when we return to Yorkshire to meet King Swein's ships. There is much to consider."

"You are confident they will arrive?"

"I am. What Swein has promised, he will see done. While I was still in Jelling, he ordered the building of more longships."

Cospatric set down his wine. "He was most eager to reclaim the heart of the old Danish lands."

Malcolm leaned forward. "In that, Scotland may have an interest. We were planning to invade Yorkshire last year on Edgar's behalf, but alas, the Norman got there first."

"He has come and gone again from York," Maerleswein informed the king, "leaving yet another of his castles and more of his French knights. While he is away is the time to strike."

* * *

York, England

Emma gazed into Geoffroi's face, as they lay together amidst the lavender flowers at the edge of the meadow that abutted the woods, content as she had never been. In the background she could hear the melodious song of the ruby-breasted linnet.

The world did not intrude into this part of the forest. It was a special place, theirs alone. It had not been easy for her to steal away unnoticed to meet him in the flower-filled meadow, but she had done so. And she came willingly, though not as often as either Geoffroi or she would have liked.

Sunlight filtered through the trees to fall across his straw-colored hair. One arm bent under her head for a pillow, she reached up with the other to touch his cheek, letting her fingers caress his now familiar face, relishing the weight of his body lying across hers.

He bent his head to kiss her, brushing his lips over hers. She heard him take a deep breath.

"I love your smell," he said, nuzzling her neck, sending shivers down her spine and awakening other parts of her body. "I noticed it the first time you rode with me."

His tongue slid over her skin and she turned into his caress.

"You taste like honey," he murmured.

She turned her head to kiss his temple.

"Would that we could always be together like this," he said, raising himself on one elbow to brush tendrils of hair from her brow. "Only I would prefer a bed," he added with a grin, "and you naked. The times I have seen your lovely form have been too few."

She smiled up at him, her hand curving around his chiseled jaw. He turned his head to kiss her palm. The warmth of his lips sent an aching need coursing through her. She loved the touch of this man. His hands were rough but his lovemaking tender. Yet, at times, his passion had risen to take her in a furious storm. She had reveled in his unleashed strength.

"'Tis a dream I, too, wish were real," she murmured. But she knew it was only a dream, one that would never be realized. In this place she ignored the allegiances that would one day tear them apart. She forgot the father she loved who led the rebels. If this was all she had of her knight and his love, she would accept it and be grateful for the gift.

His face was mere inches from hers when he whispered, "I meant when I said I would have no other, Emma. Do me the honor of becoming my wife and when I return to Talisand, come with me."

She let out a breath. How she wanted to go! Somehow she must find the words to tell him she could not. "My life is here, Geoffroi. The twins, my home, Inga." *My people, my father, my future.*

"Bring Inga and the twins with you," he said undaunted, sitting up to cast her a mischievous smile. "Even the hound! Talisand has room for all and I have a manor and land of my own. Even Artur and Sigga would find a home there with us."

"If only…." She gazed into the depths of his blue eyes. If only her father did not plot with the Danes to recapture York. If only she was not a thegn's daughter with all the attendant responsibilities to her station and to those who depended upon her. If Geoffroi knew her father and his allies planned to send the Norman king running, he would have nothing to do with her. His love might even turn to hate. If her father knew she had taken a Norman knight as her lover, he would kill that knight. Torn between them, she could tell neither of the other.

"You need only say 'Yes', Emma."

She sat up and began to brush the grass from her tunic, avoiding his eyes. "I cannot. Not... now."

He was silent for a time and then he said, "I know it would mean an upheaval in your life, but I will give you time, Emma, as much as I have to give. It may be that at summer's end I will return to the Lune River, to Talisand. I pray you will go with me. We belong together."

She felt a shiver run up her spine. At summer's end, he and the other Normans could be dead, slain by her fellow Northumbrians or their Danish allies. Mayhap even her father. The weight of the knowledge she bore crushed her. How could she tell him the battle for York was not over, as he might believe, but had only just begun? How could she face the prospect of losing him in that battle? Geoffroi could not die. No, he must live to return to his beloved Talisand, even if it were without her.

He stood and helped her to rise, then kissed her. She welcomed his kiss, desperately clinging to their few moments together. Each of his kisses was precious, for she did not know how long she would have them.

They brushed the grass from their clothes and walked hand in hand from the meadow, the ache of regret lodging deep within her heart for what she knew could never be and for fear of what was coming.

* * *

'Twas the middle of August when Malet found Geoff in the bailey where he had been speaking with Mathieu about the horses. The sun overhead was warm, heating his mail and the skin beneath his tunic. He was hoping for a cup of ale, but he could see by the sheriff's face, set in stern lines, he carried the weight of the world. The tankard of ale would have to wait.

Sending Mathieu on his way with a wave of his hand, he turned to Malet. "What is it?"

"A messenger has arrived from the king."

"He is returning?" Geoff guessed. "I thought William was hunting in Gloucestershire."

"He was," said Malet. "That is where the news reached him that more than two hundred Danish ships have been sighted off Dover. Since then, the Danes have attacked Ipswich and Norwich in East Anglia, destroying William's ships and plundering the towns."

For a moment, Geoff was too shocked at the news to speak. When he found his voice, he said, "The Danes are attacking England?"

"Aye, sailing north and pillaging along the way," came Malet's grave reply.

Regaining control of his thoughts, Geoff raked his hand through his hair, hardly believing that after three years the Danes would choose to sail to England. "Why would they do that when William has taken control of the land? Are they testing our defenses?"

"Mayhap they are. Think of it, Sir Geoffroi, more than two hundred longships, their warriors plundering the coast and moving north."

Staring into the distance, Geoff pictured the ships with their red and white striped sails, the curved stems carved into dragon heads. In his mind, he counted the warriors each would carry, some as many as a hundred. All together it would be thousands more men than they had knights.

"Does William believe they are headed to York?" Even as he asked, Geoff realized if the Danes were plundering the southeast of England, they would not fail to come north with a treasure as rich as York in their path.

Malet nodded.

"What are the king's orders?" Geoff asked.

"He orders us to resist and asks how long we can hold out."

"That will depend on whether the Northumbrians join them," said Geoff. "Remember, we are not so many compared with their greater numbers. York is not a small city and the warriors they have would add greatly to the Danes' numbers and their fighting skills. Worse, the Danes would give the rebels courage to fight on."

"I believe we can hold out for a year were we to take in sufficient food," said the sheriff, "but FitzOsbern wants to discuss it. That was my purpose in seeking you out. He has called for a meeting at the evening meal."

"I will be there," said Geoff.

Malet strode away, mumbling about sending a page to tell Gilbert of the meeting. In Geoff's mind, he saw Emma. *I must warn her.*

* * *

At the far end of the garden where Artur had built benches, Emma sat telling the twins the tale of Beowulf, one she had told them many times before but they had pleaded to hear it again. Beside her sat Inga, just beginning to show her rounding belly. The twins, with their upturned faces, were sitting cross-legged at Emma's feet, Magnus between them. They had spent many afternoons in such manner after their chores were done since the weather was warm and the days long.

The children loved the tale, so she told them what she knew, what her father had told her years ago, the tale of the great warrior who had come to the aid of the Danish king to slay the monster Grendel and later a dragon. The twins' eyes grew large at the daring exploits she described.

Inga, sitting next to her, looked at the twins with an amused expression. Her friend showed great patience with the children, making Emma think she would make a good mother.

"He lived to slay the dragon only to fall, fatally wounded in battle," Emma told the twins. "'Twas a crushing blow."

"I do not want him to die," said Finna mournfully.

"Ah, but 'tis the way of warriors," said Emma, tapping Finna's small nose.

"A great warrior expects to die in battle," Ottar sternly informed his sister as if he were an authority on great warriors and intended to become one himself. She supposed he did. His fascination with the knights had not diminished with the battle he had witnessed. The twins had just turned ten the week before and she regretted that the innocence of their childhood was being cut short by the times in which they lived.

"'Tis best to avoid battles, Ottar, and live in peace," she chided. Even as she said it she knew one sometimes had to fight for what was important and to defend one's home, one's honor. To live peaceably sometimes meant playing the coward. She would not want that for Ottar.

Artur strode into the garden. "Mistress, the squire has come on a matter he says is urgent."

"Squire?" It took her a moment to realize he meant Geoffroi's squire. "Oh, yea… Mathieu. I will come." She rose. "Inga, can you tell them another tale? Mayhap the tale of Cnut the Great?"

"Of course," said Inga, smiling at the children.

The twins settled down to hear more and Magnus left his place between them to follow Emma into the house.

The squire stood next to the hearth, his young face somber.

"Will you have something to drink?" she asked.

"Nay, my lady. I come in haste and must return. Sir Geoffroi sent me to warn you. We have word the Danes are sailing north towards York with hundreds of ships, mayhap only weeks away from the Humber."

She let out a sigh. *So it begins. Thank God Geoffroi knows.* She thought of the danger for him and her family on different sides of a fight that was surely coming. Would they survive such an onslaught?

"Please tell Sir Geoffroi I am grateful that he sent you, however unwelcome the news may be."

"Aye, my lady." With that, he bowed and departed.

She did not move but stayed next to the hearth, listening to the pounding of the horse's hooves as the squire galloped down the street to return to his master, her Norman lover. From the open door leading to the kitchen and the garden beyond, she could hear the twins' chatter.

Magnus nuzzled her hand with his cold nose. She patted his neck, having nearly forgotten he was there. Inhaling deeply, she steeled herself for what must be faced in the days ahead.

* * *

"How did she take it?" Geoff asked Mathieu, regretting he could not have gone himself to see Emma, to embrace her, to love her. It had been days since he had been able to get away and he sorely missed the woman who had become the light of his life.

"It was odd, sir. She did not faint or cry, as I dreaded she might. She was calm, saying little. Just thanked you for the warning. It was almost as if..." His brow wrinkled. "... as if she expected to hear what I had to say."

"Many of us have been expecting the Northumbrians to muster another attack. I have often spoken to her of my concern. But I never mentioned the Danes. I would have thought they were gone with Hardrada's defeat three years ago. But Emma is a strong woman. Mayhap she was trying to be strong for the children."

The meeting that evening was boisterous, each man having a different opinion.

"We must let William know we need more men and soon," urged Gilbert.

"The Danes are experienced warriors," said FitzOsbern, the gray in his dark hair suddenly speaking loudly of his years at William's side. "One wonders why they waited so long." He had fought them before, Geoff knew. "Why do they come now?" FitzOsbern's need to understand the why of it was not unlike Geoff's own but there was little to gain by pondering the Danes' motives at this late point. They were coming.

"No one knows," Geoff said, "but it hardly matters now."

"William asks how long we can hold out," said Malet, bringing them back to the message from the king. "Mayhap he means to send us more knights." The sheriff sent a hopeful glance in Geoff's direction.

"We must begin immediately to take in food stores and water," argued Gilbert. "I have room in the new castle's bailey for pigs and cattle enough to see us through a long siege."

"We must do that, of course," said Geoff, "but food and water will not be our only concerns. With one torch, the Danes could set the castles ablaze. And then there is the very real possibility the Northumbrians will aid the Danes by filling up the moats to ease their crossing."

"Aye," said Malet, "they might use timber from the houses that ring the castles. What do you suggest, Gil?"

"I would burn the houses that surround the castles," replied the castellan.

"Fire is a dangerous tool in our hands as well as the enemy's," warned Geoff. "Be careful what you do." He did not see how burning one row of homes would prevent others from being torn down, their timbers used to fill the moats. And he liked not using fire in such a way.

They argued for some time, but in the end, Malet decided to send the king word they could hold out for a year, as he believed. Geoff thought it unlikely. He would have asked the king for more men at once.

In keeping with his idea, Gilbert was dispatched by FitzOsbern to see to the firing of the homes near the castles.

"You do intend to warn the residents of York who live in those houses?" Geoff asked Fitz.

"For all we know they may succor rebels," insisted FitzOsbern. The Earl of Hereford's reputation was that of a harsh overlord, so the suggestion did not surprise Geoff. If it were left up to FitzOsbern, the people would have no warning at all.

"Fitz, there are women and children in those homes," argued Geoff. "They should at least be allowed to leave with what they can carry."

"Very well," FitzOsbern conceded. "We have time yet. You take a group of knights to warn the people in those homes, Sir Geoffroi." To Gilbert, he said, "We will give them five days to get out before you set the torch."

Geoff did not relish the task of telling people they were about to lose their homes, but he would see it done. Better he risked his men to warn the citizens of York who were threatened than allow innocents to die in the flames.

* * *

Maerleswein rapped on his daughter's door, anxious to tell her of all that would take place. Already he tasted victory on his tongue, knowing thousands of Northumbrians would join the Danes when they arrived at the mouth of the Humber.

The door opened and Emma stood there, smiling, but he sensed an underlying tension that spoke of worry. In her eyes he saw something else, mayhap fear.

"Father," she said, as he entered, "from whence do you come?"

He kissed her on the forehead. "The Humber most directly, where my army assembles. 'Tis where Swein's ships will meet us and soon, but before that I was in Scotland with Cospatric and Edgar."

She beckoned him to sit. "Are you hungry? Thirsty?"

"'Tis a warm day. Some ale would be welcome."

She fetched the drink herself and when she had returned and he sat on the bench, she pulled up the stool she always sat upon.

He took a drink of his ale and wiped his mouth.

"I have heard the Danes are coming," she said, "plundering their way north."

"I expect they are; you know they love their plunder, Emma. But how did you learn of this?"

"The Normans know, Father. Their king sent them word."

"Did you hear this from the Norman knight you spoke of?"

"Yea, he meant to warn me. He knows nothing of you."

"As I would have it. If they knew you were the daughter of the thegn who once ruled the North for King Harold, and now leads the uprising, they would as soon see you dead."

"Some of them, mayhap." She looked down at her hands entwined in her lap.

When he recalled her friendship with the French knight, his forehead creased with concern. He brushed it off, knowing the man would soon be dead. Glancing about the room, he suddenly realized how quiet it was. "Where is your brood, your hound, your servants?"

"Artur took Thyra to the blacksmith to have a loose shoe tightened. Sigga went with him to shop in the market—we want to have as much food on hand as we can—and the twins are in the garden with Inga and Magnus, tending the new plants. Why?"

"'Twould be best if you stayed close to home for the next fortnight. Thank God the house is far from the center of town. The Danes and our allies know to stay away from this street but with thousands of men, I cannot guarantee they will abide by their orders. I will post guards on every side and come to you when I can."

A shadow crossed her face.

"Do you worry still?" he asked.

"For you and my family, yes." Then looking up at him, "And for my friends in the city. Even for the Normans who have shown me kindness."

"Friends among the Normans?"

"You know the ones I have spoken of… the ones who brought Ottar home, who rescued Feigr and Magnus. I owe them much, Father."

"No matter, the Normans must go. We would again see an English king in the North."

Emma sighed and looked away. "I wish they would leave without all the killing."

"'Twill never happen, Emma. William wants Yorkshire as he wants all of England. To think we can stop him without a fight is to want something that can never be."

"Aye, I know it well," she said.

Seeing her sad face, he thought to cheer her. "Cospatric asks after you, Daughter."

She turned her beautiful eyes on him, the eyes of her mother. But her expression was not one of gladness as he had hoped. "The earl is a nice man," she said with no great enthusiasm. "Please give him my best."

"I am certain you will see more of Cospatric once York is again ours. We stopped at his estate at Bamburgh on our way sailing south from Scotland. 'Tis a grand place."

"Would you like to see the twins?" she asked, changing the subject.

"They miss you."

He heaved his large frame off the bench. "Aye, let me at the little mischief makers." He would have to speak of Cospatric another time.

* * *

Emma was happy her father was home, at least for a time, but she was restless and unable to gain any peace for her anxiety over the battle that grew ever closer, like a great, roaring beast stalking its prey.

Who would live and who would die? Should she and her little family flee or should she trust her father to guard them? He had many Northumbrians at his command. Surely they would protect her and the children, but what of Sir Geoffroi? And her friend, Helise Malet, and her sons?

When her father suggested they visit the old archbishop together, she leaped at the chance. Mayhap he would have words of wisdom to share.

"Can we go, too?" Ottar asked.

Inga looked up from where she sat on the bench at the end of the garden, the children and hound at her feet. "You and Finna can stay with me, Ottar," she said, seeing Emma's shake of her head when the boy wanted to go. "I do not think Emma will take Magnus either."

"Nay," said Emma's father, "the beast stays. We go to the Minster on business. I doubt the archbishop would want the hound sniffing around his sacred relics."

"You can go with me to Mass, Ottar," said Finna. "'Tis not as if you never go to the Minster."

"Oh, all right," the boy reluctantly agreed. "I would rather hear another tale anyway."

Emma tousled his hair with her fingers. Then thinking of how young, how vulnerable they still were, she took them into her arms and held them close. "I will be back soon and then we can make some more berry tarts."

The twins exchanged eager glances and, placated by the promise of tarts, settled down to listen to Inga as she began a tale of a Danish warrior of long ago.

Emma and her father walked to the Minster. They were far enough from the castles where the knights congregated that she felt confident her father was safe from recognition by any, save for his friends.

The sun was bright in the cloudless sky and the day so warm she needed no cloak. Since they went to see the archbishop, she wore a gown of dark green linen finely woven and a belt of cloth embroidered with golden thread. Halden had traded for much fine cloth and she had a store of gowns saved for special days and feasts.

People passed them on the streets, going about their business. Some recognized her father and bid him welcome. He was well liked in York.

"'Tis odd to think that these streets, filled with people plying their trades and shopping for their families, will soon have to deal with thousands of Danes," said Emma.

"The people will see them as coming to their aid. The Northumbrians and the men of York will join the Danes to defeat the Normans. The people will rejoice at the victory the Danes will allow them."

When they were nearly to the Minster, it occurred to her to ask, "Why do you want to see the archbishop? Do you seek Ealdred's blessing?"

"Nay, though I would have it if he offers. My purpose in coming is quite different. Cospatric will meet us at the Minster. We want the archbishop to agree to crown Edgar king, if not of England, then at least of Northumbria."

Emma knew the archbishop well enough that she did not think he would agree. After all, it had been he who had crowned the Norman king three years before. And it had been the archbishop who had warned against further rebellion.

They ascended the steps of the great cathedral and Cospatric pulled away from the shadows to greet them.

"My lady," he said taking her hand and bowing over her fingers, "I was hoping Maerleswein would persuade you to come."

She recognized the noble countenance and the handsome face of the Earl of Bamburgh. She had not seen him since winter but she had long known him. "Earl Cospatric, how good to see you." Was that interest she detected in his brown eyes? There was certainly something new in his gaze. She believed Cospatric to be a fine man, but she had given her affection to a certain French knight. Once her heart was given, she would not change.

They strolled into the cathedral. Cospatric's guards waited at the door.

"Do you share my father's confidence for the outcome of the uprising?" she asked the earl.

"The outcome is not in doubt, my lady. The Danes sail with their hundreds of ships and, not only them, but others have joined our cause from Poland, Frisia and Saxony, even Lithuania—men-at-arms, ready to fight."

"I have long wanted the Normans and their castles gone from York," she said, "but I shudder to think what it may cost us to see it done."

Before he could answer, the archbishop's assistant approached. "His Lordship is expecting you. Please follow me."

Her father raised a brow to Cospatric.

"I made certain he was available to see us," explained the earl.

The monk led them to a room behind the nave near the great library. He opened the door and bid them enter.

In a carved chair set to one side, the archbishop sat clothed in a fine, white linen tunic belted at the waist. His countenance was drawn and pale. His body slumped against one side of the chair. He did not look well.

Her father introduced Cospatric, though he was known to the archbishop.

When her turn came, Emma greeted him as "My Lord Archbishop" as was her custom, yet he had never insisted anyone call him more than "Father".

With a frail hand he bade them sit. Then he waited, studying their faces.

"Do you know why we have come?" asked her father.

"I know that Danish ships sail toward York. FitzOsbern has told me."

"Yea, 'tis true. And soon we will meet Edgar."

"So, the Ætheling returns from Scotland," the archbishop said with a sigh. "I do not think it wise."

"But he is the rightful king of England," protested Cospatric. "We would have you crown him as such."

"I once thought to do so," said the archbishop, sinking deeper into his chair. His face was lined with sorrow. "But no more. I crowned William and now he is king. And king he will remain."

"Even of the North?" her father asked, his brows drawing together in a frown.

"Yes, even here. The time has come for peace, Maerleswein. Do not fight what you cannot change. It will only lead to many deaths."

"We must fight," her father insisted.

"Many rise with us, Good Father," Cospatric said, his expression hopeful. "Not just the Danes and others from Europe. All over England there are those who want an end to the Normans. People whose lands have been seized, who cannot pay his egregious taxes, people who refuse to become his serfs."

The archbishop looked troubled as he let out a deep sigh. "I feared it was so."

A long silence hung in the air. Emma thought the archbishop might fall asleep he appeared so weak, so weary.

At last, her father spoke. "So you will not name Edgar king, even if we are victorious, as we are certain to be?"

The archbishop let out a sorrowful breath. "Nay, I will not."

The two men rose and she with them. What more could they say? Her father and Cospatric said their goodbyes and turned on their heels to leave, disappointment clear on their faces.

She told them she would join them shortly and remained with Ealdred. She had thought to seek his advice but seeing how frail and pale he was, she did not want to trouble him. "You do not look well, My Lord. Is there anything I can do for you?"

"Nay, my daughter," said the old man, patting her hand with his ancient, bony fingers. "I am old and it is time for me to leave this life for the next. I do not wish to see what will follow this day. But I will pray for you."

She gave him a small smile before taking her leave. "God bless you, Father, for the good you have done."

"And you my daughter," came the feeble reply.

Before she left the cathedral, Emma stopped at the altar and said a prayer for the man who had faithfully served God for so long.

CHAPTER 11

"Archbishop Ealdred has passed from this life," Artur somberly announced as he stepped through the front door a few days later.

"I am sorry," Emma said, looking down at the golden tapestry stretched on the frame. She had been working on it for some months as a gift for the archbishop. It depicted him riding on a black horse, his head held high as he traveled through an English village. She had hoped it might bring him memories of happier days. It was finished. She rolled it up and rose from the bench, giving Artur a sympathetic smile. "This will keep for another day."

It was not just the passing of a good man but the ominous end of an era. She was sorry her father had left for the Humber and was not here to share the loss. She had known the archbishop was old and frail, yet she could not help wondering if he had died of a broken heart. The look of despair she had seen on his face when she had left the Minster a few days before spoke loudly of his sadness at having failed to persuade the people of York to submit to the Norman king. All his pleading had been for naught.

A sigh escaped her lips as she took the tapestry to her chamber and placed it in a chest with some others. Mayhap it was best he had passed, for the city Ealdred had longed to see at peace would now see only war.

She decided to go to her garden where Sigga was harvesting vegetables. It was September and harvest time for all of Emma's fields, too.

"'Tis a dark day," said Sigga, patting down the dirt around the herbs from which she had taken cuttings.

Emma joined her servant in the work, grateful for something to do that took her mind from more troubling thoughts.

"The archbishop was a voice of reason," murmured Sigga, glancing at Emma from where she was digging out a weed.

Sitting back on her heels, Emma wiped her brow. "He was old, Sigga. His death was not unexpected. But you are right; such a faithful servant of God will be sorely missed."

They were watering the plants with the buckets they had carried from the well when an acrid smell rose in Emma's nostrils. "Do you smell smoke?" Her eyes met Sigga's. "Something is burning."

Alarmed, she sniffed the air and hurried through the kitchen and into the hearth room, detecting nothing amiss. But the faint smell of smoke persisted. Seeing no one, she shouted up the stairs, "Inga, where are the children?"

"Here with me," said Inga coming to the top of the stairs.

Emma's heart raced with fear as she threw open the front door. The bitter smell of burning wood was stronger. Fire was dangerous in a city made of timber, wattle and daub. Stirred by the wind, it could quickly leap from one structure to another, rapidly destroying an entire street, even the entire city.

"Inga," she shouted, "there is fire somewhere. Keep the children inside until I return."

Ottar appeared at the top of the stairs. "I want to see, too!"

"You and Finna stay here with Magnus until I learn what is happening."

The hound suddenly appeared next to Ottar to stare down at her. "You, too, Magnus."

Outside, she raced across the streets that lay between her house and the Minster. She arrived out of breath. Panting, she stood in front of the cathedral, looking south toward the castles, shielding her eyes as she stared into the distance. A huge cloud of black smoke rose high into the sky above where the castles stood. *May God have mercy.*

Artur came to her side, his chest heaving from running after her. "My lady, is it the castles?"

"I cannot say for certain, but its source must be near them." Feeling the breeze on her face, she said, "The wind is coming this way. It will bring the fire to the Minster. It will bring the fire to us!" She faced her servant. "We must prepare to flee."

With haste born of fear, they ran back to the house.

* * *

"What in God's name was Gilbert thinking!" shouted Geoff. He pointed to where the flames leapt from one thatched roof to another. "See there," he said to FitzOsbern, standing beside him on the tower's battlement, "the fire spreads beyond the houses he torched. It roars into the city."

"Aye, the wind carries the blaze north," replied the earl in dismay. His lined face a mask of worry, he gazed north. "The Minster lies in its path."

"It has not rained for days. At the speed the dry wood will burn, it will no doubt reach the cathedral." Geoff gritted his teeth, furious Gilbert's men had not been more careful. It was just as he had feared. For a moment, he watched the flames engulf another house, disturbed at how fast the fire was spreading.

It had been foolish for Gilbert to set fire to the homes. Surely destroying them would not prevent the rebels from finding sufficient timber to fill the moat. The forests of York were full of wood. But Gilbert had been intent on torching the homes nonetheless.

Smoke filled Geoff's nostrils until it made him cough and he had to cover his face with a cloth. Emma's home lay in the path of the fire though some distance east of the Minster.

"I must warn Emma," he told FitzOsbern. He had to help her and her family escape the inferno.

Minutes later, Geoff launched himself into the saddle and tore out of the gate and over the bridge with Alain following. Galloping through the smoke, they sped down one street, then another, avoiding the path of the fire, burning straight through the center of town.

People scattered in all directions before the hooves of their powerful horses. Panicked by the spreading fire, they shouted to their families and serfs to help carry away their goods.

Pulling rein in front of Emma's house, he and Alain slid to the ground. Their horses' coats were soaked with sweat and lather from the hard ride. "Can you stay with the horses?" he asked.

"Aye." Alain accepted the reins Geoff handed him.

Geoff stormed to the door, preparing to knock, when it opened.

"My lady is upstairs packing, sir," said Artur.

"'Tis well she does. The fire is headed this way."

"Are the castles burning?" the servant asked with a look of concern.

"Nay, 'tis the homes around them but the fire has spread." Geoff glanced up the stairs, anxious to see her, to assure himself she was safe and had a place to go. "Artur, I must speak with your mistress. Can you help Sir Alain with the horses? We ran them hard."

"Aye, I will take care of them."

The servant left and Geoff raced up the stairs.

In her chamber he found Emma scurrying around, shoving things into a tapestry bag. The hound came to greet him, wagging its tail, unaware of the danger that had all of York on the run.

Emma whirled around and her eyes lit up. "Geoffroi!" She ran into his arms and, for a moment, there was no fire, no threat, only the comfort he drew from knowing she was safe. Inhaling her fresh woman's scent above the smell of smoke that permeated his clothing, he felt the tension in her body. Looking up at him, she said, "I was terrified to think the fire might be coming from the castle. That you might be in danger."

"Nay, my love, 'tis homes burning, torched to prevent their wood from being used to fill the moat. A witless idea. Now the whole city is threatened."

She pulled back from his arms, terror in her eyes. "I must finish packing. We are leaving."

"Where are the young ones?"

"With Inga. They are helping her to pack." She reached for some clothing on the bed and stuffed it into her bag.

"Where will you go?" he asked, already knowing where he wanted her to go. Though taking her to the castle had its own risks.

She reached for some jewelry, the gold glimmering in the dim light, and dropped a necklace into a small velvet bag. "In truth, I know not. I just want to be certain we are free of the fire. If need be, we can stay in the fields. There are those who will shelter us."

"Will you come to the castle? The wind blows away from it. You would be safe there."

She hesitated, her blue-green eyes speaking of her distress. "Nay. I would rather not be surrounded by so many of your knights. And Inga will not return there again. Besides, Feigr is on his way, bringing friends who will flee with us."

Geoff did not want to leave her but he knew he must. "I cannot stay but I will come tomorrow. Where will you be?"

"If the fire is out and my house still stands, I will be here. Otherwise, I will be on the other side of the River Foss, among the crofts to the north."

Geoff had seen the cultivated fields to the north and east of the River Foss and remembered the cottages that dotted the countryside. "We can take you there. Alain is with me."

"Nay, there will be too many of us. I have Thyra and she can carry what we cannot."

He had always known she had courage. Now, intent on helping the others, she calmly accepted that she must flee her home. "All right, but please take care, Emma. And hurry." Drawing her into his arms, he kissed her. It took all of his resolve to pull away. "I will come tomorrow or the next day. Keep the hound close."

Worry clouded her eyes as she stared up at him. "I will."

He patted the hound's head as he departed. Geoff felt certain that his life was bound up with Emma's. Somehow they had to be together, no matter the fire, no matter the Danes.

As he and Alain rode back to the castle, the shouts of the people fleeing the onrushing flames echoed all around them. Not a few of them threw curses at "the Norman swine".

* * *

Two days later, Maerleswein stood on the deck of the longship rolling beneath his feet, his eyes on the waters of the River Ouse as they sailed toward York. It was the same ship on which he had sailed to Denmark and Scotland, the same ship he had sailed to meet the Danes at the mouth of the Humber.

Turning his head, he glimpsed Osbjorn and his nephews, Harald and Cnut, proudly standing on the deck of their dragon ship, sailing beside him, the square sail taut with the wind. The black raven on a red banner flying atop their ship's mast was the symbol of the victory they believed would soon be theirs. Behind the two ships were hundreds more.

Maerleswein's spirits soared. Soon York would be theirs once again.

They had left the mouth of the Humber the day before, accompanied by King Swein's ships with their colorful round shields hanging from the side of the sleek hulls, their square sails billowing with wind. Marching apace along the riverbank were Northumbrians, rejoicing as they went. It was all he had asked for, save that Malcolm of Scotland had yet to appear.

But he had the leaders he needed. He had the Danish ships and he had the men.

Next to him, young Edgar braced his hands on the rail and gazed back at the hundreds of ships in their wake. "I have never seen such a sight."

"Nor I," said Cospatric, standing next to the Saxon heir.

"'Tis the Danes who will see us the victors," said Maerleswein. "Swein does not come himself, but he has thrown the might of his people into the fray."

"What is your plan?" asked Waltheof, the tall, blond Earl of Huntingdon, who appeared every bit the Dane as he leaned on his tall axe, his powerful legs swaying with the ship's movements.

"Unless Osbjorn has a better idea, I would make camp and attack at first light," said Maerleswein.

Waltheof nodded, a grin spreading across his face. "Your plan pleases me."

Another hour brought them within sight of the city. Gazing off the leeward side of the ship, Maerleswein stared in shock, for where there should have been the city, there were only tendrils of smoke rising from scorched ground. The only structures he could see above the blackened earth were the castles of the Norman king.

"What goes here?" Cospatric asked, his face showing the shock Maerleswein felt.

Anger such as he had never known surged through Maerleswein's veins. "Have the Normans destroyed the city?"

The crews rowed their ships to the bank of the river where a crowd so great he could not number it poured forth to greet them, shouting their welcome and joining the Northumbrians who had traveled the bank of the river all the way from the Humber.

"You there!" Maerleswein shouted to one of the men coming to greet them, "What has happened to cause this devastation?"

"'Tis the Norman scum's doing," said the man as his lip curled in a bitter scowl. "They thought to keep us from filling their ditches by burning the homes that ringed the castle. 'Twas bad enough they took so many homes, but then the fools let the fire escape."

"My God," breathed out Cospatric.

"I must see my daughter," said Maerleswein. He gave orders to his men and soon tents began to rise on the bank of the River Ouse. "I leave you in charge, Cospatric, while I go in search of Emma."

"Do you think Emma is safe?" the earl asked, his face speaking his disquiet. It pleased Maerleswein to see the look of concern in the earl's eyes. Mayhap he already considered Emma as a future wife.

"Aye. You know as well as I, Emma is a resourceful woman. She would have fled the blaze. I but go to see for myself how she fares and to leave guards who will assure no Dane thinking to pillage comes close to her. I will return ere long."

Taking some of his most trusted men, Maerleswein mounted the dark bay horse he had brought with him on the ship and left Osbjorn and Cospatric to organize the camp.

* * *

Geoff joined FitzOsbern on the battlement, looking north into the smoldering ruin of the city. Malet and Alain stood with them. The cloud of smoke had mostly cleared now and the blue sky reappeared in places in stark contrast to the black ash and charred timbers. It saddened Geoff to think of the destruction.

In the distance, what was left of the tall Minster rose from the ground, a charred hulk whose bell was now silent. Ravaged by fire, the wooden parts of the church had burned, but bits of its skeleton remained to signify the terrible loss. He was glad the archbishop had not lived to see it.

The fire had raged for two days, cutting a swath through the city from the castles north toward the cathedral, destroying homes and shops along the way. Small fires still lingered where there was fuel. Oddly, the blaze had left some buildings undamaged, a home here, a shop there, as if it had carefully selected which structures would be its victims.

Consumed with fighting the fire's incursions into the outer palisade fence, he had not been able to return to Emma's house. From what he had heard, it was possible that, lying so far to the northeast, it might have been spared. It was his fervent hope and his nightly prayer she was well. She was his heart and he could not live without her.

From the other side of the battlement, a great hue and cry suddenly arose. He and the other men quickly crossed to the other side to look down at the point where the River Ouse met the River Foss.

His heart sank as understanding dawned. As far as his eye could see, longships were unloading at the banks of the river. "The Danes have arrived."

"There must be hundreds of them," said Alain beneath his breath.

"And thousands of warriors," said Geoff. As they watched, the Danes, armed with axes, swords and spears, poured forth from the ships to be embraced by Northumbrians waiting on the shore.

"*Mon Dieu,*" gasped Malet, gaping at the Danes swarming ashore.

FitzOsbern said nothing but the scowl on his face spoke loudly.

Geoff watched the scene, dismayed. Even knowing they were coming had not prepared him for the sight. He turned to Malet. "Would that you had not sent word to William telling him we could hold out for a year."

"Mayhap I was wrong," admitted the sheriff in a stunned voice.

"Surely William has received word of their numbers," muttered FitzOsbern. "He knows they have been plundering their way north."

"Even if he has," Geoff said, "his army cannot move as fast as we require. I would not count upon his aid. Best we prepare for the siege that will soon be upon us."

* * *

Maerleswein first stopped at Emma's house, pleased to find it untouched by the fire as were all the homes in that section of the city, but many were empty, including Emma's. He ordered his men to ride on, northeast of the city walls, to where he thought she might go—the cottage of Jack and Martha, two of her villeins. Emma was fond of the couple and he knew them to be trustworthy, loyal to his daughter.

When they arrived, he was relieved to see the twins playing in front of the cottage. He dismounted, telling his men to wait.

The twins rushed to greet him and he swept them into his arms.

"Have you come to save us, Godfather?" asked Finna.

"From the fire, you mean?"

"It was awful," interrupted Ottar. "The smoke burned my eyes."

"Mine, too," added his sister in a small voice.

"I have come to take you and Emma home, and to see you are safe. There now, is not that a fine thing?"

The twins grinned. It brought joy to his heart to have cheered them. A fire sweeping through the city must have been terrifying to one so young. It would be terrifying to anyone.

The door of the small thatched cottage opened. Emma appeared, her long flaxen plaits trailing down the front of the simple, brown tunic, one he thought she kept to work in her garden.

"Father! I heard voices and wondered who it was the twins were speaking with. I am glad to see you."

He put the twins down, walked to his daughter and kissed her on the cheek. The twins ran at his side to keep up with his long strides. In truth, he was glad to see they were all here. He stopped in front of his daughter and studied her face. "You are well?"

"Yea, Father. We escaped the fire as you can see, but we have watched the smoke and people fleeing tell us the city lies in ruins. Did you see my house?"

Finna clung to Emma's tunic and looked up at him.

"Aye. It stands." At that Emma's face brightened, Finna's did as well. "I have come to bring you home. Are Sigga and Artur with you?"

"Sigga and Inga are in the cottage and Artur is helping Jack with the lambs."

"You must see them, Godfather," urged Finna. "They are much bigger now."

"I will visit the lambs," he agreed, not wanting to disappoint them. "Then we must go while we still have light."

"I see you do not come alone," Emma remarked, her eyes taking in the five men who had come with him sitting atop their horses some distance away.

"Nay, and not just these, four of which I will leave to guard you. The Danes have come with their many ships. They camp on the bank of the River Ouse along with the Northumbrians who have joined our cause. Cospatric and Edgar are with them. Think of it, Emma. Hundreds of ships and thousands of men. All of Northumbria has risen to fight the Normans."

"When does the fighting begin?" she asked anxiously.

"We attack at first light."

* * *

Geoff had spent the night preparing his men and his weapons. From the tower's battlement, he had watched the hundreds of fires in the Danish camp on the bank of the river, wondering if fire would be the Danes' chosen weapon. None in the tower castle had slept even after the campfires died down.

Dawn broke in the cloud-streaked sky as he gazed toward the city. The flames still lingering in isolated places added to the hellish nature of what Geoff knew might be the place of his last battle. He had faced death many times and knew well the fear before a battle. But he could not recall a time when William's forces had been so greatly outnumbered. Even so this was not the first time he had considered the day might be his last.

He did not want to think he might never see Emma again. He wanted a life with her, one day even a child. He did not worry for her safety since she was a Northumbrian, but the Danes' presence added an uncertain element. Would they seek to pillage what was left of the city? *Will Emma and her family be safe?*

Geoff was standing at the top of the motte looking into the bailey when the Danes' fierce war cries echoed through the air as they attacked the castle in a great rush. Their shrieks sent an icy chill snaking down his spine. He had fought for William in Maine and Normandy against the French, at Hastings and Exeter against the English and the year before in York at the side of the Red Wolf, but if he survived the day, he would never forget the shrieks of the Danes as they tasted blood they had yet to shed.

Arrows flew from the castle battlements in a great whooshing sound. The Danes raised their shield walls where the arrows struck in the thickest part of their numbers. A few of the Danes fell but not many. The archers on the battlements of both castles fired another volley. Once he and his fellow knights engaged in close fighting, the arrows would no longer be of use.

Geoff rushed down to the bailey and mounted his destrier Mathieu had waiting.

"*Dex Aie*!" God aid us! Knights shouted as they poured forth from the castle to engage.

"I want you and your knights with my own and those of FitzOsbern, Sir Geoffroi," shouted Malet coming alongside Geoff.

"As you wish," Geoff said and signaled to his men to circle Malet's and FitzOsbern's guards. Protecting the two noblemen, Geoff and Alain led the knights into battle.

Immediately they were confronted with the Danes' axes and swords flying in all directions. With his long shield, Geoff blocked an attack from a blond, bearded warrior on one side of his horse, then with his sword sliced the neck of a dark bearded man on the other. The Danes screamed in exaltation and their victims grunted in pain. It was almost like Hastings where they had faced the elite huscarls of the Saxon army.

Geoff and Alain fought side-by-side keeping the nobles protected from the most vicious attacks. Around them, the other knights sought to cut down the bearded rebels, but they swarmed like bees over the ground.

What seemed like hours later, Geoff felt fatigue sapping his strength. He had lost track of the rebels that had fallen to his sword as the clash of steel with shields and blades gave way to the groans of wounded and dying men. He was coated in the blood of the slain. His own arm had suffered a gash and only now did he feel the pain.

Finishing off one rebel, he surveyed the field of battle. While they had killed many of the Danes and their allies, too many French knights had fallen. Their mail-clad bodies littered the grass now soaked in blood. The knights protecting the nobles had dwindled to a precious few. Concerned he could no longer afford Malet and FitzOsbern the protection needed, he gave the order, "Fall back!"

They managed to shield Malet and FitzOsbern as they retreated across the bridge to the palisade gate, fighting off Danes and rebels as they went. The nobles and the small group of knights plunged into the bailey, past the guards still holding the gate.

"Into the tower," he shouted to Malet and FitzOsbern, fearing it would only postpone the inevitable.

They dismounted in the bailey where Mathieu met them. "Stable the horses, then follow us into the tower."

Mathieu nodded and took the reins of their horses.

A short while later, Mathieu joined them in the hall. Geoff knew the squire was disappointed not to have seen his share of fighting but the battle was too intense for Geoff to allow it. He would not risk the Red Wolf's faithful squire.

"I need you here," said Geoff, "but keep to the shadows. You may have need of escape."

"Aye, sir," replied Mathieu.

Minutes later, Geoff stood at the door of the great hall looking down into the bailey when the Danes broke through the line of knights defending the gate.

"Bar the door!" he ordered the few men inside the tower. "Then fall back to guard the sheriff and the earl."

* * *

Gripping his round shield in one hand and his spear in the other, Maerleswein and his men surged forward with their swords and spears to inflict a bloody assault on the Normans. Grudgingly, he admitted the French knights fought well but they were sorely outnumbered and the people of Northumbria unforgiving in their revenge.

No mercy was given, no quarter offered. They fought with a purpose, not for the love of battle like the Danes, but to take back their city and to thrust out the Normans who had viciously oppressed them.

At one point, he crossed paths with Feigr, the sword-maker, wielding one of his silvered blades, crying aloud his vengeance as he slew a Norman knight. "This," said Feigr, piercing the knight's throat and thrusting his sword deep, "is for my daughter." Maerleswein wondered how many men of York had come seeking reprisal for their daughters' stolen virtue. *Too many.*

He was surprised when some of the Normans left the protection of the walls of the new castle on Baille Hill, venturing forth on a sally, only to be cut down as they passed through the gate. Waltheof had placed himself there like a Nordic harbinger of death. As each Norman drew near, Waltheof let his giant axe fall in a move that could only be called an execution. In a steady stream, the severed heads of the French knights fell to the earth and rolled down the hill to form a large pile below. Even to Maerleswein, it was gruesome.

The fighting went on for hours, battle lust carrying Maerleswein and his men forward until, with the Danes' help, they had captured the castles and nearly every Norman lay dead. Hundreds of bodies were strewn about the baileys, at the base of the massive, square towers and on the banks of the rivers.

Some Danes and Northumbrians had fallen to the long French swords and lances as they fought on the riverbanks, but their losses were few compared to the number of French knights slain. In such tight spaces the knights' horses had not given them much of an advantage. And their numbers were not so many as the Danes.

When the battle was theirs, Maerleswein's men surged through the gate and broke down the door of the first castle built the year before, a hated symbol of Norman domination.

Soon after, with Cospatric at his side, he strode into the great hall where his captain told him he could find the nobles they had taken prisoner: Gilbert de Ghent, whom Osbjorn had brought over from the new castle where he'd been captured, William Malet, the Sheriff of Yorkshire and his family, and William FitzOsbern, Lord Hereford.

He knew the three men from his time as Sheriff of Lincolnshire. And he could see from their faces, they remembered him.

A small group of French knights surrounded the nobles, their stance oddly proud given they had just lost thousands of men and been stripped of their weapons.

Osbjorn swaggered into the hall with Swein's two sons and walked toward him, all three bearing wide grins. "We have won!"

"Aye, so we have," said Maerleswein.

"We go to join the men," said Osbjorn. "They seek their plunder and we would have our share. Even now Norman helms and swords lay on the ground for the taking. What do you have here?"

"A few prisoners I must see to."

Osbjorn nodded and cast a glance at the nobles behind Maerleswein.

"Go, then." He waved the Dane off. "But take no booty except from the Normans and keep your men clear of the far northeast of the city where lies my daughter's home, else your men will die by my sword."

"Of course," Osbjorn said, tipping his head. "I will see you later when we return for the evening's feast."

Maerleswein rolled his eyes at Cospatric. The Northumbrians might be there to take back their city, but the Danes were there to plunder its riches. King Swein would not have been so shortsighted.

Swein's brother and sons departed as Maerleswein's captain approached. "What would you have me do with these?" He gestured toward the group of nobles and the knights who stood with them.

"We will keep the nobles as prisoners. They may yet be useful to us. The rest we will slay." Smiling at Cospatric, he said, "Mayhap Waltheof's axe is not yet dull."

CHAPTER 12

Emma anxiously paced as Artur stirred the hearth fire, grateful Inga watched the twins in their chamber. Knowing the battle had been underway for some hours, she prayed for the safe deliverance of the men she loved, hearing in her mind her father's words. *It will be a time of celebration, not mourning*. How could that be true when the two men she cared for most fought on opposite sides? The people of York might celebrate a victory this night, but would she?

She had explained to Ottar and Finna what was happening as best she could. They knew of the fire, had seen the destruction on the walk they had taken with Emma after the conflagration had ended.

Finna had stared at the smoldering ruin of the Minster and wrinkled her little girl forehead. "What happened?"

How could she explain to a child that the place in which she was growing up—her home—was changing, that men fought and died to control it? None of the answers she had to give told the whole truth, nor could they, but she had tried all the same.

A pounding sounded on the door, scattering her thoughts.

Artur went to open it. To her shock, one of the men her father had left to guard her home stood with his knife pressed to the neck of Geoffroi's squire.

The burly guard forced Mathieu through the door. The squire's hazel eyes were wide with fear, his cheeks flushed. He had obviously ridden hard to get here. "This one says you know him, my lady. Claims he brings you an urgent message. Should I slay the Norman offal and be rid of him?"

"Nay! I do know him. Take your knife from his neck. He is a friend."

The guard gave her a skeptical look but lowered his knife. "I have already removed his weapons, my lady."

"You may leave us, sir," she said, ignoring the guard's incredulous look.

"Come Mathieu." The squire looked bedraggled and frightened, his brown hair tangled around his face, his mail soiled. "Artur, get Mathieu some ale."

Artur fetched the ale and the squire took a large swallow, wiping his mouth with his sleeve, then handed the tankard back.

She gazed at him with concern. "How goes the battle, Mathieu? I have had no word."

"The Danes and the rebels have their victory, my lady, but at a terrible cost. Thousands of the king's men lay dead, nearly the entire garrison of both castles."

Emma was stricken, torn between the Northumbrians' success and the stark reality of the slaughter that had secured it. "Sir Geoffroi?" she asked in a faint voice, almost afraid of the answer.

"He lives but mayhap not for long. That is why I have come. The rebels now in charge of the castle threaten his life and that of Sir Alain. I only escaped through the postern gate to seek your aid. I do not know if you can help but if you have any influence with their leaders, please come. The nobles they have taken prisoner, but the knights they intend to kill."

Emma did not know who held the nobles, but certainly if not her father then Cospatric or Edgar. Even King Swein's brother, Osbjorn, would know her. "I will go." She turned to address Artur. "Call the guards and saddle Thyra."

Her father's guards were not happy to accede to her request. "The Danes are now controlling the city, my lady," said the one in charge. "They may be allies but 'tis still dangerous. We cannot defend against so many."

She knew what he meant. He was worried they might see her as an object of their lust. Dismissing the danger she could do nothing about, she said, "I must go. A man's life is at stake." Glancing at the squire, she said, "Remove anything that shows you to be a Norman. Artur can give you a plain tunic. You will ride pillion with me."

The guards did not like it but, in the end, two of them rode with her and Mathieu and two remained behind to guard her family. Emma left the house with a word to Artur to keep Sigga, Inga and the children safe. Magnus whimpered as they left, the look in his dark eyes telling her he wanted to go. She would not risk his life.

* * *

When they were surrounded by the rebels and their weapons taken, Geoff had placed himself in front of Malet and his family. His arm was still bleeding but not badly. Alain had taken a sword point in his shoulder and now dripped blood onto his mail. Undaunted, the Bear stood in front of Gilbert and FitzOsbern. The few other men who had been in the castle when Geoff had ordered the doors barred now huddled with the nobles. Without their weapons they would be of little use but Geoff still thought of himself as a protector. His death might at least delay that of the others.

He had not witnessed the end of the battle but he had heard the shouts of the great victory claimed by the rebels. He heaved a bitter sigh knowing the rest of his knights and men-at-arms must now be dead.

"Who is the tall one who gives the orders?" he whispered to FitzOsbern over his shoulder.

"Maerleswein," he spit out, "the former Sheriff of Lincolnshire, a thegn who once swore allegiance to William. Beside him, the younger one with the dark hair is Earl Cospatric. He was once the Earl of Northumbria. Rebels both."

"The leaders?"

"Aye, most likely, along with the Dane who just left."

The one FitzOsbern had named Maerleswein pulled his long seax from its leather sheath at his waist and strolled toward Geoff and Alain. The tall Northumbrian was coated in dried blood, even his face and beard were streaked with it.

In Norman French, Maerleswein said, "You and the other knights are of no use to me." Then he took a step toward Geoff and pressed the knife's edge to his throat. Geoff felt a trickle of blood course down his neck and both fear and resolve streaked down his spine. He would not cower. If die he must, then die he would.

The blade was suddenly withdrawn and the rebel leader's head jerked toward the front of the hall where a tall woman wearing a dark cloak ran through the door.

Geoff would have recognized her anywhere. *Emma. Mon Dieu. What is she doing here?* At her side was Mathieu, dressed as a Northumbrian, followed by two warriors, their swords drawn.

"Father!" she shouted, letting her hood drop and hurrying toward Maerleswein.

Father?

Maerleswein sheathed his blade. "Emma, why have you come? 'Tis not safe."

Emma's eyes were fierce as she shot Geoff a glance before drawing near to the man she had called father. Panting, she breathed out, "I come to save a friend."

Maerleswein frowned at the guards behind Emma, his harsh glare chiding them for having failed in their duty. Facing his daughter, he demanded, "What friend could you find in a Norman castle?"

"These two knights and this squire you would slay," she said to the blond giant she had claimed as her sire.

Geoff remembered the large shoes he had seen in the room where they had laid the sword-maker and his gaze shifted to Maerleswein's feet. Emma was his daughter? The leader of the rebels was her *father*? Disbelief gave way to rising anger that settled into his gut. All this time she had known her father plotted with the Danes to slaughter William's knights, yet she had said not a word. She had allowed Geoff to aid the family of the rebel leader, even feeding them. For Christ sake, she had even welcomed him to her bed!

To betray me?

"Father, remember the Normans I spoke of who came to my rescue? The ones who helped Ottar, Feigr and Magnus?"

Maerleswein cast a glance at Geoff and Alain. "*These* are the French knights?"

Emma nodded. "The ones who stand before you, guarding the Norman nobles, and this squire who summoned me. I would ask you to spare them."

Maerleswein's face hardened into a scowl, his eyes narrowing as if he would deny her request.

"For *my* sake, Father," she pleaded.

Maerleswein let out a breath and his countenance softened when he looked into his daughter's anxious eyes. Geoff had experienced those same blue-green eyes turned on him. He did not doubt her father would relent.

"All right, Daughter. It will be as you say. They are not many and I suppose 'twill not hinder us." Then to one of his soldiers, "Put the knights in the tower chambers and post guards at the doors. Malet, his wife and sons can take another chamber and FitzOsbern and Gilbert a third."

"Aye, sir," the warrior dipped his head, "it shall be done."

"Thank you, Father," said Emma, casting Geoff a glance that spoke of regret.

"Helise, I am sorry," Emma said to the woman.

Malet's wife regarded her coolly and looked away.

Geoff felt empty, sickened at the thought Emma could accept his kisses and his trust while carrying on a grand deception. He had been well and truly deceived. Now, like the Valkyrie he had first imagined her, she would choose to give him life. *But for how long?* He could not imagine they would keep him and the others alive when they had already slaughtered the garrisons. Mayhap once she was gone, Maerleswein would see to their deaths as well.

Malet had been right the night of the feast when he had warned him. *Could she be a rebel spy?* Geoff had not thought so then, but now the evidence was laid before him, too clear to deny. Lured like a fish to the line, baited by her beauty and her winsome smiles, he had never considered Emma might be one of the rebels, much less the daughter of their leader. He had believed her only a widow he could win. He had been wrong.

Geoff grew bitter remembering the hundreds of knights and men-at-arms the rebels and their Danish allies had slain. Some had ridden with him from Talisand, good men and true. Like him, they were younger sons who served the king hoping to gain lands of their own in England. Now they were gone, their voices stilled forever.

* * *

Riding Thyra back to her home, accompanied by her father's guards, Emma carefully picked her way through the bodies and charred debris scattered over the streets of York. It was an unholy sight. The tension that had gripped her not knowing if she would be in time to save them ebbed with the relief that came, knowing her father would spare Geoffroi and his companions. But the look of hatred on Geoffroi's face would haunt her forever.

She had never lied to him but she had not told him who her father was or that he had gone to the Danish king, who was his friend, to seek aid for the rebels in York. The revulsion she had glimpsed in the knight's eyes was so unlike the warmth she had always seen there before it chilled her.

He held her responsible for what had transpired. But what could she have done? She loved her father and her people who suffered under the Norman yoke. Her own hatred for the French knights had been strong. Yet into her life had come one who was not like the others, one who showed her kindness at every turn. One whose laughter had brought joy into her life, even love. His kindness had softened her heart and made her want to love again.

But how could she have told him of the coming battle?

She had never believed Geoffroi would lose his life. To her he was invincible, destined to return to his beloved Talisand. And he *had* survived the battle while most of the Normans had died.

On her way to the castle, she had seen hundreds, mayhap thousands of bodies strewn about the streets and near the castles, Normans mostly by their clothing and long shields, but Northumbrians and Danes as well. Even horses had fallen.

Vultures circled overhead, some descending to the bodies to pick at the corpses. The stench that had drawn them made her want to vomit. She could never get used to war's leavings and hoped to never see them again.

The victors were removing swords and knives from their victims and piling up the corpses to be burned.

Though some of the slain knights and men-at-arms had undoubtedly inflicted evil upon her people, treating the citizens despicably and defiling young women as if their virtue was of little consequence, the sight of so many dead was still horrible and one she had never seen before.

They rode down Coppergate, past the ruined stalls that had once been the shops owned by Feigr and Auki. Feigr's forge had survived the flames, a blackened monument to a once prosperous business, but the rest of his shop was a mound of ashes. At least Feigr had fled before the flames destroyed the wooden structures. Even now, many of Feigr's goods were stored in her home. *Had he survived the battle?* Inga would ask her.

Glancing at the two rough looking guards riding on either side of her, she was glad she had apologized to them for her part in their having to face her father's wrath, but she would not change what she had done. She could not have left Geoffroi to die, not just because he had oft rescued her and those she loved, but because she cared for him.

Did she love the Norman? Yes, her heart told her, for she dreaded life without him, his cheerful presence, his tender touch. His smile and his love had been gifts she had never thought to have. Into her mind came the picture of his face as she had departed the castle. It had been twisted into a grimace, so harsh it had made her recoil. She had always known he was her enemy; now he knew she was his.

What would become of him and the other Normans her father held prisoner? Would they be ransomed? She hoped so. At least that way they would live.

Questions swirled in her mind as they neared her home. With the city reduced to a burned out shell and only a few structures still standing, where would the people go? The wealthy, she knew, could flee to other places. Mayhap they already had. But what of the shopkeepers, freemen and villeins? Would the Danes remain to defend them when the Norman king returned, as he surely must? Could the Northumbrian warriors hold York without them? From all her father had told her about the Norman king, she knew he meant to rule all of England.

She shuddered when she considered the ruthless methods he might employ to see it done. Surely when he heard the news of his forces' defeat, he would seek vengeance.

* * *

Geoff peered out the small arrow slit in the chamber high in the tower where he, Alain and Mathieu had been confined. The fires from the Danes' camp along the riverbank burned strong in the late September night as the sounds of their revelry drifted up to him and he remembered Emma as he had last seen her.

He had loved her, had even wanted her for his wife. But seeing her with her father cast a shadow on all they had shared. She was a beauty who had captured his heart and then tossed it at his feet. How long would Maerleswein keep his promise to her and allow them to live?

Hours had passed with no word. They had tended their wounds as best they could. Alain's was worse than Geoff's but they were finally able to stop the bleeding, clean the wound and make a bandage out of what cloth they had found in the chamber. If the Bear did not come down with a fever, he would heal.

Alain went to the door and pressed his ear to listen. "The sounds of celebration from the hall grow loud. Let us hope they have forgotten us in their feasting and drinking."

"At least they have allowed the servants to bring us food," said Mathieu, picking up a piece of bread from where it sat on the tray with cheese, fruit and a pitcher of wine.

Geoff sighed, his thoughts on the far side of the city where Emma might be sitting by her own hearth fire. How could she have betrayed him?

He felt Alain watching him. He was not surprised when he spoke words of advice. "Forget the widow. There will be other women."

Geoff said nothing. It might be wise to forget her, but he was not so sanguine as to believe it was possible. There would be no other woman like Emma. He wanted to hate her for her treachery. Mayhap for long moments he had. But then he remembered their afternoons together in the meadow, her sweet response to his lovemaking, her kindness to the orphaned children, the girl Inga, even the hound, and his hatred turned into a longing, a desire for what he had lost. How could he still desire a woman who had sold him to the rebels?

Alain picked up his goblet of wine and threw back a large swallow. "'Tis our wine they give us, the last we shall see, at least for some time."

"Aye," said Geoff, helping himself to the French wine, hoping it would make him forget.

Alain stared at the goblet, turning it in his hand. "'Twill soon be October. Aethel's babe was to be born in September."

Geoff knew the big knight worried for his wife. Childbirth could mean the death of the mother or the child, or both. "She will be well, Alain. Did not Maugris see your little girl growing up with the Red Wolf's son?"

"Aye. For that reason Aethel chose a name before I left."

"What is it?" asked Mathieu from where he sat eating some of the cheese.

"Lora," the Bear said with a smile that suggested a pleasant memory.

"'Tis a beautiful name," Geoff remarked. Then seeing the wistful look on Alain's face, he added, "You will see them, have no worry." He had his doubts of their returning to Talisand, but he would not share them with his friend.

"When was Lady Serena's babe expected?" asked Mathieu.

Geoff recalled Maugris' words to Serena. "'Twas to be in the spring, April, I think. If all went well, as Maugris' vision told him it would, she has been delivered of the Red Wolf's cub, his heir."

"They were to name him Alexander," said Alain.

Geoff grinned thinking about the Red Wolf as a father. Missing his friend and wanting to cheer his companions, he lifted his goblet. "A toast! To Alexander and Lora and to our seeing them before this year is done."

Alain and Mathieu lifted their goblets and the three drank in somber celebration in the midst of a castle where a clamorous revelry celebrating their defeat echoed from the hall below.

* * *

"Tonight the Norman hall rings with the sounds of our victory," Maerleswein announced, lifting his goblet of mead to Cospatric and Edgar who sat on one side of him at the high table. Osbjorn, King Swein's sons and Waltheof sat on his other side. "Tomorrow we will tear down these walls, these symbols of Norman tyranny."

"Aye," said Cospatric raising his goblet and taking a long drink.

"'Tis a long time in coming," said Edgar.

The great hall glowed with torches and candles. Hundreds of Danes and Northumbrians sitting at the long trestle tables lifted their cups, goblets and tankards in toast to the victory they had won that day. When the fighting was over, they had bathed in the same river that had brought their dragon ships to York, washing themselves of the blood of their victims.

In the center of the room over the hearth fire, a side of beef roasted on a spit, a lad turning it often. Outside, other fires played host to roasting meat and other celebrations. The smell of beef and melting fat mixed with herbs filled the hall, making Maerleswein's mouth water. No food had touched his lips since first light, and then only dried beef to sustain him.

Along with the beef, there was to be roast pork and several varieties of fish. The servants were already setting cooked vegetables from the castle gardens and bread and honey upon the tables. The serving wenches flitted about, obviously happy to be waiting upon the warriors who had freed their city. The Danes eyed the women with lusty gazes. The women were quick to offer sultry smiles in return. He was glad Emma was not here.

Osbjorn, who sat in the center of the high table with King Swein's sons and Waltheof on his other side, filled his drinking horn with ale, then got to his feet and lifted it high. "To those in the hall," he loudly proclaimed, "we celebrate a great victory! York is once again ours!"

The Danish warriors and the men of Northumbria stood and raised their drinking cups, echoing Osbjorn's pronouncement before downing their mead.

Lowering his hand, Osbjorn made the sign of the cross over his drinking horn, as was tradition. It was Thor's hammer and not the Christian cross Osbjorn paid tribute to, while Bishop Christian of Aarhus, who King Swein had insisted come with them, sat on the far end of the high table. It did not surprise Maerleswein. The Christian God had come to the Danes decades before, and though most were now Christians, some still observed the old ways.

The men were in high spirits as they downed their mead. Maerleswein was pleased. How could they not be happy? They had taken back York and slain the Norman usurpers. But as Waltheof's Icelandic skald lifted his lyre and took his place before the dais to sing his lord's praises, Maerleswein reflected on what was to come, knowing the battle for York was not yet over. William would not easily accede to their rule in the North.

* * *

The next day, Geoff and the other prisoners were moved from the older castle to the Danish longships. He, Alain and Mathieu were put in chains and guarded by Danes armed with axes and swords.

Malet and his family, together with Gilbert, FitzOsbern and their few remaining guards, were consigned to other ships. He could not imagine the valuable noble prisoners being kept in chains. Guarded yes, but Maerleswein had once considered them colleagues. And Malet was half Saxon. At one time, the two men might have been friends. Geoff could not see the prisoners once they were taken to the other ships, so he did not know for certain if they received different treatment. He could only wonder at their fate.

What followed next did not surprise Geoff. Standing at one end of the deck of the dragon ship where he and the others were confined, he watched as the rebels attacked the castles with hammers and axes. The sounds of vicious pounding and the splitting of wood echoed in the autumn air from morning through afternoon.

The next day, what the army of Danes and Northumbrians had not torn down, they burned.

They spared the stables, but the smoke caused the horses to rear and scream in fright so they led them away until the fire died down. Most of the smoke was carried north into the city, but the bitter smell was everywhere. Charred wood floated in the air, landing on the longships anchored in the river and falling into the slow moving water like a storm of gray snow.

Mathieu stared at the castles, now reduced to rubble. "What will be left for them to defend with the castles gone?"

"'Tis a reasonable question," said Geoff. "Their actions may appear foolish to us with the city nearly destroyed and nowhere but the ships and their camps to take shelter, but you have to remember, to them, the castles represent our sire and his claim to York."

In the days that followed, Geoff and his two companions were moved again, this time to an abandoned home that had not been destroyed in the fire. He did not know what became of his other knights or the noble prisoners.

The Danes shoved them into a large chamber on the first floor of the house, then boarded up the windows. A few cracks allowed shafts of light through. Geoff and his companions also had candles, which they used sparingly, not knowing how long they would have to last. The chains they still wore chafed their hands and feet, but Geoff did not complain. At least they were alive.

Before they lost the outside light, Geoff studied the chamber. Like Emma's home, it was well appointed with tapestries hung on white-washed walls. It had once been the dwelling of a leading citizen of York.

"Could be worse," said Alain the next day as they sat pondering their circumstances. "We have pallets to sleep on and each other for company."

"Aye, we have a roof against the night's chill and the Danes feed us," said Geoff, "but I can tell by their glares and the ribald jesting we hear through the walls, they would sooner run us through."

"Mayhap the lady's pleas to her father protect us still," said Mathieu.

Geoff said nothing. Dreams of Emma cursed his nights. He did not want to remember her beautiful eyes, her smile nor the feel of her skin beneath his hands. Likely Mathieu was right, but Geoff could hardly feel gratitude for the time her guilt had bought them. Who knew how long they would live?

* * *

Emma sat by the hearth fire as night settled in around her small family, drawing her lap robe over her legs, happy for the warmth it provided. The chill that had come with November told her winter would soon be at their door. She had done what she could to provide for her family. The garden's vegetables had been harvested and they had a supply of the apples produced from the orchard, stored in an alcove off the kitchen. Added to those were the dried beef and salted fish and the walnuts from this year's crop. Even without the market, they would eat.

The city was still mostly in ruins though on her infrequent excursions, accompanied by the guards, she had noted some rebuilding had occurred in the months before on Coppergate.

She let out a sigh as she threaded the needle for the border of flowers she embroidered on the small, linen tunic Sigga had made for Inga's babe. Inga sat nearby on a bench near the hearth. With one hand on her large belly, she silently stared into the fire.

If all went well, the babe would come before Christmastide. Her villein, Martha, had said she would help deliver the child. For that, Emma was grateful for it was with sadness she reflected that she had never experienced a birth herself. Some days when she had allowed her mind to wander, she had thought of a fair-haired child that might have been hers one day, a child born of her love for a French knight. She shook off the thought. That was a dream best forgotten.

Emma's father had told her that Feigr had survived the battle and was with the Northumbrians camped on the banks of the River Ouse. Having gained a reputation among the Danes for being a superb craftsman, he was kept busy repairing their swords. Inga was happy for him.

At Emma's feet, the twins sat cross-legged, playing a game with her father who was stretched out on a fur laid on the floor. He was teaching them the game of *hnefa-tafl*, King's Table, a game played on a wooden board inlaid with walrus ivory and carved soapstone pieces that each player tried to capture from the other.

Ottar pointed to the dark pieces. "Why are the king and his men outnumbered by the ones attacking them?"

"It has always been so," answered her father. "But remember, the king has an advantage. He can only be captured when he is surrounded on all sides."

Emma thought of the Norman king, curious if he knew the castles he had built now lay in ruins. She had tried not to think of Geoffroi but she had failed. His face was ever before her. She knew he was being held somewhere in the city. Her thoughts often returned to the summer days they had spent together. When she asked about him, her father had assured her the prisoners were being well cared for. She had stubbornly tended the garden she and Helise had planted, which had survived the destruction of the castle on Baille Hill. When she and Sigga had harvested the vegetables, she made sure the guards saw that some were given to the prisoners.

Finna sat on the floor observing the play of the game. In one hand, she clutched a new poppet, the cloth plaything that Maerleswein had given her that was Finna's very image in a red tunic with long plaits made out of yarn. The child's other hand rested on Magnus, curled up at her side with his head on his paws. Tucked in next to Ottar was his new wooden sword, a gift from her father, who had said it was time the boy learned. She supposed he was right though it pained her to see Ottar, only ten, training to one day take his place with the warriors.

Maerleswein looked up at her. "Osbjorn wants to winter on the Humber where his men will be fed by the Northumbrians in the marshes."

"Will you leave with them?"

"Aye, 'twould be wise for me to keep an eye on them since Cospatric, Edgar and Waltheof want to winter in the north closer to Bamburgh. Someone must watch Osbjorn. He is not constant." Her brow furrowed and he added, "You need not worry. The city will be left with the Northumbrians who remain. And the guards will stay to see no stray man comes near the house."

"We will miss you."

She studied the faces of the children. They loved their godfather who, years ago, had taken the place of their own father who had died.

"I will not be so far I cannot check on you now and then, weather allowing. Now that the Danes are gone, I will leave you two guards. When the winter is over, the Danes and I will return."

* * *

She stood on the shore of the great North Sea, watching the twins frolic in the shallows, dipping their toes into the white sea foam brought to shore by the rushing waters. The sun at her back cast her shadow onto the warm golden sand. Without warning, the waters suddenly pulled far out to sea and a wave taller than any castle rose in the distance towering above them, turning the sky dark. As she stared, unable to move, the great wave came toward them. "Run!" she shouted, even as she realized with sudden dread, it was too late.

Emma startled awake, every nerve on end, her heart racing as she blinked, then stared into the darkness of her bedchamber. The images persisted causing her to shiver even though she was nestled under the bedcover. At her side, Inga slept. The fire in the brazier, banked when they had retired, provided little light. The terror of the dream, for that is what it was, would not leave her. It was too vivid, too real. Dread encircled her like a heavy black cloak. What could it mean?

The few dreams she had experienced in her life had always portended some coming disaster. Those in the last few years, though rare, had been no different. The dream of a ship swirling in the ocean as it was pulled into the depths only days before Halden was lost, the dream of the bodies in the clearing… and now this.

Unable to sleep and wanting to fill her mind with other, more normal images, she slipped from her bed, donned her clothes and redid her long plaits. Magnus followed her out of the room and down the stairs to the kitchen.

As she entered the warm space, Sigga looked up from where she was stirring gruel over the fire. "You are pale, my lady. Is aught amiss?"

Emma sat on a tall stool, still trying to calm her heart pounding in her chest. "I have had a dream…"

"Oh, no." Sigga stopped stirring and removed the kettle from the fire. She knew Emma's dreams to be omens of ill and had come to trust the warnings.

"Aye. And I fear what it portends. Something dreadful is about to descend upon us, Sigga."

Emma's gaze locked with the servant's. Both spoke at the same time. "The Norman king."

Silence hung in the air as Emma faced the one thing that had occurred to both of them. She could think of nothing more terrifying. "Aye, the Norman king and his army, they will come and none in York will be safe."

"We must be prepared to flee, Mistress."

"Yea," she said on a sigh, "but I wish it was not winter we were facing. The Humber is too far and the fields too open to go there. This time it will have to be the forest, where the dense stands of trees can provide shelter and Magnus can hunt."

"What about that cave the twins discovered last summer?" Sigga asked. "It was in the forest."

Her gaze met Sigga's. "I had forgotten about that. Yea, it might serve. We must take the villeins, Jack and Martha, with us. And we must prepare for bitter cold, for winter is nearly upon us."

Sigga's brows furrowed. "What about Inga?"

"We will go slow and she can ride Thyra. I will make her a soft pillow to sit upon. But Sigga, we must tell her the truth of it. It may be that her babe, like the Christ child, will be born in a cave."

* * *

Geoff awoke to a silence he had not known since they were taken captive. Always there had been the sounds of the Danes coming and going, drinking or loudly speaking in their harsh tongue. In the gray light of dawn filtering in through the boards across the window, a thought came to him and he whispered it aloud. "They are gone."

"Who has gone?" Alain asked in a sleep-filled voice that told Geoff the Bear was not quite awake. He had recovered from his wound, as had Geoff from his, in the many weeks they were held prisoner.

"Our captors." He stood up from his pallet and crossed the room to shake the still sleeping Mathieu, the rustling of Geoff's chains sounding loud in the stillness of the early morning.

They had slept in their clothes since the day of the battle so he did not need to dress. Their mail had been taken from them long ago. By now, what they wore smelled rank, some of it bloodstained. He walked to the door the Danes had kept barred. He tried the latch and it opened.

In the main room, the hearth fire had been allowed to die. The front door stood ajar. "Aye, they have left, mayhap in a hurry."

"Why?" Alain said, approaching with Mathieu.

"I know not why they have gone, but the better question is why we still live. They could not hate us too much for they have left us our lives. And the keys," he added, seeing on the table the ring of keys he had seen one of their guards carry.

After several tries, he managed to get the key into the lock. Once he was free of the heavy chains, he quickly unlocked those that bound his companions, the metal rings slipping from their hands and feet.

Alain rubbed his bruised wrists. "Mayhap your widow's pleas did not go unheeded."

Geoff shrugged. He did not want to think about Emma. She was gone, most likely with her rebel father.

He strode through the main room to the kitchen of the well-appointed home just off Coppergate where they had been kept prisoner. They needed to eat. "Food!" he exclaimed when he saw the remnants of a meal scattered about the kitchen.

Alain picked up the bread on the worktable and broke off a piece. "They must have left in a hurry and could not take it all." He brought the hunk of bread to his mouth and chewed. "Not old either."

"Mayhap they did not think to need this food," suggested Geoff.

"Looks like they had roast chicken last night," observed Mathieu, looking at a half-eaten fowl sitting on a side table. "'Tis not what they served us."

"Well, 'tis ours now. Might as well eat while we can," urged Geoff, even as he realized food no longer appealed as it once had. The long days of imprisonment with only the memories of the slaughtered garrison and Emma's betrayal to haunt him had robbed him of his desire for food. But they had to eat to survive and survive he would. "We can carry enough for the next meal while we search the city."

He ate some of the chicken but his own smell was ruining what little appetite he had. "I want out of these bloodstained clothes. Mayhap they left us water to wash. Mathieu, when you have finished, take a look at the chests in the chambers above. See if there are any clothes we can wear. Since we have not shaved and our hair has grown long, we look more like Northumbrians than Normans."

"With your fair hair, you could pass for one of the Danes," said Alain, piling a plate with food.

"The Danes might have difficulty understanding me," said Geoff with a grin, "and you know I would have difficulty keeping silent. Besides, I suspect the Danes are gone, at least for a time. If we wear the Northumbrians' clothing, mayhap we can go among them unnoticed. I doubt the city is deserted."

"We will need weapons," said Alain.

"We might find some knives here in the kitchen," Geoff suggested and began looking on the shelves. In a basket on a shelf next to some clay jars, he found a supply of knives. "Ah, just what we need. And a sharpening tool!" Geoff had never been so happy to see such crude weapons and idly wondered who was wearing his fine steel sword.

An hour later, cleaned up and garbed in the clothes Mathieu had found in the chambers above, they cautiously stepped from the house. Each had a knife tucked into his leather belt. With their fine woolen tunics and leggings, and cloaks fastened around their shoulders with metal brooches, they appeared like good citizens of York, save for their more powerful builds that, to a discerning person, would identify them as warriors.

Dark clouds told Geoff rain would soon fall. They ambled down Coppergate, trying to appear as unthreatening as possible. The street was not empty but many structures lay in ruin. Only a few people now had reason to traverse the street that had once been home to many shops and homes. In a few places, he observed new buildings had risen from the rubble.

The tower castle, or what was left of it, was not far, but it was not Geoff's destination. He wanted to see if the dragon ships still occupied the River Ouse.

They reached the bank of the river and he peered down its course as far as he could see. Nothing. "'Tis as I suspected. The Danes have deserted York. I wonder why."

"Mayhap they have what they came for," Alain suggested, his voice dripping sarcasm. "They took much plunder in Ipswich and Norwich and a horde of armor from the knights they killed here in York, horses as well."

"Whatever the reason, I am glad to be rid of them," said Geoff.

"'Tis as if every man went to his own home," observed Mathieu staring at the river with nary a ship on it. "… the Danes to their ships and the Northumbrians to their woods."

And where has Emma gone? Geoff wondered.

CHAPTER 13

Something in Emma warned her they had little time. It was the same feeling she had when the sky grew dark just before a storm. And so it was with haste and a quickening pulse that she hurried about packing what they would need, what she must take should they not be able to return. Magnus lay on the floor, his intelligent eyes watching her every move. It seemed only days ago she had gathered the same things when the fire threatened their home.

Finna walked into the chamber and stood next to the chest at the foot of Emma's bed, gripping her poppet tightly to her small chest. She watched Emma stuff clothes into the familiar tapestry bag. "Emma," she in her little girl voice, "are we going to Jack and Martha's again?"

Emma paused and came to kneel in front of the child. Taking her into her arms, she held Finna close, then kissed her on her forehead.

"Yea, we will go to their cottage and then all of us will have an adventure in the forest."

"The forest?" Ottar asked from the open doorway where he'd been listening.

"Aye," said Emma. She stood and resumed her packing. "Do you remember the cave you found last summer?" she asked him.

"It was a splendid cave," he said.

"Well, you can lead the way," said Emma, "for that is where we are headed."

"It was dark," said Finna, a frown forming on her face.

"You need not worry, Finna. We shall make a warm fire and there will be candles for light."

Finna's brown eyes were full of trust, but Emma sensed she was not as eager as her brother to take to the woods.

"Do we go for the day?" Ottar asked, his tone revealing his growing excitement.

"Yea, for the day. But we will also stay for a time." She did not want to tell the twins they were fleeing the Normans, or that they might have to live in the cave for the winter with the ground covered with snow. For now the sun lingered in the trees and it was not so cold a cloak failed to provide adequate warmth.

"Why not see if you can help Sigga and Artur pack the food we will take to make sure she includes your favorites?" The kitchen would be the best place for the twins. Inga was packing the twins' clothes and those for the coming babe. She did not need the two children underfoot.

Ottar, followed by Finna, raced from the chamber, Magnus on their heels, leaving Emma alone to gaze about the room, realizing how much she must leave behind, the chest of tapestries, the fine gowns she would not wear in the woods, her father's things in his chamber, things too heavy to carry. She did not like the idea of leaving her home, of fleeing into the forest with her small family, but she would not ignore the warning. To do so would be folly. The Normans, even her lover, now considered her one of the rebels though she had yet to lift her seax against any of them. If the Normans returned, she and her family would be first on the list of those to be killed. Or, they might take them prisoners to use against her father.

The two guards her father had left with her had not wanted to leave their post but it hardly served to guard an empty house. Still, she gave them a choice.

"Return to my father on the Humber or go with us. We cannot remain here for the Norman army is coming."

They chose to go with her.

Inga appeared at her door, her hand on her swollen belly. "I have finished, but I fear we will have much to carry."

"It will be all right. Thyra will carry you as well as our bags. And the guards—though they will surely complain—will carry those things we cannot give to Artur, Jack or Thyra. We will go slow, Inga."

Inga had never complained, but now Emma saw fear in her beautiful gray eyes. Placing the last of her things into the bag, Emma walked to where Inga stood and hugged her as close as she could, given the child that was between them. "Oh Inga, you will not be alone," she said into the girl's honey hair. "I will be with you. And Martha has midwifery skills. She and Sigga will help deliver you a healthy babe if we have not returned by your time." She wanted to encourage her friend and hoped with all her heart the words she spoke were the truth. Her only experience with birth was the babe she had lost.

When Emma pulled away, leaving her hands on Inga's shoulders, there were tears in both their eyes.

* * *

Geoff felt certain William would come. The king's ego would demand it if not his desire for revenge. Other rebellions in the South might have demanded his attention, but he would not fail to return to York.

Geoff spent a part of each day standing on the top of the motte gazing south to where the River Ouse flowed into the distance, watching for William's return. At those times, he thought of Emma. He had been to see the garden she had planted with Helise on Baille Hill, a sad reminder of happier days. The wooden fence was torn down on one side and the vegetables had been harvested. What remained of the herbs was now crowded with weeds. He did not go to her home to see if, per chance, she was there. His heart and his body ached for want of her yet always there was her betrayal between them. Besides, he could not imagine she was still in York. If Maerleswein had left with his Danish allies, he would have taken her with him.

Much of the city was deserted and lay in ruins. With winter coming on, the people remaining in York would take shelter in the homes that still stood. Each night he, Alain and Mathieu returned to the house they had been confined in.

They spent most their days securing food and seeing to the horses. He was glad the Danes had left the stables and many of the Norman horses and their saddles. To his great relief, his first search had revealed Athos in a stall in the rear of the stable, next to Mathieu's black palfrey. But Alain's tall gray stallion and Geoff's fine destrier he rode only into battle were missing, likely claimed as booty by some Dane. Alain found another horse to his liking and Geoff contented himself with his chestnut stallion that was his favorite after all.

Geoff stroked Athos' neck, brushing off the coating of dust that dulled the horse's rich chestnut color. "You need a good curry, boy."

"Aye," said Mathieu from behind him, "I will see to it."

Geoff shook his head. "Nay. For the time being, we will each tend our own."

Geoff found a horse comb and curried his horse until its coat shone. In his days as a squire he had enjoyed the task.

Mathieu and Alain set to work tending their horses. Hay and oats had been stored for the winter, so there was sufficient feed.

They found a few village boys milling about who, when asked, told them they had been enlisted by the departing Danes to care for the horses. Mayhap the Danes intended to return after all. The thought did not please him. He could only hope William arrived first.

The job of caring for the horses was a large one for the boys, and so he, Alain and Mathieu joined in feeding and grooming the other horses as well as their own. Fine horses required much care. And the horses would serve William's army when they finally reached York.

Not wanting to give away their identity as knights, Geoff told Alain and Mathieu not to ride the horses, but to lead them around the bailey for exercise. The boys were happy to have the help and seemed to accept them as Northumbrians.

Geoff and his two companions were careful to speak only English, even to each other.

In late November, in the midst of a cold, spitting rain, Geoff stood on the motte, looking south when a dark cloud appeared moving over the ground. *Horses!* A cavalry rode in formation followed by hundreds of marching men-at-arms.

William had finally arrived in York.

Now Geoff had no qualms about riding the horses. With Alain and Mathieu at his back, he mounted and sped over the bridge they had managed to repair, meeting William on the other side of the River Ouse.

As they approached the king, his personal guard closed ranks in front of their sovereign. "Hold!" said the captain raising his gloved palm in front of Geoff.

Geoff reined in his stallion and Alain and Mathieu pulled up on either side of him. "My Lord," he shouted over the guard to William, "'Tis Sir Geoffroi, your knight and two who rode with me from Talisand."

William shouted to his captain, "Let them pass!"

The knights of the guard parted, leaving Geoff a clear path to the king.

Beside William on a handsome steed sat a younger man, noble in appearance with the familiar look of William about him, the same sun-streaked brown hair, prominent nose and blue eyes. Both he and the king wore fine tunics with much decoration and purple woolen cloaks trimmed in gold thread.

When he reached William, Geoff bowed his head and, in a quieter voice, explained, "My Lord, I apologize for our appearance. We have been hiding among the Northumbrians who remain in York. Our numbers are too few to allow them to see us as French."

William laughed and wiped the rain from his face. "And so you fooled even our guard who should have recognized one of our knights by the way he sits a horse, no matter his apparel or the length of his hair." The king's gaze paused on Geoff's face. "You will need a sharp blade for that beard, sir knight."

Geoff grinned, fingering the ragged beard he had grown in the last few months. It was darker than his hair and now wet with the rain. "Aye, sire, I will see to it straight away."

"Robert," said William to the younger man riding at his side, "this is Sir Geoffroi de Tournai, the one who rides with our wolf."

And to Geoff, the king said, "Our brother, Robert, the Count of Mortain."

Geoff dipped his head to the brother, trying to remember what he had heard of him. As he recalled, Robert was a half-brother who had gained many lands from his royal association. Geoff's memory of the man was vague but there was something at the back of his mind. Then he remembered. This half-brother was rumored to beat his wife. A side-glance in Alain's direction told him the Bear had also heard of it.

William gazed toward what had once been the tower castle, where now stood only a bare motte. "We have heard that our castles are destroyed, our garrisons overrun."

"Aye, My Lord," Geoff sadly admitted, "'tis true. The Danes came with their hundreds of ships and joined the Northumbrian rebels to attack the castles. Your knights fought hard but, in the end, they were defeated."

"We would have been here sooner," said Robert, "but we were delayed three weeks by violent resistance, swollen rivers and a downed bridge."

"How is it you have survived?" demanded William.

"We were spared when the daughter of Maerleswein, the rebel leader, pleaded for our lives." The king's brows lifted in question, but not wanting to discuss Emma, Geoff went on. "There were a few other men and guards who were also spared, but I know not what became of them. We were separated and I did not see them again. When the Danes left, the keys to our chains remained behind."

"And what of Malet, FitzOsbern and Gilbert?"

"Your nobles were taken captive, along with Helise Malet and her two sons. As far as I can determine, they are no longer in York."

William's eyes flashed. "Damn the Danes! We would send them and their ships to Hell." The frown that formed on the king's face was deep, his lips set in a thin line, his eyes cold. Dropping his royal speech, he spoke in a tone that sent a chill down Geoff's spine. "By the splendor of God I will have my vengeance on the North!"

Casting a glance at his brother, William said, "Robert, you will go to the Humber where, no doubt, the Danes have retreated to their ships and get our nobles back."

"Mayhap I can negotiate the Danes' removal as well," said Robert in a manner that suggested he had dealt with his brother's anger before.

"Their history," said the king, "is one of accepting gold to leave England's shores. If we must, we will deign to pay it. We do not wish to see the pirates again." Returning his gaze to Geoff, the king clenched his jaw, his eyes narrowing. "Our army will rebuild the castles, but we will personally punish the rebellion of York's people. You will ride with us, Sir Geoffroi. And when we are finished, there will be no more rebellions in the North."

At the king's gesture, Geoff, Alain and Mathieu turned their horses to join William's guard. Mayhap the king had always known conquering England would not be accomplished in a few years, but did he anticipate that his reign would be so vehemently resisted?

"Now," said William, "we would see the city, or what is left of it."

* * *

Geoff was amazed at the king's energy. Before the day was out, hundreds of tents dotted the far bank of the River Ouse and meat roasted on spits over fires. The next morning, Robert and a part of the army left to chase the Danes to the Humber with orders to negotiate the release of the nobles and to pay whatever gold was necessary to send the raiders home.

Another group of men was consigned to rebuild the castles. But, true to his word, William took up the hunt for the rebels himself.

"With God's help we will hunt them down!" shouted the king to the group of knights assembled in his tent. His blue eyes were fierce as they narrowed their focus. "Like hounds after a fox, we will find the holes they hide in and kill them all. Then we will destroy the holes." Studying the map of England before him, William swept his fingers from York north to Durham. "We will not return until this land is a waste." Raising his eyes to his men, he said in a commanding voice, "Burn it all!"

The knights standing around the king were somber as they nodded their acceptance of the king's orders. Some had lost friends, some brothers to the Danes. They wanted revenge. Wasting the North was not too high a penalty for the rebels' treachery.

"Word has it," said one of William's men, "that the Ætheling has sought refuge in the valley of the Tees north of York. Here," he pointed to an isolated area on the map.

"Then that will be our first destination," said the king.

The next morning, Geoff, Alain and Mathieu rode north with William and his army. It was not to be an easy path. At times, they crossed ground so rough they had to dismount and proceed on foot. Each day the weather grew worse, as snow fell and a harsh winter closed around the knights huddled beneath their cloaks.

When they finally arrived at the place where Edgar was supposedly encamped, he was gone. But the trip was not without its rewards.

They cornered the rebels and after fierce fighting, defeated them, slaying all those who had not fled or were taken prisoner. Earl Waltheof, who had led his own men, wielded his axe with powerful strokes, but ultimately even he surrendered and agreed to make his submission to William. The tall, blond Northumbrian swore his allegiance, kneeling before the king. Geoff remembered the axe-wielding giant from the battle in York and was amazed to see that William granted him mercy.

It was from Waltheof they learned that the Ætheling had retreated to Scotland and King Malcolm's court.

Cospatric also made his submission to the king, but he did so by messenger. It was clear to Geoff the Earl of Bamburgh did not trust William. The fact that the king accepted the submissions, even the one by proxy, told Geoff that William must need the earls if he was to hold the North.

After the rebels had been slain or captured, the knights took their vengeance on what was left, burning every village and cottage, slaying even the serfs. Geoff had no taste for such vengeance. But William had told them never again would the Danes use the North as a base from which to attack. In the villages and alongside the roads the knights left rotting corpses lying where they fell. The stench of death was so thick he could have cut it with a knife. There was no one left alive to cover the bodies with earth.

"Mark our words," William said to his senior knights one evening in his tent. "We shall be feared as none before us, for we mean to destroy not only the rebels' hiding places, but also their means to survive."

Geoff understood the king's aim, even the reasons for it, but he was sickened by the slaughter and the destruction of a land so beautiful it often left him in awe. And much to Geoff's regret, William ordered his men to salt the land to assure that nothing would grow. Beyond that, the king was ruthless with the hostages they had captured, ordering the torture of many. Geoff and Alain were thankfully spared such an order and turned away in disgust.

To Geoff, the decision to destroy an entire people was a stain on his sire's honor, for the innocent died along with the guilty. Never before had William showed such cruelty. Geoff's own taste for vengeance on those who had slain his fellow knights had waned with every mile they traveled, every village they burned, every acre of land laid waste. In the end, he and his fellow Normans had proved just as vicious as the Northumbrians who had slain Robert de Comines, the Earl of Northumbria, and Richard FitzRichard, the first castellan in York. He could not help but wonder what the people who had fled and still lived would do to survive the harsh winter. To survive the years to come. He wondered if survival was even possible, for he had heard the wolves howling in the forest at night.

What would Emma and her children do? The king had not spared York or the lands around it. Before they had left for the north, William had given orders for his remaining knights to lay waste the land.

After nearly a fortnight, satisfied with the results of his march to Durham, William turned his army south. The return march to York was a treacherous one, as winter descended with a cold fury and the king chose a perilous route through forested mountains and snow-covered valleys. Even the hardened knights and men-at-arms suffered.

"'Tis freezing," said Alain, crouched on his saddle beneath his thick, woolen cloak as they rode side-by-side down a treacherous mountain path.

Mathieu followed behind them, the hood of his cloak pulled down over his eyes.

"I could wish for that beard I had when we lived as Northumbrians," Geoff wistfully remarked. Even his gloves had not prevented his fingers from going numb. He could no longer feel his feet. "The cold pierces like an arrow. I even heard trees cracking last night."

"And wolves howling," said Alain.

The talk of wolves reminded Geoff of an earlier time and place. "The last time I lived through such a winter was the one Ren and I endured in the County of Maine when he was attacked by the red wolf."

"I once heard him tell of it," said Alain. "He remembers that night as if it were yesterday."

"'Tis not a thing he or I would ever forget," said Geoff. Nor was the fifty-mile swath of destruction William had cut from York to Durham. Geoff would remember it always.

As his taste for vengeance subsided, Geoff's love for Emma returned. Perhaps it had always been there, for Emma was too much a part of him. Removed from his rage that day he'd discovered she was Maerleswein's daughter, he could now see she had been caught between opposing forces, a father she loved and a man to whom she had freely given herself despite his being a French knight. It was a position thrust upon her by circumstances not of her doing. Circumstances that made them enemies from the beginning.

She had not lied, just never disclosed her noble lineage or that her father was chief among the rebels. He could hardly blame her. And in the end, she had saved his life. In his mind he heard Maugris' words. *You will find an ally where you least expect it.* The daughter of the rebel leader was an unexpected ally indeed.

He had once believed Emma was all that was good. But that conviction had disappeared at her betrayal. Now, that inner conviction of her goodness returned. *I love her. I will always love her.*

William's war on the North had brought them together and then it had torn them apart. He had lost her.

With cheerless effort, they straggled on to York. Nearing the city, Geoff said to Alain, "I would rid myself of the blood that stains my mail and tunic. I find I crave a wash even more than food."

The Bear chuckled. "Now that is a change all at Talisand would find amusing."

"Aye, well, food will come after. I would have roast pork tonight and some of that hot bread dripping in butter. Surely they must have found a stray pig or a wild boar somewhere." His mouth watered. "And wine. Much wine." He wanted to forget the horrible scenes he had witnessed in the past week and he wanted to forget the haunting image of Emma's beautiful face that had never left him in the ride south to York.

"Do you think William would have brought a supply with him when he came to York?" asked Alain.

"I have never seen him travel without—"

"Look," shouted Mathieu, "the castles!"

In the distance, Geoff saw what appeared to be new square towers rising from the snow-covered mottes. William's new castles. *"Dieu Merci,"* he said on a sigh. "A place to sleep other than the cold ground."

As they neared York, the tents of William's encamped army filled every space of level land near the castles. Palisades circled the baileys, the wooden stakes repaired where they had been knocked down or burned.

Having destroyed his enemies, William was once again asserting his authority over York.

"I grow tired of the fighting," Geoff said to Alain, "if that is what it was. 'Twas no even match with William's ordering the slaying of mere serfs."

"I could not find any honor in it," said his friend, "and was glad when you steered us away from the burning of the cottages. I long for the peace of Talisand and Aethel and our babe."

"Mayhap William will release us if the Danes do not return."

With that happy thought, Geoff dismounted and left the horses to Mathieu, telling the squire they would see him at the evening meal.

Once Geoff and Alain had what sufficed for a bath, they donned the clothes and weapons supplied by their fellow knights, then took their places at the new trestle tables. There was no head table as yet so the king sat among them, his half-brother on one side and Geoff on the other. The hall smelled of new wood, the hearth fire and roasting meat.

Mathieu, along with the other squires, helped serve the king and his knights since there were few servants to be had.

Over a dinner of roast boar, Robert, who had returned from the Humber, told them of his encounter with the Danes.

"We kept a close watch on their ships where they were anchored on the north shore of the Humber. With us there in large numbers, they could not leave to forage for food."

"Were the rebels supplying them?" asked William.

"Indeed," said Robert taking a drink of his wine. "We found their camps in the marshes but we soon cut that line of supply."

"Men cannot eat treasure," said William. "They would soon grow desperate. But what of our nobles?"

"I sent a messenger," said Robert, "asking to talk. Left with the prospect of a miserable existence and little food for so many men, their leader, Osbjorn, agreed. After much haggling, he was persuaded to accept your gold in exchange for our nobles' return and the Danes departure at winter's end."

"We do not like leaving our nobles with the raiders for the winter," said the king, "but 'tis not surprising they demanded it of you. Do you believe the pirates will keep their word?"

"Aye, I believe Osbjorn means to return them at winter's end. He wants your gold and he did not seem to want to face your army."

"They will not leave empty-handed," William ruefully acknowledged. "In addition to our gold, their ships are full of treasure taken from East Anglia."

"My men will remain," said Robert, "allowing only food to pass to the ships. The Danes cannot endure the winter without a few hunting trips."

"Then you have done all we could ask," said the king.

Relieved to hear the Danes would not be returning to York when William and his half-brother took their leave, Geoff lifted his cup to Alain. "To our soon return to Talisand!" While the thought pleased him, inside he was not all gladness, for he had never believed he would return to Talisand without Emma. Their days in the meadow had convinced him she would finally agree to become his wife. How wrong he had been.

Later that evening, on his way to his chamber, William, who stood at one end of the hall with Robert, stopped him.

"We are determined to celebrate Christmas in York," said the king, "no matter it will be amidst the Minster's ashes. But after that, we ride to Cheshire. And you will accompany our army, Sir Geoffroi."

Geoff bowed his head. "As you wish, Sire."

"You will be pleased to hear that after Cheshire," continued William, "since we will be near the Red Wolf's den, you and your companions may be released. If all goes well, I might even pay our wolf a visit."

Geoff watched the king stride away, thinking of the awful punishment he had inflicted upon the North, hoping to never see the likes of it again. In his mind echoed Maugris' words.

William is a great king, but terrible in his wrath.

CHAPTER 14

Emma woke to the call of a thrush, its flute-like song one she could not ignore even inside the cave. The long days of summer were gone. No longer did the linnet send its melodious notes over the green meadow that had once provided a soft bed for her and her Norman lover. No longer did the lavender flowers bloom at the forest's edge. Now the brown thrush with its spotted chest trilled its solitary song over the bleak, winter forest.

A longing filled her heart for those earlier sun-filled days of love, so strong at times it caused her to shudder. She missed her gallant knight, his easy smile and his welcoming arms. He had brought laughter into her life. Now it was gone. But 'twould do no good to ponder what could not be. She had her little family to care for and protect.

Ottar had shown them the way to his cave. Once Artur and Magnus had chased away the small animals that dwelled there, its chambers, leading deep into the limestone cliffs, became their home. The main chamber was very large, at least fifteen feet in height. Deeper into the cave, the chambers were smaller and devoid of light. They always took candles when going into them. They stored food in one of the chambers. The twins, Inga and Emma slept in another, Artur and Sigga in a third and Jack and Martha in yet another. Inside the cave, the ground was hard, coarse rock but their pallets and furs made it tolerable.

A boulder and a dense stand of trees hid the opening of the cave, which was large enough near its entrance to provide shelter for Emma's mare. At night, the two guards slept by the fire they made inside the main chamber, giving Emma a sense of safety, though she well knew if the

Norman army discovered them, the guards would afford little protection.

From the guards, who scouted far afield, she had learned the Normans had returned to claim York and now a large part of the army was headed north toward Durham, destroying all in its path. She was glad for the dream that had allowed them to escape. Were there others who had fled? She had warned her neighbors but was not certain they would heed her plea to leave.

Living in the forest required everyone to do their part, but the duties were not onerous. Ottar fished in the stream near the cave and foraged for plants with Sigga. Magnus hunted for hares and squirrels, but Emma would not allow him to leave the cave at night for it was then the wolves howled. The women cooked and saw to the needs of the children. Finna helped. The guards, who grumbled that they had been turned into serfs, helped Artur and Jack to hunt and kept the fire going. During the day, all of them gathered wood. Each night before they took to their pallets, the men laid heavy brush across the cave's entrance.

With December and the onset of winter, the days grew short and the air so cold, Emma could see her breath. The frost on the morning ground did not always melt in the midday sun and seeing the thick coats of the squirrels, she knew it was only a matter of time before the forest was blanketed in white.

Hearing the twins stirring, Emma rose and fumbled to light a candle. Once it burned brightly, she donned her woolen tunic over the undertunic she slept in, and pulled on her woolen socks and leather shoes. She let Inga sleep, for the babe had given her a restless night. By Emma's counting, in a sennight Inga would become a mother.

Emma found her way to the main chamber where Sigga huddled under her cloak, tending the cooking fire. "Artur and one of the guards have gone for water. Magnus is with them."

Emma added a log to the fire and sat beside her servant who had begun to measure out grain for gruel. Sigga had been a stalwart soul throughout the ordeal. "Thank you, Sigga, for your faithfulness. We would not eat so well if I were to cook our meals."

The servant gathered her cloak around her with one hand while she reached for a bowl with the other. "Mistress, you are the one who holds us together. You carry the weight of us all. If it were not for you, we would not just suffer the cold, we would be long dead by now. You have kept us alive and safe."

Emma reached for the dried berries to add to their morning meal, wondering how long any of them would be safe. "God and the archbishop's prayers that live beyond him protect us, Sigga. I can think of no other reason. Did not God send the dream to warn us?"

Sigga's hazel eyes held a glimmer of hope. "I believe He did."

"Once winter has passed, we will find a new home," Emma encouraged, all the while knowing it would not be anywhere near York. Sigga said nothing, mayhap because, like Emma, she did not know where they would go.

Since the guards had cleared the brush away from the entrance and let Thyra out to be watered, the cave took on the faint light of the new day, making it easier to see using only the light of the cooking fire.

Finna was the next to rouse from the rear chambers, stumbling out as she rubbed sleep from her eyes while clutching her poppet. The cloth plaything had become her constant companion, its red tunic now soiled from being dragged everywhere with the child. It occurred to Emma the poppet was, to Finna, a symbol of happier days.

She held out her arms to Finna who came to sit in her lap. "Are those your warm socks?" she asked the child.

"Yea, and my warmest tunic, but I'm still cold."

She hugged the girl to her. "Soon the fire will warm you and we will have some hot gruel in our stomachs." She rubbed Finna's belly making her laugh.

Artur and the guard returned carrying water and more wood. Magnus, trailing alongside the men, trotted over to greet Emma and Finna. The child stroked his rough fur as he plopped down next to Emma.

"I think your hound likes living in the forest," said Artur, handing his wife the wooden bucket, water sloshing over the sides. He took the wood from the guard and stacked it next to the cooking fire. "Magnus was a happy fellow, running in circles around us."

Magnus' tail beat against the ground as if he were anxious to tell her of his morning adventure.

As the men sat around the fire, Jack and Martha came from their chamber to join them, reaching out their hands toward the warmth of the fire. Jack scratched his belly, then ran his fingers through his mussed hair. "I sleep right well in the cave," he remarked with good humor.

"Speak not for me, husband," said Martha, rubbing her back. Her brown plaits were graying but she was not old. "I can nay get used to the hard ground."

Once Ottar and Inga had risen from their pallets, they all sat together around the fire, breaking their fast. Emma was glad for their company, for each had given to her in his or her own way. And she had given to them all she could.

When they had finished the meal, they went about their chores.

Emma set aside her half-eaten bowl of gruel. Her stomach lurched and her head suddenly began to pound. She did not feel at all well. Raising her palm to her forehead, she felt her burning skin. Unlike the others, she had not felt the cold.

* * *

Two weeks before Christmas, because rumors persisted of rebels around York, William ordered Geoff to lead a group of knights to make a sweep of the buildings that still remained in the city and to scout out the surrounding countryside. Geoff selected nine knights to accompany him, Alain and Mathieu, who was nearly a knight himself. All had been with him on the march to Durham.

Inside the city walls, there were enough homes and shops remaining, even some that had been newly rebuilt, that it seemed prudent to Geoff to divide the men into four groups of three, each taking a different section of the city. He reserved the quadrant containing Emma's home to search for himself.

With Alain and Mathieu on either side of him, he rode through the debris-filled streets of York, past the burned out Minster, to the part of the city where Emma had lived. A rain had melted much of the snow but patches of white remained. The homes in that part of the city had not fallen victim to the fire, but as they began their inspection, it was clear they had been ransacked and were devoid of people.

Entering Emma's home, Geoff was assaulted by memories. It was cold now, but he imagined a blazing fire in the hearth ring and Emma sitting beside the flames. In his mind, he heard the laughter of the twins. He could smell the stew they had shared. He could taste the honey wine. *Where had Emma gone?*

"'Tis a mess," said Alain when they discovered the chests in Emma's chamber, the remains of their contents scattered on the floor, the things the departing Danes or arriving Normans did not want.

Geoff stared at Emma's bed, remembering the first time she had brought him here and their first coming together. He turned away, but not before Alain had seen his regret.

"At least with her father, she is safe," the Bear said.

"Aye," was all Geoff could manage to say.

They walked through each room, taking more time than they might have with another dwelling. The house had more memories for him, each room bringing a picture to his mind of the twins or Magnus, Sigga and her berry tarts, even the sword-maker and his daughter.

He could see by the gloomy expressions on the faces of his companions that he was not the only one with fond memories of the times they had spent in this home. "Come, let us be done with this," he urged Alain. "We still have the woods to search."

Before he left the house, Geoff retrieved one thing he had hidden there under some boards beneath the work table inside the kitchen.

As had been his plan, sometime later they joined the rest of the men on Coppergate. Other than a few villeins who had taken shelter in some of the homes, they found nothing of note. There were no warriors and no rebels.

"You did not kill the people you found, did you?" he asked the others.

"Nay," replied one of the knights. "Done enough killing of serfs."

"*Bien*. I too would have spared them. Now for the woods."

To better enable them to cover the surrounding countryside, Geoff divided the twelve men into two groups and chose for himself the woods to the west of the city.

"We will meet back at the castle before the evening meal."

The one appointed to lead the other group waved as his group of six rode off toward the east.

Geoff turned Athos toward the woods.

* * *

"Her fever still rages," Sigga informed the worried Martha, standing at the entrance to the chamber where Emma lay at the back of the cave. Candles lit the dark space but added little warmth. Magnus lay close to the pallet his head on his paws. "This wet cloth does little to cool her even with the chill in the air." She reached out to bathe her mistress' face once again, despairing of hope. As soon as she laid the cloth on Emma's forehead, it became hot to the touch. "She is out of her mind most of the time. Once she awakened but she was so confused I do not think she recognized me. She takes no nourishment. Martha, I am scared."

"At least she no longer spews up her stomach," encouraged Martha.

"That is because her stomach is empty, poor mistress. I made her some ginger tea but even that she would not touch." Looking up at the villein who had come to inquire after Emma, Sigga chided, "You should not be here, Martha. You cannot become ill; Inga will need you for the babe. 'Twill be here any day. If you were to come down with the sickness that has befallen our mistress, it would leave only me and I do not have your skills."

Martha hesitated, her worried gaze fixed on Emma. "Ye think we might lose her?"

"I refuse to consider it. She will recover. She must."

Three days had passed since Emma had fallen ill. Sigga was gravely worried. She had friends who had died of such fever. Emma had lost weight for lack of food. And she was weak. They had moved her to a chamber deep in the cave to isolate her from the children and Inga. Only Sigga had spent any time inside the chamber where Emma lay too fevered at times to know where she was.

Emma moaned in her sleep, mumbling, "Geoffroi, Geoffr—"

Sigga dipped the cloth in the bowl of cold water, wrung it out and placed it on Emma's forehead. "It will be all right, Mistress." *I know you miss him.*

"Who is it she calls for?" asked Martha.

"Sir Geoffroi."

"A… a French knight?" Martha stammered, disbelieving.

After all they had lived through, the question did not surprise Sigga. "Aye, but one to whom we owe much." *One whom her mistress loved.* Sigga had observed the inner light that had shown from Emma's face whenever she was with the Norman. After each of her trips to pick flowers last summer, her eyes had sparkled with some secret knowledge; her face had glowed with happiness. Sigga had known from the beginning that it was not the flowers that drew Emma to the meadow. It was the French knight. Sigga was certain the two loved each other. Sadness overcame her as she thought of the pair. Her mistress had found love only to lose it.

"You should go, Martha," Sigga urged the woman.

"All right," Martha said at last. "I will leave… for Inga's sake."

"'Tis best. Will you ask Artur to take Ottar to gather some pine needles and herbs? Some garlic root, chickweed and St. John's Wort? Even in winter they can be found buried under leaves beneath the snow. Ottar has picked those herbs with me before. He knows where to find them. I must have them to make a tea for the fever. She cannot go on like this. If I can get her to take the tea, it may help."

"Aye," said Martha, her brows drawn together as she gazed down at Emma. "I will send Artur and Ottar with the guards. Jack can stay with us."

What neither acknowledged was that if the Normans found them no man could save them. But they kept to the belief they were well protected. Life was easier that way.

As the villein departed, Sigga lit another candle and set it on the rock ledge to replace the one that had burned to a stub. Although her mistress' fever raged, Sigga kept the fur cover ready because when Emma was not burning up, she was shivering with chills. Remembering the last time, Sigga shuddered. She could not bear the thought she might lose the mistress she loved.

* * *

The sound of clashing swords rang through the forest startling Geoff. A side-glance at Alain told him his fellow knight was equally bewildered. They were far from the practice yard and, to his knowledge, he and his men were the only ones dispatched to search out rebels around York.

With a shouted, "Follow me!" Geoff spurred his horse into the woods toward the direction of the tumult. Alain, the three other knights and Mathieu followed closely behind.

Geoff emerged from the trees into a snow-dusted clearing.

A scream rent the air. *A child's scream.*

Drawing rein, he quickly slipped from his horse and stepped into the bleak space of winter-shrouded ground. Patches of snow lingered in the shadows under the surrounding trees. In front of him lay the bodies of two men, bloody upon the ground, Northumbrian rebels by their beards and weapons. He caught a sudden movement and jerked his head to one side. Two Norman knights stood, their swords drawn and dripping blood.

Clutched in the hand of one was a tearful, squirming Ottar. Shaking the boy, the knight pressed his sword to Ottar's neck. The other Norman had a horrified Artur pinned to the ground with a sword pointed at his heart.

"Hold!" Geoff demanded, drawing his sword, his eyes narrowing on the knights.

At his side he heard Alain yank his sword from its scabbard. Behind them the sliding steel of other knights rang in the clearing.

The two Normans paused. They would not have expected their fellow knights to draw swords on them, but Geoff was not in the mood to explain.

"What goes here?" Geoff roared as he stomped toward them.

Ottar whimpered, his young body hanging limp beneath the knight's grasp. The boy's eyes darted to Geoff and in them he saw recognition.

"Let the boy and his servant go!" Geoff commanded.

The Norman looked down at Ottar and moved the sword back from his neck but did not release him. "Why should I not kill this rebel spawn when the king has ordered all their deaths?"

The voice of the knight was familiar to Geoff, but since the knight wore a helm, Geoff could not be certain. "Who are you?" he asked in a gruff voice.

With his sword poised once again above Ottar's throat, the Norman said, "Sir Eude—not that my name is any concern of yours."

Eude. Geoff had never liked the knight who had raped Inga and now he threatened the boy Emma loved. His thoughts scattered. If Ottar was here, Emma must be near. *But how had Eude come to be here?* The day of the Danes' attack no Norman had been spared, save for those taken prisoner. And Eude was not one of them.

Before he could pursue his questions, Eude asked, "Which of William's knights are you?"

"Geoffroi de Tournai."

Eude fell silent, as if pondering the name. "Ah, Sir Geoffroi. I recall you."

"How did you survive the Danes' slaughter, Eude?"

"The rebels are not the only ones who can hide in the woods. Murdac and I escaped into the forest and have only just rejoined William's army."

"Then you and your friend are cowards, Eude. For none ran, save you." Geoff had fought men like this one before, braggarts who were sure of their ability against a lesser foe. A Northumbrian rebel, ill-trained and ill-equipped, he might easily defeat. But a Dane's powerful arm, wielding a deadly axe with skill, Eude would not have wanted to face. Only a coward would prey on a defenseless girl like Inga.

"Yet *you* live," said Eude, his tone sarcastic.

"I was prepared to die but instead I was taken prisoner. My men and I did not run from the field. You are worse than a coward, Eude, for you defile innocents. Did you know that one of York's maidens now carries your bastard?"

"I care not how many bastards I drop in England. 'Tis the way of the conquered to submit. I doubt she is the only one. As I recall, you had your own York wench, one you refused to share."

"I would not take a woman against her will," said Geoff. He felt a twinge of regret for the show he had put on that night, but he had done it to spare Emma the lust of the others. "You are unworthy to be a knight."

Eude sneered. "Stand aside while we dispatch these rebels."

Geoff held his stance, his drawn sword speaking loudly. "Nay you will not slay them and I will not stand aside." Anger welled in his chest. This knight had brought much dishonor on the king. Mayhap such a one had even spurred the people of York to rebel. It was going to give Geoff great satisfaction to finally deal with Eude.

"You would defend our enemies?" Eude asked, incredulous.

"They are not my enemies. They are innocents."

Even with his helm hiding half his face, Geoff saw Eude's scowl. "Then you have turned traitor," he spit out.

Geoff raised his chin, his shoulders squared. "I adhere to the code to which I was sworn—to protect the innocent—while you would defile and slay them. For that, you will meet my sword."

Eude and his friend, Murdac, turned from their intended victims.

"Run to Mathieu, Ottar!" Geoff shouted, his eyes fixed on Eude. Out of the corner of his eye, Geoff was relieved to see the boy and the servant circling around behind him.

Eude's eyes darted to the knights with drawn swords behind him and then to Alain at his side. "I would accept your challenge, but there are six of you and only two of us."

Geoff looked over his shoulder. "Sheathe your blades," he ordered Mathieu and the knights. "This is a matter of honor for Alain and me to handle."

Four swords slid back into their sheaths. Tension hung thick in the air as Geoff returned his gaze to Eude and silence descended. Not a bird or forest creature stirred as Geoff slowly advanced.

"For Inga and the innocents!" he cried and swung his blade, striking Eude's raised sword in a bone-shattering clash of metal.

Eude lumbered away then lunged.

Geoff deflected the long blade, so like his own. The clash of metal against metal filled the air as each sought mastery over the other.

To his right, Alain grunted as his sword met Murdac's blade in a rapid exchange.

Minutes passed as the four swords vied for control in the clash of well-trained knights. But this was no swordplay; this was a fight to the death. One Geoff welcomed to avenge the innocents in York.

Eude was tiring, his swings slowing, becoming less precise. Geoff backed up, feigning his own fatigue, luring Eude into the trap his mind had been conceiving as he'd made note of Eude's weaknesses.

In his arrogance, Eude lunged again but his swing was too wide, leaving his midsection vulnerable.

Geoff swung the broad side of his sword into Eude's ribs.

With a groan, Eude stumbled to the side. At that moment, Geoff eyed Eude's unprotected neck and swung. Blood spurted from Eude's neck and his eyes went wide as he fell to his knees and then to his face, his blood turning the snow-dusted ground crimson.

Heaving a sigh of relief, Geoff wiped his blade on Eude's back. It was over.

A side-glance at Alain revealed the huge knight standing over the body of Murdac. "Seems to me you toyed overlong with the refuse."

Geoff chuckled at Alain's humor. "At least the job is done."

Ottar ran to Geoff and he embraced the boy. "You are safe now."

"You were magnificent!" Ottar said, looking up at Geoff in wonder.

"Nay, Ottar. 'Tis a knight's duty I did, nothing more."

"Someday I will be a knight," he proudly proclaimed.

The boy was older than Geoff when he had become a page. He would not discourage him. "Aye, someday you will. Be an honorable one. Not like these." Geoff had crossed a line in killing William's knights. He could argue he had done so to save the boy, yet he knew it was more. He resented corrupt knights like Eude who betrayed their oath, making the king's mission more difficult by raising the ire of the people.

Over Ottar's head, Geoff saw the other knights and Mathieu approaching, their swords now sheathed. Artur stood close by, waiting.

Without being asked, Mathieu collected the dead knights' swords and helms. "We can add them to the armory."

"I would have done the same, Sir Geoffroi," said one of the knights who had ridden with him that day. "There have been too many innocents killed."

"I agree," said another. "I will say nothing of this encounter."

Grateful for their support, Geoff dismissed the three other knights to return to the castle. "The day's business is done. I will join you later."

Since he had entered the clearing and seen Ottar and the servant, Geoff had known the slain Northumbrian rebels must have been guarding Emma's family. He looked into Ottar's dark eyes and asked the question that had been screaming in his mind. "Where is Emma?"

Ottar's expression grew sullen. "She is in the cave, sick."

The word "cave" immediately caused Geoff's heart to speed. Sweat broke out on his forehead as he remembered a rocky hillside and a chamber so black it inhaled light. Where the only sounds were those of dripping water and animals scurrying in the dark. Where as a boy Ottar's age his brothers had left him for three days until he was starving and nearly out of his mind.

As he stood there, frozen with the image of the cave in his mind, Artur spoke beside him. "Sir Geoffroi, we owe you our lives."

"Artur," Geoff managed to say with difficulty, "... your mistress?"

"Emma is unwell. She burns with fever. The lad and I were gathering herbs for Sigga to make potions for her." He gestured to a small sack lying at the edge of the clearing.

Emma so close. "Is the cave far?"

"Nay," said Artur.

"Show me," said Geoff and followed when Ottar ran ahead.

Artur picked up the sack and joined him as they took off through the woods. At Geoff's signal, Alain and Mathieu followed with the horses.

Minutes later they arrived at a brush-covered hillside of gray rock.

Ottar stopped, out of breath, and pointed toward the face of the cliff. "'Tis just there."

Geoff blinked, his eyes searching the rock, but he could see no opening.

The boy took off running. As Geoff and Artur neared the cliff, Ottar disappeared behind a large clump of bushes. Geoff followed with Artur. On the other side of the bushes was a wide entrance to a cave.

A gaping invitation to Hell.

Geoff came to a sudden halt and stared at the large opening in the rock. His mind raced back to when he'd been trapped in a cave much like this one. Frightened out of his mind, he had not entered another since the day his older brothers had returned and freed him, calling him a coward when they saw his tears.

You will have to face the fear you have carried from your youth, the one you keep hidden even from the Red Wolf. Maugris had seen this day in his visions.

Not even the sight of a man's chest spurting blood could cause him to vomit, as he wanted to now. He fought the overwhelming urge to turn and run. Inside this cave was the woman he loved, sick with a fever that for all he knew could take her life. He took a step toward the darkness, feeling his gorge rise. Then another.

Artur looked intently at him. "Are you also unwell?"

Geoff swallowed. "Nay." He forced himself to face the entrance of the cave, imagining Emma within. "Lead on." He was about to follow the servant when Alain drew close.

"'Tis best you and Mathieu wait outside."

Alain nodded and Geoff followed Artur.

Inside the cave, Finna sat by a fire, clutching something to her chest. Smoke ascended to the roof of the cave. He forced himself to calm. The chamber was large, the roof high. And there was light. "Finna," he said, trying to keep his eyes on the girl and not the dark walls around him.

"Sir Geoffroi!" She leaped up to run to him. When she would have hugged him, he put out a hand, stopping her. "Best to wait until I can clean the blood from my mail."

"You look like you did the first time I saw you," she said.

"Aye, but not for long. Where is Emma?"

Finna pointed to the back of the cave. "In the chamber where Sigga sits with her. Magnus, too."

Artur handed him a cloth. "Here, this will help until you can do more."

Geoff thanked him and wiped the blood from his mail.

A man and woman Geoff did not recognize emerged from the back of the cave. The woman gasped when she saw his bloodstained hauberk. Before he could speak, Artur said, "He is a friend, Martha. He and his fellow knight just saved our lives, defending us against Normans who killed the guards." Turning to Geoff, he explained, "These are Emma's villeins, Jack and Martha. They came with us when we fled."

It was obvious from the woman's doubtful expression Martha was reluctant to consider any Norman a friend. He did not think ill of her for such a view given the circumstances.

The villein, Martha, spoke to Emma's servant, Artur. "Inga has begun her lyin' in; already she cries in pain. She has confessed her sins. I came to fetch salve fer her belly." She stooped to pick up a clay jar and retreated into the depths of the cave.

Geoff kept his eyes on the fire, avoiding the brooding rock walls that surrounded him. "Show me where Emma is."

Ottar picked up a candle and handed it to him. "Finna and I are not allowed to go into Emma's chamber. Sigga is worried we might get sick, too."

"I can show you where she lies," said Artur.

The man named Jack kept his eyes on Geoff as he followed Artur. The servant clutched his sack of herbs in one hand and a candle in the other.

They walked deeper into the cave, over the uneven ground, past smaller chambers carved by nature into the rock. The ceilings were lower here and the space to walk narrowed as they went on. Shadows cast by their candles created ominous images on the cave walls. Geoff forced himself to inhale a deep breath and let it out. He had to do this for Emma.

From one chamber they passed, he heard a woman moan. "'Tis Inga?"

"Aye," murmured Artur. "The babe comes."

"I wonder if it would please her to know Eude is dead." Geoff spoke his question aloud.

"I cannot say, but I think she wants the child. I believe the mistress has finally convinced Inga we will be family for both her and the child. 'Twould be hard not to love a babe that is Inga's."

Geoff kept his eye on his candle as they continued on. Finally, the servant turned into a chamber. Candles lit the small space not more than eight feet in length. Sigga knelt beside a pallet, wiping Emma's reddened face with a cloth.

On the far side of the pallet lay Magnus, his head on the edge of the pallet, his dark eyes looking forlorn. When Geoff entered, the hound raised his head but did not leave Emma's side.

Setting his candle on a ledge, Geoff dropped to his knees beside the pallet. Emma's eyes were closed and she tossed her head in her fevered sleep.

Sigga moved the cloth away as he reached out to touch Emma's forehead. The reddened skin burned under his palm. "Emma?"

"She will not wake, Sir Geoffroi," advised Sigga. "But in her dreams she has called for you."

He wrapped his fingers around Emma's frail hand. She was thin and there were dark shadows under her eyes. He brushed the stray tendrils of damp, flaxen hair from her forehead. His heart ached for love of her, for fear he would lose her. He longed to tell her he understood what she had done, that he still loved her.

"She carried so much of the burden for us," said Sigga. "She wore herself down." Guilt shadowed the servant's face. He could tell by Sigga's grief-ridden expression she did not believe Emma would live.

"How long?"

Worry creased the servant's brow as she gazed at her mistress. "'Tis the fourth day since the sickness came upon her. At first she could hold nothing down. Then came the chills and the fever. For the last day she has not been in her right mind. She grows ever weaker."

From behind him, Artur said, "Sigga, I brought the herbs you asked for."

Sigga stood. "Will you sit with her, Sir Geoffroi? I must prepare a tea for the fever."

He nodded. "Has she eaten?"

"Nay, but in the first days, in the times she was near awake, I was able to get her to take a bit of broth."

Sigga glanced at his mail still bearing some bloodstains, then raised a brow at her husband.

"Sir Geoffroi and his fellow knight saved us from two Normans who killed the guards and would have killed us."

"Oh, no," Sigga said, raising her hand to cover her mouth.

Her husband put his arm over her shoulder. "'Tis all right now, Sigga, but 'twould distress Emma to know her father's trusted men were killed."

"There should be no more knights wandering in the woods," Geoff assured her, "but still, you must show caution when leaving the cave. There will be hunting parties from time to time."

After Sigga had gone, Artur explained, "We have kept Emma separated from Inga and the twins. We were afraid her fever might spread."

"Aye, you did well, but Emma should not be in this cold, dark cave. I will take her to her home. It has already been searched and will be safe, at least for a time."

"My wife might not like it, but if Emma's home still stands and you think it safe, I agree. We cannot care for her here as well as you could there."

Geoff had been fighting the urge to flee the cave since he'd first entered it. For Emma's sake he had not. "As soon as Sigga has prepared the tea, I will leave with Emma."

"You will guard her from your fellow knights?"

"Aye, with my life."

CHAPTER 15

Even before she opened her eyes, Emma knew she was no longer in the cave. The scent of herbed rushes and the occasional sound of a coal shifting in the brazier spoke of another place. *Home.*

The effort it took to open her eyes told her she was still weak. The room was dimly lit but the face looming over her had familiar blue eyes and an anxious expression. "Geoffroi."

His face softened into a smile. "Yea, 'tis I. And you are finally awake." He let out a breath. "I believe the fever has gone."

"But how—"

His warm hand wrapped around hers. "I found your hiding place in the cave. Actually, Ottar led me to it. When I saw you were sick, I brought you here. I have no fondness for caves and the cold was doing you no good."

"The others?"

"They remain in the cave. I could not bring so many without attracting unwanted attention and Inga was just giving birth."

"Is Inga…?" Emma despaired of the answer. Giving birth could lead to the death of both mother and child. It was why a mother confessed her sins before giving birth and why Martha, as a midwife, would be allowed to baptize the babe.

"Mathieu brings me reports as well as food, potions and your tea. Inga gave birth to a girl child she has named Merewyn. Both are well."

Emma closed her eyes as gratitude flooded her heart. *Inga lives. Thank God.* Remembering Inga's fears for the appearance of the child, she asked,

"Did Mathieu happen to see the babe?"

"He did. He says 'tis a lovely child with the look of her mother: gray eyes and a head covered with a soft, honey-colored down." He grinned. "Mathieu is quite smitten with the child and mayhap with Inga as well."

Emma sighed, content at least for the moment. When she swallowed, her throat was parched. "Can I have something to drink?"

Geoff reached for a cup. "Sigga made you a special tea for the fever. I have forced a little down you every few hours. The fever has left you, but I would have you drink the rest of it. Then, if you feel hungry, I have some broth."

"A knight who plays cook?"

He laughed. "Hardly. Sigga made the broth. I only serve it." Lifting her head to help her drink, he said, "I could have brought Sigga but she wanted to stay to help with the babe. I even let Magnus remain with them. I trust you do not mind."

"He will protect them where I cannot," said Emma, laying her head back on the pillow.

She studied his face seeing no hatred in his eyes, no hostility. The knight who had lain with her in the meadow had returned. "I am so sorry, Geoffroi. I wanted to tell you, but I could not seem to find a way."

"I know."

"You forgive me?"

"Aye. When I was deep in the snows of Durham I realized what it must have been like for you, torn between your father and me."

"Durham?"

"Much has happened." Then he told her of his king's dreadful revenge on Northumbria. "My men and I did not take part in the worst of it when cottars and villeins were killed and their cottages burned." At her look of dismay, he added, "We helped some to escape."

"The archbishop warned us," she said on a sigh.

"William was determined to destroy the rebels' base so they could not rise to challenge his rule again. It was unlike anything I have ever seen, Emma. Worse than the Danes' slaughter of the garrisons in York, for the end of it was not a battle among warriors."

"I cannot imagine…" Her voice trailed off as she thought of the women and children, her father, Cospatric and the others—men she had known from her youth. "What of the leaders… my father?"

"I have heard nothing of Maerleswein. If he was with the Danes, they are still on the Humber where William blocks their return to York. They have agreed to accept the king's gold to leave in the spring."

"Father will not like that, but then he never trusted Osbjorn's motives. They had planned to return, you know, or so my father told me."

"I suspected. Undoubtedly so did William."

"And the other leaders of the uprising?"

"Earl Waltheof and Cospatric live and have submitted to William. He has accepted them back into the fold."

"I am glad for it. I know them both."

A thought came to her mind. He had said that Ottar had showed him the cave. "How did you find Ottar?"

"He and Artur had gone in search of herbs for you at Sigga's request. I came upon them when your guards were attacked by Eude and his companion."

"Eude? He lived through the Danes' attack?"

"Aye. A coward, he ran to the woods."

"Does he yet live?" *Inga might be dismayed to hear he is in York.*

"Nay. When he threatened Ottar and your servant, I managed to kill him. Were it known I killed my fellow knight, in the eyes of some, I would be a traitor. Eude called me as much when I stood against him."

In his eyes she saw regret. But surely not for killing Eude. She squeezed the hand holding hers. "You are a man of honor. I could not respect you otherwise."

"Your respect means much."

She remembered their last encounter and the bitter hatred she had seen in his eyes then. It was not there now. "So, you do not hate me after all?"

"Nay, Emma." He bent his head to kiss her forehead. "I did try," he said with a slight smile, "mayhap I even succeeded for a while, but I found such a feeling toward you impossible to sustain. It seems I love you."

Joy filled her heart such as she had not known since the summer afternoons they had spent together. She smiled up at him glad their love had somehow survived. "I love you, too. And I have missed you so."

When his lips touched hers, they were gentle. If she had not been so weak, she would have pulled him onto the bed. The irony of it made her chuckle.

He pulled back and gave her a puzzled look. "What is it about my kiss, pray tell, that renders you so merry?"

"When you wished for a bed, we had none. Now that we have one, I am too weak to enjoy it with you."

A gleam came into his eyes. "There will be other times. You will not always be so weak."

"Are we safe here?"

"Aye, at least for now. The homes that remain in York have been searched and William's army is encamped outside the city."

* * *

In the days that followed, Geoff cared for Emma, at first despairing she would recover and then, as she improved, finding joy in seeing her gain strength with each day. At first she remained abed but occasionally he would let her up for brief periods. Even then she tired easily.

"Another cup of broth and I will let you sleep."

"You torture me with your potions and brews," she teased, but her eyes told him she was pleased he was here. She sat up and drank the broth. "Do you not have some knightly business to attend to?"

He chuckled. It was a familiar exchange. She was not truly annoyed, nor did she wish to see him go, but he knew she felt guilty for taking him from his duties. "I have seen enough of fighting and I need no more time in the practice yard." Soon she would be able to return to her family, to the cave. What then? He would have to go with William. It pained him to think of leaving her in York but it could not be helped.

She handed him the cup and lay back on the bed, closing her eyes. He leaned over her and kissed her forehead. She had rested well this day.

Without opening her eyes, her hand reached out and wrapped around his neck, pulling him toward her, bringing his lips to hers. "Kiss me, sir knight."

"With pleasure." He kissed her and it was summer again with a meadow of fragrant blossoms surrounding them no matter winter swirled outside the house. He tasted her lips and inhaled her woman's scent, wanting more. His passion for her had not faded with time. To be with her and not be able to touch her had been torture. He wanted to love her again. This time in a bed.

He broke the kiss and looked at her, wanting to know if she was ready. She had been so weak for days he had feared for her life.

"What are you waiting for?" she asked. "We have a bed and we are alone."

He needed no more invitation than her words and the knowing twinkle in her eyes. He shed his clothes—her eyes following his every move. Already his groin swelled in anticipation. He slipped under the bedcover to lie beside her. Pulling her slim body into his arms, he felt the warmth of her breasts through the thin linen shift as she pressed them into the hard planes of his warrior's chest.

Passion was not the only thing that rose between them.

"I can feel how you missed me," she said. "Why did you wait so long?"

He nuzzled her neck and kissed his way back to her lips, his hand sliding under her shift to stroke the silken skin of her thigh.

"You have no idea how much strength it took not to touch you, to wait until you were recovered."

He slid her shift higher and then removed it altogether. Her naked breasts pressed against his chest. He pulled back so that he could admire them. "Smaller, mayhap, but still lovely."

"You tease me."

"I do." He nuzzled the valley between the rounded mounds, breathing in her smell. It was like coming home. He covered one breast with his palm as his mouth moved to lick the other. Her taste was sweet and made him harden all the more.

They had never been able to linger with the preliminaries but tonight he wanted to go slowly, to savor what he might have to live without for a long time and to make it an experience she would not forget. One she would want to repeat for the rest of her life.

As he kissed her breasts, he slid his hand to her hip, then the top of her thigh. She held his head to her.

He pulled from her grasp to kiss his way down her body, to the flat plain of her belly. She gripped his shoulders writhing beneath him.

"Emma..." It came out as a moan though he had intended it as an endearment.

He kissed his way back up to her mouth and slipped his leg between her thighs, opening her to his touch. He was gentle, not sure how strong she was. But after only a few strokes through her damp, ready flesh, she nudged away his hand. "I can wait no longer."

Geoff raised above her, positioned himself at her entrance and in one thrust sank deeply into her warm, tight sheath. She wrapped her legs around him and threaded her fingers through his hair as she pulled his head to her, kissing him with abandon.

Her tongue tangled with his as they moved together. She broke the kiss to press her cheek to his, holding tightly on to his shoulders. "Geoffroi," she whispered, as she clung to him, "oh, Geoffroi."

He was surrounded by the woman he loved, happily drowning in his passion for her. Their bodies grew slick with sweat as they moved more swiftly.

He felt her muscles constrict with her release. It was all he needed to send him over the precipice. His own release came with a storm-like violence.

Coming back to awareness, he kissed her temple and rolled to the side, bringing her with him. For a time he drifted, content just to hold her.

She tucked her head into his shoulder and laid her hand on his chest.

"Are you all right?" he asked, hoping he had not been too rough.

"Oh, yea. I am," she said, moving her fingers through the smattering of hair on his chest.

Geoff began to drift toward sleep. The knock on the door below sounded loudly in the quiet of Emma's bedchamber, startling him from the twilight just before sleep.

He gave out an exasperated sigh. "I had best see who comes before they storm the door and find us like this."

With great reluctance, he climbed from the bed and donned his braies, leggings, tunic and leather boots.

Running a hand through his tousled hair, he descended the stairs and unlatched the front door. Alain stood next to Mathieu, their cloaks dusted with snow. The Bear's arm was draped over the squire's shoulder.

"Remember us?" Alain asked with a grin.

He managed only a droll smile, knowing his hair was likely mussed and his color high. "Aye, how could I forget? What brings you here?" He gestured them inside where he had kept the hearth fire going and shut the door, closing out the bitter winds of winter.

Reaching for a pitcher on the table, he was about to pour them some mead when Mathieu took the pitcher from him. "I can do that, sir."

Geoff tipped his head to the squire and allowed the squire to serve the knights.

"William asks for you," said Alain, taking a drink of the honeyed wine Mathieu had poured him. "He would have you attend the crown-wearing ceremony he intends to hold tomorrow as a part of his Christmas celebration."

"In the ashes of the Minster, no doubt," observed Geoff, running a hand through his tangled hair, trying to imagine such a ceremony.

"I suppose he must make his show," Alain replied.

"He sent men to retrieve his crown and king's robes all the way from Winchester," said Mathieu, setting down his empty cup.

Geoff's companions had never questioned his love for the daughter of the rebel leader. They did not question him now. But they would remind him of his duty. The crown-wearing ceremony was yet another demonstration that William was the lawful King of England. Geoff must attend.

"At least the ceremony will not be far from here," he said, "and Emma is nearly well." Looking at Alain, he asked, "Will you stay with her while I pay homage to the king?"

"Aye. I will take the watch while you are away," Alain replied.

"If you need me, I am at your disposal," said Mathieu.

Geoff placed his hand on the squire's shoulder. "I could not have tended Emma without your help. You, too, Alain. I am in your debt."

Alain smiled, the genuine warmth of it eclipsing the scar on his jaw. "The mead is much appreciated."

The next day, Geoff was present amidst the blackened walls of the Minster for the ceremony. The king, wearing crown and robes, sat in a newly built chair, looking as regal as if he were in Westminster. To Geoff it was a dim shadow of what might have been had Archbishop Ealdred lived and the fire not destroyed the church. But despite the miserable setting, William was announcing his rule in the North. It mattered little to him that he did so among the ruins of a once proud cathedral.

The ceremony was brief. William had made his point and clearly did not wish to linger among the ruins of the once beautiful edifice. He and his men, Geoff among them, retired to the hall in the new square tower to eat the Christmas feast.

The roast goose was served on silver plates that William's men had retrieved from Winchester along with the king's crown and royal robes. Geoff was certain the feast paled in comparison to what William would have enjoyed in London, but it was not the food that was important to his sovereign. It was the record history would make that it was King William who dined in York this Christmas, not Edgar Ætheling or Swein of Denmark.

After the meal was finished and they had toasted the day, William disbursed vast tracts of land to his loyal followers, for he was rich with demesnes from those he had claimed as king. Geoff was among those rewarded. He was relieved the lands were not in the wasteland that was now Yorkshire. Instead, William awarded him lands abutting the great demesne of Talisand. His friend, the Red Wolf, would be pleased, as was Geoff. But the price had been high. Not just the decimation of Emma's people, which he would regret forever, but he had to wonder if the price had included his honor. He believed he had turned from the brutality William inflicted on the North before it was too late, and in doing so, had saved the lives of innocents, but he would always wonder if he could have done more.

As he rode back to Emma's, he longed for only two things: Emma as his wife and peace. Both were very much in doubt. Emma might love him, but would she come with him to Talisand? He already knew William was not finished putting down rebellions and would demand Geoff's sword arm.

* * *

Heated male voices woke Emma from sleep.

"She should come to Talisand where she will be safe." *Geoffroi.*

"She should come with me to Scotland where King Malcolm welcomes us." *Father.*

"I have asked her to be my wife," Geoffroi intoned.

"Should she wish to marry, my daughter has many suitors… *noble* ones."

"I may be a younger son, but my family is of noble rank," Geoffroi protested.

"Your family is Norman French," her father spit out. "We are noble Danes. Well half, in any event," he said in a softer tone. Emma knew he was thinking of her mother. "Julianna was an English thegn's daughter, but that matters little to my point. Emma's future lies outside of an England ruled by a Norman king."

Rising up on her elbow, she said, "Will the two of you stop arguing about my future? I have a mind that is no longer so fevered I cannot decide my own fate. Besides," she fell back onto the pillows, "I have a family to care for."

"You can bring them to Talisand," said Geoffroi, casting her a glance from where he stood at the foot of her bed next to her father.

"They can come with you to Scotland," her father declared, his voice deep and commanding.

Pushing herself higher onto the pillows, she said, "I will hear no more of this tonight. It is bad enough I am not with my family at Christmas. I would at least have peace in my house."

At her chiding, both men looked sheepish. She loved them both. Yet they were sworn enemies. She was glad that tonight they warred only with their tongues and not their swords.

"I will look in on your little family before I depart for the Humber," said her father. "None of you can remain in York."

"On that, at least, we agree," said Geoffroi.

"How were you able to leave the Humber, Father?"

"I was not with the Danes and their ships, but in the marshes nearby. It was not difficult to slip away." He gave Geoffroi a look that said he thought little of the Normans who guarded the marshes. "Were it not for Osbjorn's poor planning, we would hold York still. King Swein would not have made that error."

Geoffroi ignored him and came to the side of her bed. "Emma, I must go with the king when he leaves for Cheshire in a day or two. Duty compels me. But he has promised to release me after that to go to Talisand north of Cheshire. Send word and I will come for you. Tell me now you want me to come and I will make plans."

"She need send no word from Scotland," her father insisted. "I will make plans for her and her family. You need not come, Norman."

* * *

Before Geoff left York with the king, he and Emma spent one last night together. The memory of it warmed him even in the relentless cold of winter as he, Alain and Mathieu rode southwest toward Cheshire. She had given herself to him in a way that told him her love was sincere, but he was still uncertain if she would come to Talisand. It was not as simple as just the two of them. She served her family like he served his king. And then there was her father…

He thought back to the night he had sat watching her sleep, shocked when the rebel leader managed to sneak into her chamber.

"What do you do here, Norman?" the tall Dane demanded as he had stepped from the shadows.

Startled, Geoff had turned, drawing his knife at the harsh, unfamiliar voice, damning himself for leaving the chamber door ajar. Recognizing the man as Emma's father, his words had been curt. "I am taking care of your daughter. She has been unwell, but recovers." Geoff had sheathed his knife and turned back to Emma. He did not worry her father would kill him. Having spared Geoff's life once at Emma's request, it hardly seemed likely he would take it now.

"Does William know you are here?" asked Maerleswein.

"Nay. And, for Emma's sake, I would not tell him. He knows only I sit by the side of a sick friend."

"Where are the others? The twins?"

"Hiding in the woods, in a cave. When I discovered Emma, she was there, sickly and suffering from fever and chills. I thought it best to bring her here. You should know your guards gave their lives to protect her."

"You killed them?" Maerleswein demanded.

"Nay, I killed the Normans who did."

The tall Dane came closer to the bed and peered down on his daughter. "I am grateful for what you have done for her."

"I could do no less for the woman I love."

Silence hung in the air. Maerleswein broke it. "Does my daughter return this love you speak of?"

"She has spoken the words and there is much between us. I have offered her marriage."

And then began the conversation that had awakened Emma. He had gone over that night in his mind many times. Maerleswein had been adamant she should go with him to Scotland, where Earl Cospatric had again sought exile even after William had restored his lands and title.

Now, as he turned Athos into the cold wind, heading toward Cheshire, he wondered. Emma was loyal to her father, but would she follow him to Scotland? Geoff could not be sure. She would do much for her family. Then, too, when he had sought marriage, she had demurred. Had she only wanted him as a lover? Was he too far below her? The thought did not sit comfortably on his mind. Emma was not one to judge a man by his birth. Remembering their times together in the meadow and in her bed, he did not believe she only wanted a lover, for she had given more than her body. She had given of her heart.

But something held her back. She had not asked Geoff to come for her when the king released him. Instead, worried about her family, she had insisted he take her back to the cave, which he had done. When he had returned to the castle, he found William giving instructions to his half-brother, Robert, to deal with the rebels in York and the Danes on the Humber. Then the king had turned to the captains of his army, ordering them to prepare to march to Cheshire. When he finished his instructions to them, he turned to Geoff, reminding him, "We expect you and your men to join us."

* * *

Emma sat by the fire in the cave one early morning holding Inga's babe so the young mother could sleep. She gazed into the face of the sweet child who, Emma was relieved to see, would one day look very much like Inga.

Artur added another log to the fire as his wife, Sigga, stood at the mouth of the cave, looking out. Winter lingered, but as Emma looked into the eyes of Inga's babe, her thoughts drifted to the spring that would come. What would she do?

Though she had stubbornly resisted both her father's and Geoffroi's plans for her, Emma's heart longed to be with her knight, her Gabriel who had ridden to her rescue so many times. An enemy who turned out to be more than a friend. He was her lover. For three years, no man had touched her woman's heart. She decided that a woman did not always choose the man to whom she gave her love. But if Emma had consciously chosen, she could have chosen no better.

Whether she had realized it at the time, she saw it clearly now. Even before the first time they had lain together, she had loved him. War had drawn them together and then it had torn them apart. Having received his forgiveness for her part in the rebellion, there was only one place she wanted to be—with Geoffroi. But she could not go to Talisand alone. She would not abandon the family she loved. If she were to go, she wanted the twins, Inga, Artur and Sigga and Jack and Martha to come with her. Until she knew they would agree, she could make no promise, for she would not leave them, not even for love of her knight.

When her father had said goodbye before returning to the Humber, she had not encouraged him to expect her to go to Scotland in the spring. He argued Cospatric's case as the suitor he wanted for her. She had confessed that she liked the earl.

"But I do not love him, Father."

"Love can grow between two who share respect," he had said, "I will call on you before I leave. In time, you will come to see what I want for you is best. Be careful, Emma. The woods are full of Normans."

She waved goodbye as he faded into the protection of the woods he knew so well to join his Northumbrian rebels. Having led the failed rebellion, once he joined Cospatric in Scotland, she did not think he would ever return to England.

A cold wind whistled into the cave, making the fire flutter wildly. Sigga wrapped her cloak tightly around her and left the mouth of the cave to sit by Emma. Now that she was no longer fevered, Emma felt the cold as the others did, shivering whenever she left the comfort of the fire.

Both Geoffroi and her father had counseled against taking her family to her home in York, for it was too easy a target should the Normans again search the town. Before he left for Cheshire, Geoffroi had told them York's stores of food not taken into the castle to be consumed by William's knights had been destroyed. The Norman king had also ordered the burning of farming tools, cottages and everything else in Yorkshire. Even the fields had been salted so the land could not be farmed in the spring. Never again would she stand on the hillside outside of York's walls to watch Ottar and Finna play among the flowers. Never again would she watch with pleasure the ripening grain.

Sigga raised her head, looking toward the mouth of the cave. "Magnus has returned but without the usual hare."

Emma looked up from where she sat holding Merewyn, now asleep in her arms. The weary hound walked to her side and dropped to the ground. She patted his head. "'Tis all right, we have enough food for today."

"I will hunt," offered Artur from where he tended the fire.

"If you go," counseled Emma, "take Jack. The woods are not free of Normans. Even more dangerous than the knights are the people who must be starving by now, willing to kill you for any game you bring down."

Artur darted a glance at Thyra, Emma's mare standing just inside the cave. They had talked about the horse. Emma refused to think of Thyra as food, but many would and she was certain that both horses and dogs would be eaten before people gave in to starvation.

A short while later, Jack and Martha came from their chamber to join them around the fire. Not long after, Artur departed with Jack, the two of them vowing not to return empty-handed.

Magnus stood as if he would go with them, but she forced him to stay. "You are worn out and I would have you with us should a stranger find the cave." The hound lay down as if in understanding.

Inga came to the fire from the chamber where she had been sleeping and Emma handed Merewyn to her.

"I will feed her," said the new mother and disappeared with the babe into the back of the cave.

It was time, Emma decided, to take stock of what food they had. With Sigga beside her, she went to examine their stores. In the rear chamber, she held her candle high as she opened the roughly woven sacks, inspecting each one. "We've grain enough for gruel until spring and, thanks to what Sir Geoffroi carried to the cave, we've mead enough. He even brought hay for Thyra, bless him."

Sigga peered into another group of smaller bags. "There are dried berries, nuts and herbs, but only enough other vegetables for another month. Oh, and we've some cheese and apples."

"Spring is two months away," said Emma, thinking out loud. "'Twill have to do till then."

"Mayhap the men will be fortunate in their hunting," Sigga encouraged, as they returned to the main chamber.

A few hours later, Emma's spirits lifted when the men trudged into the cave carrying three red squirrels. Magnus sniffed them and walked away as if unimpressed. Emma had to smile. Sometimes the hound spoke loudly even though he lacked words.

"You did well," she told the men. "As I recall, Sigga makes a fair squirrel stew."

Sigga, who was a very good cook, smiled. "Aye, I will make short work of them. A few onions and turnips with spices 'twill make a hearty dish."

It was a few weeks later when a small family of three freemen found the cave in which Emma's family lived. In truth, it was Ottar they found, gathering wood just outside. Perhaps the boy had been drawn to the man's son for they were nearly the same age.

"They are hungry, Emma," Ottar announced, leading the small family into the main chamber. Emma was sitting by the fire putting her embroidery skills to work mending the twins' clothes.

"You are welcome to share what we have," said Emma rising to greet them. They must have fled with little more than their clothes and those not in good condition. Their tunics and cloaks were soiled and threadbare, their faces dirty and gaunt beneath their hair. "Come, sit by the fire."

"I'll fetch them some mead," said Sigga, hastening to where they kept the wine.

The small family introduced themselves as Sker, his wife, Drifa, and their son, Hunlaf. Both the father and son had red hair and ruddy complexions; the mother's hair was golden like Inga's. If they were to be cleaned of dirt, they would be a handsome family. "We had only a little notice," said Sker, "but it was enough to save our lives. We grabbed what we could carry as we fled. I am a farmer, unused to hunting. We have been surviving on what we brought with us until recently."

Seeing the hungry look in their eyes, Emma inquired, "How long has it been since you ate?"

"The day before yesterday," Drifa said, looking around the cave as she reached her hands to the fire. "It is warm here. You have prepared well."

"I had a dream that warned us," said Emma. "We came here before the Normans returned."

They did not question her dream, only nodded. Such were the beliefs of the people they gave credence to warnings, visions and dreams.

Without being asked, Martha served bread and cheese to their visitors and Sigga brought them cups of mead.

"The bread is stale," Emma explained, "but 'twill fill your stomachs. Our men caught some squirrels this morning, so there will be stew for dinner. The water in the stream is good, too."

"We are most grateful," said Sker as he and his family greedily ate the bread and cheese, washing the small meal down with the mead.

Finna came to sit in Emma's lap, her brown eyes watching with interest the family across the crackling fire.

When Jack announced he was leaving to gather wood, the two boys happily went with him. "Mind Jack, Ottar," Emma said.

"You, too, Hunlaf," Drifa said to her son. Since the woman had first entered the cave, her eyes kept darting to where Magnus lay by Emma's side, his head on his paws.

"The hound will not harm you," said Emma, relieved when the woman appeared to relax at her words.

"All of our friends fled when the Normans came to burn the cottages, but we became separated," said the father, Sker. "No one is left in York, save those who may be hiding in the homes that remain. And that is dangerous should they be discovered. If the Normans had waited until spring or summer for their revenge 'twould not have been so bad, but now it means starvation for most."

His wife shuddered and, with a look of pain, turned her head away.

Inga, holding little Merewyn, came from the back of the cave to join them by the fire. Merewyn was a contented babe, blithely unaware of the desperate times into which she had been born. Would she be better accepted in Talisand than Scotland? Merewyn would not be the only half-Norman babe born in England this year.

Looking at the freeman and his wife and thinking of three more mouths to feed, Emma worried about the dwindling stores of food. Their small band of survivors now numbered twelve, including the babe.

While Martha helped Sigga prepare their meal, Emma decided mayhap it was time to broach the subject of where they might go in the spring.

"My father would have us go with him to Scotland," she told them. "He will come in the spring to see if that is our desire." Those huddled around the fire listened intently. "But we have another choice I would ask you to think on." She waited, feeling their eyes upon her. "We can go to Talisand." To the newcomers, she explained, "'Tis the home of our friend, Sir Geoffroi, and lies a few days' journey to the west, longer with us walking."

"A Norman?" asked Sker, aghast.

"Aye, a French knight," acknowledged Emma, "but a noble one. Talisand is the demesne of a former English thegn whose daughter is wed to the Norman who is lord there. We have been assured we will be welcome."

They stared at her, then began to mumble among themselves.

Emma interrupted them. "Whatever we do will mean a hard journey." She glanced at Inga who held the sleeping Merewyn in her arms. "And if we travel to Talisand, 'twill be dangerous. Not just because the Norman army garrisoned in York would kill us if they found us, but the wolves we hear at night might set upon us in the forests and there are people so desperate for food they would stoop to violence for what little we have." She was not telling them anything they did not already know but she felt she had to warn them.

"We cannot stay in York," said Inga.

They all nodded. The horrors of war had come home even to the children.

"I would choose Scotland," said Sker's wife, "but I know nothing of it."

"I want to go where Mathieu is," Finna insisted. "He will go to Talisand."

When the new arrivals looked to Emma for an explanation, she said, "Sir Geoffroi's squire."

"He is very kind," added Inga.

"And I would go with Sir Geoffroi," said Ottar. "He might let me be his page!"

"We will go with you," said Artur, taking his wife's hand and looking at Emma. "Sigga and I have discussed it. We are part of your family. Wherever you go, we will go."

"Aye," said Sigga. "We are fond of Sir Geoffroi and if you choose Talisand, we are with you. I would not have you go without us. Maerleswein would never forgive us."

Emma smiled. To hear such words warmed her heart. Her servants, her twins and her friend were her family. She wanted them with her. But she wanted them to know the risks they faced. "We would have to cross the fells and rivers swollen with spring rains. We could not forage for food until we passed the salted lands. It would be especially hard on the little ones but they can ride Thyra."

She reminded herself this time they would have no guards. For all their grumbling, her father's men had been faithful protectors. What did Artur, a house servant, and Jack and Sker, who were farmers, know of guiding women and children over such obstacles? Even she did not know Talisand's precise location, only that it was in the Lune River valley to the west. Would they be able to find it?

As she stared into the bright flames, the responsibility for the others weighed heavily upon her.

Jack spoke into the silence. "We would go wherever we can farm."

"I remember hearing Sir Geoffroi speak of the wondrous place called Talisand," said Sigga, "where the English live in peace with Normans. There is land to farm there."

"Must be land in Scotland," said Sker's wife.

"Aye, but colder winters than in England," said her husband.

"I wonder if 'tis possible to live in peace with Normans," Inga muttered beneath her breath but Emma heard it. Inga's reaction did not surprise her. The decision to live among Normans would be difficult and she had voiced such concerns before. Given her being unwed, Inga would face disapproval and shame wherever she went. At least at Talisand, she would have friends who understood.

"We do not have to choose today," Emma reminded them. "I know some will want to think on it." Her gaze fell upon Inga and her babe. "Scotland is far but with my father guiding us, 'twould be safe. Talisand is closer but the journey will be difficult."

CHAPTER 16

Geoff and his men, along with that part of William's army not left in York, were driven mercilessly across England, heading southwest over the snow-covered peaks lying between the cities of York and Chester.

They rode through barren hills and dales and splashed through icy streams. The middle of England was a vast wilderness with few inhabitants. Their food consisted of meager pickings except for the few times they managed to hunt and the pace William insisted upon kept their hunting trips few.

Cheshire in the west of Mercia had yet to be conquered and William had vowed he would not return to London until all of England was his. The city of Chester in the far west of Cheshire near Wales stood like a last remaining column in a long forgotten temple, a symbol of lands still free. But, if William had his way, 'twould not be for long.

With unrelenting determination, the king pushed his men forward.

The cold took its toll in suffering and even the death of some horses. Men in William's army had begun to grumble, particularly those from Anjou, Brittany and Maine, who were neither Norman nor English. They wanted to be released, but William would not hear of it. Instead, for their complaining, the king told them they would serve another forty days.

Though he was not among those affected, Geoff inwardly groaned at the news. Having already endured one march through snow and ice, it now appeared he and his companions would have to endure another. But they did not complain. When he could, Geoff helped the men whose strength was faltering, encouraging them to go on. And he took special care with Athos to ensure his horse did not fall. When he grumbled, it was not to William, but to Alain.

"I like not this duty that takes us over so much ground claimed by winter's brutal storms. My only hope is that we will soon see the rich pastures of Cheshire."

"I remember well those pastures. We rode through them two years ago."

As it turned out, when they reached Cheshire, much to Geoff's dismay, those rich pastures were covered in snow for the harsh winter was even felt here.

More than a year before, at William's command, Geoff and the Red Wolf had ridden to Exeter in the south of England to join the king's army where they laid siege to the walled city. Like Exeter, Chester was an old Roman town with Roman walls, a fortress that would have to be taken by force.

And take it they did by William's order.

The resistance they met was fierce, but unlike William's actions in Exeter, where he granted mercy, in Chester he offered none. Instead, he inflicted the same drastic measures on Cheshire he had on York and Durham. The king ordered his knights to ravage the countryside, wasting the land to assure there would be no base for future rebellion. It sickened Geoff to see such a beautiful land treated so. But William had grown intolerant of anything save total submission secured at any cost. The king's mercy was at an end.

As before, Geoff resisted the killing of innocents. Instead, he and the few men who agreed with him helped those who were left homeless, the young and old and women and children, to escape. He had heard the Abbey of Evesham to the south was taking in those fleeing William's wrath and so he directed the fleeing toward that shelter where Abbot Æthelwig provided food to the hungry. For all his help, some still died.

If Geoff had ever had a taste for war, he lost it in the snows of England that winter.

Once William conquered Chester, to no one's surprise, he ordered the building of a castle as a sign of his lasting imprint on that city. Since it had become more difficult for Geoff to disguise his actions to help the fleeing English, he was greatly relieved to be among those knights who were then released from the king's service.

It surprised Geoff that William, who had acted so ruthlessly to force the people to submit, could then give God thanks for blessing what he regarded as his "holy work" of conquering the whole of England. Geoff believed the holier work had been that of Abbot Æthelwig. But he accepted William's thanks and words of honor and, with a grateful heart for the end of it, turned Athos north toward Talisand.

As they rode north, Emma was never far from his thoughts. *Would she have sent word? Should he go to her even if she did not?*

* * *

By the time Geoff arrived at Talisand, winter was turning to spring. Rain had followed the snow and the hills were once again clothed in green. The picture he had carried in his mind for over a year, of wildflowers dotting pastures where lambs idly grazed, was beginning to take form. There was no starvation in this valley of the River Lune for it was well tended by the Lord of Talisand and his lady, Serena.

"'Tis just as it was when we first arrived," Geoff said as they reined in their horses on top of a hill to gaze down the long slope leading toward the green meadow in front of the palisade that backed onto the River Lune.

"Only the castle you see in yon distance was not there two years before," said Alain.

"Aye, of course," he said letting out an exasperated breath. "But all else is the same, the palisade, the village, the river. I have missed this place." *How I wish Emma was here to see it.*

Spurring their horses to a gallop, the three of them raced down the hill to the palisade surrounding the bailey, the manor and the motte on which sat a timbered castle three stories high.

Aethel must have seen them coming for as soon as they passed through the gate and Alain slid from his horse, she flew into his arms.

"Ye have a daughter, husband!" exclaimed the dark-haired beauty as she brazenly kissed her husband.

"Lora?" asked Alain, sweeping his wife off her feet for a hug only the Bear could give.

"Aye," she said breathlessly, "a babe among many babes born at Talisand in the year ye have been gone. I cannot wait for ye to see her. I was so worried when the tales started coming to us from York."

Shooting Geoff a glance, Alain said, "'Twas a bad time. But we'll not speak of it now. I would see my child."

Alain took his wife off, arms wrapped around each other, making Geoff smile to see them together. Once the old thegn's leman, Aethel had become the treasured wife of the Norman knight.

Geoff dismounted and handed the reins to the waiting Mathieu. "You served me well, Mathieu. 'Tis time you were a knight and had your spurs. I will see Ren about it."

"Thank you, Sir Geoffroi. It was an honor to serve you and Sir Alain. Sir Renaud is a grand knight 'tis my privilege to call 'lord', but he is no better lord than you."

"That is quite a compliment coming from Ren's squire, but if it be so, it is because Ren and I share the same heart. We may be men of war, Mathieu, but neither of us would see innocents suffer or women ill-treated."

Mathieu bowed his head and led their three horses toward the stables, leaving Geoff alone in the bailey. But not for long.

A smile on his wizened face, Maugris walked toward Geoff, his thin frame covered by a fine tunic of dark blue Talisand wool.

"I suppose you saw our return in your visions?"

"Nay, 'twas the king's messenger. At least this one bore good news."

Geoff took off his gloves, his helm he'd left tied to his saddle. "You were right about it all, Maugris. There was more death than I ever want to see again, innocents among the guilty."

"But you return a better man, one who has faced evil and stood against it."

"Aye, at least I hope so," Geoff said, still wondering if he had done enough.

"And what of the woman?" asked the old man, the breeze blowing his gray hair across his forehead, his pale blue eyes seeing too much as they always did.

"I have no woman," said Geoff. "Mayhap I never will."

Maugris chuckled. "You would quit the field too soon."

Geoff studied the old one's wrinkled face, all lightheartedness gone from his ancient countenance.

"The Red Wolf has his jewel," said Maugris, "and, in time, Sir Geoffroi, you will have yours."

* * *

That night a great feast was held in Talisand's hall, constructed by King William's command two years earlier. Torches and candles lit the large space and fresh rushes smelling of dried spring flowers had been laid on the floor. It was the kind of welcome Geoff and his companions had talked about during the days they rode home. He was glad William had decided to ride south for another crown-wearing ceremony, this one at Winchester. Talisand would have a more intimate feast without him.

At the head table, Ren and Serena sat in the middle with Geoff on Ren's right. On Geoff's other side sat Alain and Aethel. Maugris had a position of honor next to Serena.

Serving wenches, some new to Geoff, carried platters of roast venison and lamb to the tables. There was also baked fish from the river. To this were added peas spiced with cumin, turnips boiled with thyme and dill, and all manner of cheeses. He was delighted to see the hot bread placed near him along with butter. 'Twas more food than he had seen in a long time.

"'Tis a feast for the eyes as well as the stomach," he told Ren.

"Serena says you are more welcome than the king and so she spared no effort to see you and Alain had the best."

Geoff chuckled. "Aye, your lady would welcome almost any of William's knights more than the king himself."

Serena leaned over her husband to offer Geoff a smile.

"Have you been gone only a year?" asked Ren, placing several choice bits of meat on the trencher he shared with his wife.

Serena spoke across her husband. "You and Sir Alain have been sorely missed, Sir Geoffroi. My husband has oft inquired when you would be home. Maugris was little help, only saying, 'when it is time'."

Geoff chuckled at the wise one's cryptic remark. He was happy to be home. "I feel like I have lived a lifetime in this last year, mayhap longer. I am sorry about the knights who left with me."

"We heard of the Danes' attack in York," said the Red Wolf. "For a while we worried you were dead, but despite the reports of the slaughter, Maugris insisted you lived."

"Were it not for a lady's intervention, I would have gone the way of the other knights in York."

"You must tell me of this lady," said Serena.

"Mayhap in time," Geoff said.

"You have changed," said the Red Wolf. "I cannot say how, but 'tis clear you have changed all the same."

"If I have changed, Ren, 'tis because our sovereign has changed. What we were asked to do was worse than Hastings where we fought Saxon warriors. Worse than Exeter and York two years ago where William showed mercy to the citizens. In York and Chester, he showed none. Mere serfs and cottars were slaughtered along with the rebels. Some were children and their mothers."

Then he told Ren of all they had seen, all they had lived through, his voice dropping to a whisper for some of it. Serena listened intently.

The Red Wolf's brows drew together in a scowl as fierce as the beast for which he was named. "I see why you no longer laugh as you once did."

"What we have seen," said Geoff, "would make any man lose his laughter."

"I doubt it not," said the Red Wolf. "'Tis regrettable our sire has resorted to such rough measures to establish his reign. To burn cottages and destroy cattle, food supplies and farming tools, leaving the people to starve in the midst of a brutal winter. How can he live with it? I could not."

"Nor could I, which was why I did what I did."

"As I would have done," Ren said, placing a hand on Geoff's shoulder. "I find no fault with your actions. I do feel some guilt for leaving you and Alain to take it on alone. When my leg was healed, I thought to join you, but my lady asked me to stay for Alexander's birth and then the news out of the North was not good and I wanted to go but Maugris made clear I was not needed, that you had much to do I could not share in. I have learned to trust the wise one's words."

Alain, who had been listening, leaned across to the Red Wolf. "All that Geoff has said is true. Not all of the dead lying in our path were men. William ordered his army to kill and maim not just the rebels, but any who could support them, whether they did or not."

"Word has come to us of the starvation that ravages the land in Yorkshire and in Durham," said Ren. "A few who escaped have made it to Talisand. They describe the wasteland Maugris saw in his visions."

Geoff experienced a terrible knot in the pit of his stomach when he thought of Emma living amidst such desolation, trying to survive in a cave. His appetite ebbed and he pushed his trencher away. Again, he questioned whether he should go to York no matter she had sent no word. He knew Maerleswein would see to her well-being, but it was not enough. He had to be sure. He had to know for himself.

When it was time for the musicians to be summoned to entertain them, a new bard stood before the dais, richly attired. His back to the hearth, he held a lute in his hands. Two others, wearing jewel colored tunics, joined him with psaltery and pipe. The music they made soothed Geoff's anxious soul but it reminded him of the beautiful music Rhodri had made with his Welsh harp as Serena sang.

"Is Rhodri no longer among us?" he asked the Red Wolf and Serena.

"My brother, Steinar, and Rhodri have hied off to Scotland," she said with regret in her violet eyes.

"We expected it after Steinar was wounded in the fighting in York two years ago," said Ren, "but my lady worries about him all the same."

"There was no future in England for the son of an English thegn whose lands were taken from him," Serena sadly acknowledged.

Ren took his wife's hand. "I know it is hard, my love, but 'tis the way of it. At least you are still lady of your people."

"I know, husband," she said giving him a tender look. "For myself, I am content. But for Steinar, I worry."

From where he sat next to Serena, Maugris spoke. "Steinar will make his own way, my lady. 'Twill not be easy for such a warrior, but he has known since our coming his future lay outside of Talisand. In Scotland, he may find it." He patted her hand. "Do not worry for your brother."

The music died and the Red Wolf stood and stepped down from the dais. The hall grew quiet with anticipation as their lord stood before them. Serving wenches drew to the side to watch.

"And now I must see to the knighting of one who has served me so faithfully," said the Red Wolf. "Mathieu, come forward."

The handsome squire rose from one of the trestle tables and slowly walked to stand before the knight he had served since before Hastings, for he had been the Red Wolf's page at one time.

Geoff had been prepared for what he knew would happen this night. Mathieu was of an age to take his place among the knights and none could doubt he had earned the honor. Geoff picked up the sword belt that lay behind him and stepped down from the dais. When he reached Mathieu, he strapped the sword on the young man. The superbly crafted blade had been a gift from Feigr, the sword-maker, when Geoff had helped him and he had managed to store it under the boards of Emma's house. Though Feigr typically made shorter swords, this one was long in the Norman style.

Once the belt was secure, Geoff helped Mathieu to put on a set of spurs handed him by the Red Wolf, a gift for Mathieu from his lord.

Slapping the squire on the back of the neck, Ren said in a loud voice that boomed around the hall, "I dub you knight, Sir Mathieu!"

The hall erupted in applause as everyone joined in the celebration of the new honor for the former squire.

Mathieu bowed to the Red Wolf. "Thank you, my lord." Then to Geoff, "and to you, Sir Geoffroi."

"'Tis well deserved," said Geoff. "Were it not for your quick action to summon Emma, I might not be here today."

Mathieu grinned.

With the toasts that followed, for a moment, at least, Geoff knew again happiness shared with friends. But all the while, in the back of his mind was the picture of Emma.

The next day Geoff was in the practice yard outside the bailey, trying to rid his mind of thoughts of Emma when he realized it was futile. "Enough!" he cried out, signaling Alain he was breaking off their sparring.

Wiping his brow with the back of his hand, he glanced up at the sun, nearly at its zenith. The vigorous wielding of swords in feigned combat required his concentration and every muscle to meet the Bear's challenge, but it had not spared him thoughts of the woman he wanted. The gnawing ache inside his chest was a constant reminder he'd left his heart in York.

He had held on to the wise one's words, hoping they meant Emma would choose him and Talisand. Anxiously, he had awaited a summons from her, some word, but there had been no news from York. He could wait no longer.

He reached for his shirt where he had laid it against a stone in the grassy area and looked at Alain. "I'm bound for York."

* * *

Emma gazed at the flowers shooting up through the ground, their yellow blossoms catching the light of the sun. She had always loved the crocuses that hailed the coming of spring. "'Tis time we decide," she told Sigga who walked beside her, Magnus ventured ahead of them roused by new scents. "Father will come soon, expecting us to leave with him."

"You do not look to the land of the Scots for your future, my lady, no matter the Scottish king offers refuge?"

"I would prefer Talisand as our destination, but 'twill be a hazardous crossing and I still have doubts I've not shared with the others."

"Sir Geoffroi cares for you, my lady, and I believe you care for him."

Emma had never told Sigga of Geoffroi's declaration of love. "Do you think me wrong to want to be with the Norman?"

"Nay," said Sigga. "He has proven himself many times. If he says we will be welcome at Talisand and that 'tis a place of peace, I believe him."

"Father spoke with Sir Geoffroi when I was ill. I overheard their argument. He knows Geoffroi has offered me marriage."

"Marriage?" Sigga raised a brow.

"Aye," she said and felt her cheeks heat. "I forgot to say."

Sigga tossed her a grin. "'Twas an important omission."

"'Twas in the summer," Emma murmured wistfully. Thinking back to their days in the meadow and their lovemaking before he had left with his king. She spoke her thoughts aloud. "It seems so long ago. I do not even know if he lives. What if we were to go to Talisand only to find him gone, or worse—dead?" Emma did not believe Geoffroi was dead or she would have felt something, a loss that she did not feel. He lived, she knew it.

"Nay, my lady, do not think it. He has survived so many battles. What can one more be to such a knight?"

"Aye, what can one more mean?" Her voice trailed off. Would Geoffroi always return from his battles for his Norman king? He might yet live but would the blood on his mail one day be his own?

"I wonder what Inga will decide," said Sigga. "The others are for Talisand, even Sker's wife has come around."

"I would not go without Inga," Emma retorted. "I have told her we will be a family, that I will help her raise Merewyn."

"Do not worry, Mistress. Inga may hesitate to go where there are Normans, but she oft speaks of the squire's kindness and, beyond that, she will not want to leave you."

Emma was thinking of Inga when Sigga suddenly said, "I had best see about what food there is for our dinner. Are you coming?"

"In a moment. I want to think a bit here among the flowers. Magnus and I will return shortly."

Emma did not stray far, knowing with the warmer days the knights might stir from their castles to hunt, though typically it would not be this late in the day. She idly wondered if there were any deer left for them to hunt in the forests of York.

York was not the place of her birth, but with her marriage to Halden, she had made it her home. It was here Finna and Ottar had been born and become like her own children. It was here she had ridden through the meadows on Thyra with Magnus bounding along. And it was here she had first glimpsed the fierce blond knight whose laughter softened her heart as well as his face. But her future did not lie in York.

She paused at the edge of the stream, swollen with the spring rains. Magnus wandered a short distance away. As she watched the rippling water, in her mind she saw Geoffroi's face, his blue eyes she had at first thought so stark but now remembered twinkling with laughter. She remembered his kisses, too, and the last time they had made love.

The fever had disrupted her woman's bleeding, but she was fairly certain they had made a child that last time nearly three months ago. She was still slim from her illness and the lack of food so there was only the barest hint of a change in her body and she had experienced no urge to vomit as some women did.

She had told Geoffroi she loved him and it was truer now than it was then for her love had grown in his absence. And now there was more to draw her to him. *I want this child as I want him.*

Even if she had to face the uncertainty of crossing the western fells and the thick forests between York and Talisand, she would do so to be with him. He was her heart's desire, had been since the night he'd first kissed her while saving her from his fellow knights. And if he still lived and had returned to his beloved Talisand, she wanted to be with him.

But she had to wonder. Had he forgotten her? Were his feelings still the same?

Aloud she whispered to the crocuses, "Does he still love me? Does he still want me at Talisand?"

CHAPTER 17

"Aye, he still loves you, Emma. And, yea, he wants you with him at Talisand."

Emma whirled. There before her, stood the knight of her dreams, tall and strong—*alive*. "Geoffroi!"

He opened his arms and she ran into them, no matter that Sir Alain and Mathieu stood on either side of him wearing amused smiles.

"You came!" she exclaimed as he showered her face with kisses. The tears fell, she could not stop them.

Seeing the huge knight and the squire turn away their faces, she felt her cheeks heat and started to pull from Geoffroi's arms, but he held her fast.

"You did not think I would allow you to be persuaded by your father to go to Scotland, did you? Nor would I allow you to cross the mountains and rivers alone. Nay, I shall escort you to Talisand myself. You will come?"

"Aye, I will come. But we must persuade Inga."

"I will leave that to Sir Mathieu."

She looked at the squire. "You have become a knight?"

"Aye," he beamed.

"I am not surprised," she said. "You have acted the knight many times in my presence, risking your own life for others."

Just then an impatient Magnus whimpered for Geoffroi's attention. He reached one hand down to ruffle the fur on the hound's head while holding on to her with the other.

"He still seems to think the sun rises with you," she said with a small laugh.

"I always thought him an intelligent beast," he said with an answering chuckle, never taking his eyes from her. He brought his hands to her arms and gently squeezed the slight flesh. "You are too thin."

"The north is starving, Geoffroi. We may have little to eat, but at least I am alive."

"You are indeed." His blue eyes sparkled as he drew her close and kissed her. She welcomed his mouth on hers, welcomed his embrace. His kiss was an elixir to heal the wounds of the war, to chase away her fears.

He pulled his head back to gaze at her face and her eyes caught a movement behind him.

Over Geoffroi's shoulder she saw her family and friends coming toward them still some distance away. He turned to follow her gaze, as did the two knights beside him.

"You know most of them," she told him, "the twins, Sigga and Artur, Inga and her new babe, my villeins, Jack and Martha, and a family of freemen who have joined us."

"All are welcome," he assured her, drawing her close as they watched the approaching entourage. The burden she had carried for so long lifted.

To Emma, Geoffroi whispered. "If I can have you by my side, I would open my doors to all the rebels in Northumbria."

She brushed his cheek with a kiss and spoke softly into his ear, "You shall have me, sir knight."

The twins broke from the group and ran toward them, coming to an abrupt stop in front of Geoffroi. He let go of her to sweep Finna into his arms. She looked over at Mathieu who was now a knight and smiled.

Ottar leaned into Geoffroi's side and Magnus ran circles around them and the two knights flanking them.

With Finna in one arm, Geoffroi wrapped his other arm around Emma. "It seems I have a family."

Emma could not resist the smile that spread across her face. "A larger one than you know, sir knight."

* * *

That night, talking around the low burning fire, they agreed to depart for Talisand the next morning. Even Inga had decided to go with them though Emma did not doubt that Sir Mathieu's comforting presence had something to do with the young woman's final decision, for the young knight held Merewyn while Inga sat next to him eating her dinner.

Geoffroi had anticipated their needs and brought food for them as well as two carts to help transport them and their possessions to Talisand.

Sigga made hare stew and all their bellies were full when the bowls were gathered at the end of the meal.

Just as they finished, Emma felt a breeze as the fire flickered. She turned to the mouth of the cave where her tall, proud father loomed, a Northumbrian warrior on either side of him, their hands on the hilts of their swords. With his outstretched hand, her father stilled their further movement, as his eyes scanned the occupants of the cave.

Sir Alain and Sir Mathieu stood and drew their swords.

"Nay," said Geoffroi, gesturing them to sit. "Maerleswein, come join us."

Emma walked to her father, placing her hands on his shoulders and reaching up to kiss his cheek. "Father, 'twas good you came. After tomorrow, I will be gone and these people will be with me. I would have left you a message, of course."

Her father's eyes narrowed on Geoffroi. "Is this the Norman's doing?"

"And mine," she said softly. "I have made my choice, as have the others. We are for Talisand. Come, sit by the fire. Share our mead. We still have a little."

He stepped into the cave, signaling his men to wait.

Sigga brought all three of their visitors a cup of the honey wine. "There is stew if you are hungry."

With a look at his men, her father nodded at the servant. "Aye, if you have enough to share, Sigga, we would eat."

When her father was seated next to her, eating his stew, she asked, "Will you not come to Talisand, Father, to see me wed?"

Her father shot a menacing glance at Geoffroi. From the other side of the fire, Geoffroi and his men stared back. "You would accept his offer of marriage when Cospatric has approached me asking for your hand?"

"Aye, I have accepted him. I love him, Father. He is a good and honorable man."

Her father's gaze bored into Geoffroi as the two warriors did battle with their eyes. Her father must have seen the triumph in Geoffroi's face for, after a time, he said, "I see."

"Will you not come with us?" She tried once more.

"Nay, I'm for Scotland. The price on my head is too high for me to stay in England. I'll not be back, Daughter."

She leaned her head on his broad shoulder and he wrapped his arm around her, kissing the top of her head. There was great affection between them, but her future lay with her Norman knight. "At least stay till morning when I can say a proper goodbye."

"Aye, we will stay till first light."

Her father and his two men slept at the mouth of the cave, their horses just outside the opening. She was certain they slept little, listening for wolves.

In the morning, he and his warriors took their leave, Emma and the twins waved goodbye as the men mounted their horses. Would she ever see him again?

Geoffroi reached his arm across her back and pulled her close. "He will be all right, Emma. Maerleswein is a survivor. King Malcolm will be glad to have such a man in his court. Mayhap he will even see Steinar, Lady Serena's brother."

"I told Father to ask about him," Emma said. "Mayhap we will hear of them at Talisand."

"Serena will be as anxious for news as you. Scotland is nay so far that messengers do not travel to and from Malcolm's court."

His words brought her comfort. But when her father and his men were out of sight, and the twins ran back into the cave, with a deep sigh, she turned into Geoffroi's arms and let the tears fall.

Soon after, they were mounted on the horses and some sat in the carts. In addition to the horses Geoffroi and the two other knights rode, they had brought with them three more. Artur, Jack and Sker rode but the knights led them as they were unused to being on a horse. The women, save for Emma, and the babe Merewyn, rode in the carts.

It frequently rained as they traveled over the hills and through the dales, leaving the horses to slog through the mud. Once the carts became stuck, slowing their progress until they were freed. The travelers huddled under their cloaks and did not complain, counting themselves fortunate to have survived when so many did not.

A sennight later they arrived in the Lune River valley. Geoffroi brought them to a halt at the top of a rise.

"I want you to see Talisand from here, Emma," he said.

The rain had stopped and the sun, hanging low in the sky, cast its golden rays onto the demesne before them. Ahead of her, Emma could see a river, curving through the green countryside. Though not as wide as the Ouse, it was still a grand sight.

In front of the river stood a Norman castle with its square, wooden tower on a motte high above all. Somehow, knowing it was part of Geoffroi's beloved Talisand, it did not seem so brooding and formidable. Below it was a large bailey surrounded by a palisade fence. From where she sat atop Thyra, she could see into the bailey. There were many buildings.

Emma could hardly believe all she saw. *This will be my home.*

To the north of the palisade fence, cottages in a well-ordered village were strung out along the river. The well-kept daub and wattle structures glowed in the sun's dying rays. "'Tis as I have dreamed," she whispered.

Geoffroi, riding beside her, his hand on the rope towing one of the other horses, watched her expression. "Aye, 'tis special. Did I not tell you?"

She looked into his eyes. How she loved him. "You did, but I did not imagine it as wondrous as this."

"Aye, and 'tis most wondrous for me because you will be here, my love."

EPILOGUE

A few days later, Emma was preparing for her wedding with the help of Lady Serena and Maggie when Finna rushed into the chamber.

Proudly holding a beautiful garland of wildflowers in her upturned palms, Finna said, "Inga helped me. Do you like it?" Ribbons of crimson, green and blue trailed from the fragrant crown of wildflowers.

Smiling at Finna, whose face glowed with happiness, Emma accepted the wreath and placed it on her head. "'Tis lovely."

The garland settled on her head perfectly. The ribbons cascaded down her back over her long, flaxen hair she wore loose.

Finna stared up at Emma, the child's fawn-like brown eyes wide. "You are beautiful, Emma."

She bent to kiss Finna. "I am so glad you think so. Thank you for the garland. 'Tis a wonderful gift for my wedding."

"I am glad you are marrying Sir Geoffroi," Finna said, "even if he is one of the Bastard's knights."

"Finna!"

Serena laughed. "You will not hear me scolding the lass." The lady of Talisand and Emma had quickly bonded. Each had lost much with the coming of the Conqueror, yet each had gained. They shared their dislike of the Norman king and their love for their Norman knights.

Maggie pulled tight the laces of the shimmering, blue-green, silk gown Serena had given Emma. She felt honored that Talisand's lady would bestow upon her such a fine gown since her own gowns had been left in York. She had managed to save her jewelry, some of the pieces gifts from her father, like the gold neck ring she wore today. It was comforting to know in this small way he was with her.

Finna turned from Emma to go to Alexander, the year-old heir to Talisand, who sat on a fur playing with a carved wooden horse. Next to him lay Magnus as if guarding the young child. "Alexander is always so happy," said Finna.

"When he is not in a temper," said Maggie, helping Emma into her shoes. "The babe is much like his father."

Serena smiled at her young son from where she sat on the bed watching him. "He is that. Ren is very proud of Alexander." Stroking her rounded belly, she said, "I wonder if this next babe will be like him. Alex's hair is near black. You would never know his mother has fair hair."

"Alex will be a handsome man," said Emma gazing at the babe who entertained Finna with his carved horse. "He has the look of his sire about him."

"I would like the next one to be a girl," announced Serena, "but Maugris says 'twill be another male cub for the Red Wolf."

Emma did not have the courage to tell them she was carrying Geoffroi's child, but when she had told him he was to be a father in the fall, he was pleased. 'Twas fortunate she had been thin when she came to Talisand as her condition was not yet apparent to the others.

"One thing is surely true," said Emma to Serena. "Your Alex will have many playmates."

"Aye," said Maggie, standing back to gaze at Emma's appearance, nodding her approval. "'Tis like a spring crop of lambs, Cassie's bairn, Rory, with his head of red hair like his mother, Aethel's little Lora, dark-haired and fair, and Inga's golden-headed Merewyn. They'll grow up together with the ones ye two will add to their number." She cast a glance at Emma and then at her mistress, Serena.

"The way Sir Niel is making eyes at your friend, Inga," Serena remarked to Emma, "'twill be another wedding soon." Emma had been heartened to see the way all at Talisand had embraced her friend, particularly Aethel, Sir Alain's wife. Geoffroi had noticed Sir Niel staring at Inga and told her he had been knighted four years before as a result of his bravery at the Battle of Hastings. Like Sir Alain, Sir Niel had a scar on his jaw. Emma thought it was a good thing since Inga, too, bore a scar though hers was not visible.

"'Tis time the young knight takes a wife," said Maggie, gathering up the things she had brought to the chamber. "But he may have to fight Sir Mathieu fer her. That one is also besotted with the young beauty."

"Sir Mathieu is going to marry me!" pronounced Finna, rising to her feet to face the three women. Emma was shocked at the serious tone from her young charge. But the other women laughed.

"Do not doubt her," said Emma. "If my gentle Finna has risen to announce such a thing, Mathieu can consider himself well and truly claimed. Remember, she is but eight years younger than he."

"Well," said Serena, "those brown eyes of hers could charm an angel out of his wings. Of course, Mathieu looks at her now as a child, but when she is a woman…"

"Come," said Maggie, urging Emma toward the door. "Ye'll have time to talk about the babes after the weddin'."

Emma left the chamber with the lady of Talisand, followed by Finna. Maggie stayed behind to care for baby Alexander. Magnus, too, remained. He had taken on a new role as protector of the young ones.

At the bottom of the stairs, Geoffroi waited, looking every bit like a nobleman with a dark green woolen tunic, embroidered in silver thread at the shoulders. Around his waist was a black and silver belt with an elegant, matching sheath for his sword. "My lady," he bowed. "How I have longed to see this day."

"And I, sir knight." She had thought to be calm but now her heart raced as the moment for them to be made one drew near.

He took her hand and placed it on his arm. Together they walked to the village where they would say their vows at the door of the stone church. The villagers and her friends from York had lined up on either side of their path, greeting them with smiles as they passed. Serena had told Emma that Geoffroi was one of the villagers' favorites so all had come to share their day. Most were English and happy to see a favored knight had taken a bride from York.

Behind Emma and Geoffroi walked the Red Wolf and his lady and the other knights and their wives.

As they strolled toward the church, Geoffroi leaned in to whisper, "I think I began to love you when I first saw you with your great hound. Not every knight can wed a Valkyrie, you know." At her puzzled look, he added, "That is how I saw you that first day I rode into York. You and Magnus were striding through the crowd. When your plea spared my life, I was certain. Aye, a Valkyrie."

The church came into view ahead of them and Emma saw a priest waiting before the chapel door. There was so much she wanted to say, so much she could have said. He was her life now, her future. But what she said was, "'Tisn't true. I am no Valkyrie. I am merely a woman who deeply loves her knight."

As they reached the church door, he brought her hand to his lips and pressed a kiss to her knuckles. Looking into her eyes, he whispered, "For the rest of my life, Emma, I will be glad I am that knight."

AUTHOR'S BIO

Regan Walker is an award-winning, bestselling author of Regency, Georgian and Medieval romances. Her stories have won numerous awards.

Years of serving clients in private practice and several stints in high levels of government have given Regan a love of international travel and a feel for the demands of the "Crown". Hence her romance novels often involve a demanding sovereign who taps his subjects for special assignments. Each of her novels features real history and real historical figures. And, of course, adventure and love.

Keep in touch with Regan on Facebook, and do join Regan Walker's Readers.

facebook.com/regan.walker.104

facebook.com/groups/ReganWalkersReaders

You can sign up for her newsletter on her website.

www.reganwalkerauthor.com

BOOKS BY REGAN WALKER

The Medieval Warriors series:

The Red Wolf's Prize
Rogue Knight
Rebel Warrior
King's Knight

The Agents of the Crown series:

To Tame the Wind (prequel)
Racing with the Wind
Against the Wind
Wind Raven
A Secret Scottish Christmas

The Donet Trilogy:

To Tame the Wind
Echo in the Wind
A Fierce Wind (coming 2018)

Holiday Stories (related to the Agents of the Crown):

The Shamrock & The Rose
The Twelfth Night Wager
The Holly & The Thistle
A Secret Scottish Christmas

Inspirational:

The Refuge, an Inspirational Novel of Scotland

Printed in Great Britain
by Amazon

83583095R00139